# Sex on Holiday
*A Wicked Words erotic short story collection*

**Look out for other themed Wicked Words Collections**

Already Published: Sex in the Office
Published in August 05: Sex at the Sports Club
Published in November 05: Sex in Uniform

# Sex on Holiday

A Wicked Words short story collection

Edited by Kerri Sharp

BLACK LACE

Black Lace books contain sexual fantasies.
In real life, always practise safe sex.

This edition published in 2005 by
Black Lace
Thames Wharf Studios
Rainville Road
London W6 9HA

Reprinted 2007

Typeset by SetSystems Limited, Saffron Walden, Essex
Printed and bound by Mackays of Chatham PLC

ISBN 978 0 352 33961 4

# Contents

# Introduction

The philosopher Alain de Botton writes in *The Art of Travel* that the appeal of an attractive potential partner is heightened if such a person is encountered abroad; prospective lovers then seem to adopt something of the exoticism of the country one is travelling through. Their appeal, he speculates, may spring from an ambition to 'weld ourselves more closely to the values missing from our own culture'. He may well be right but, to be prosaic for a moment, the primary aim for most travellers journeying out of the UK is usually to weld themselves to the nearest pool lounger and draw down those much-needed rays on their poor, sun-starved bodies.

But there is no doubt that an encounter away from home can provide a giddying thrill rarely found in one's own neck of the woods; a chance to indulge one's sybaritic side and give over the pull of nature. On holiday we recline that bit more luxuriously; dine a good deal more sumptuously, and bring forth our passions more readily. It's no accident that the duty-free areas in airports display such an embarrassment of beauty care and sweet-smelling riches. The departure lounge is the place where women, especially, love to treat themselve to quality cosmetics from the upper price bracket in anticipation of lavishing them on their bodies when their skin begins to bronze. We visualise our holiday selves, beautified and groomed, taking an evening walk by the sea or in the town square, flashing smiles and flirty eyes at a handsome passer-by or fellow traveller.

As you would expect from a *Wicked Words* compilation, the characters in this collection of sexy holiday stories go a good deal further than the flirting stage. In fact, none of these girls are going to let slip the opportunity to indulge in X-rated frolics, often al fresco, with their holiday flings. And what an assortment of manly charms they encounter. For those who like guys 'tanned and rugged', you are in for a treat: there's a tour guide who knows how to hit the right pleasure spots; a hotel masseur who goes that extra bit further; a down and dirty US backwoodsman and a sex-mad Aussie snake handler who brings his mates along for the ride. More exotic is a Cuban salsa dancer and a dastardly Czech spanking fan, and, an unusual addition, the story of a young man encountering a beautiful dominatrix in a ski resort. I was spoilt for choice for stories with a French setting, but one character doesn't even make it on to Gallic soil before she's in action on the ferry crossing.

All in all, it's a fabulously saucy beach read, and I bet that there'll be many a hotel room with a dog-eared copy of this compilation on its bedside table. Just be careful you don't spill your factor 15!

Kerri Sharp (Ed.)

## Want to write for Wicked Words?

We are publishing more themed collections in 2005 and 2006 – made in response to our readers' most popular fantasies. *Sex at the Sports Club* and *Sex in Uniform* are the next two collections for 2005. The deadline for the *Sports* collection has now passed but if you want to submit a sizzling, beautifully written story for *Sex in*

*Uniform*, please read the following. And keep checking our website for information on future editions.

- Your short story should be 4,000–6,000 words long and not published anywhere in the world – websites excepted.
- Thematically, it should be written with the Black Lace guidelines in mind.
- Ideally there should be a 'sting in the tale' and an element of dramatic tension, with oodles of erotic build-up.
- The story should be about more than 'some people having sex' – we want great characterisation too.
- Keep the explicit anatomical stuff to an absolute minimum.

We are obliged to select stories that are technically faultless and vibrant and original – as well as fitting in with the tone of the series: upbeat, dynamic, accent on pleasure etc. Our anthologies are a flagship for the series. We pride ourselves on selecting only the best-written erotica from the UK and USA. The key words are: diversity, surprises and faultless writing.

**Competition rules will apply to short stories: you will hear back from us about your story <u>only</u> if it has been successful. We cannot give individual feedback on short stories as we receive far too many for this to be possible.**

*Sex in Uniform* – deadline for stories end April 05

If you want to find out more about Black Lace, check our website, where you will find our author guidelines and more information about short stories. It's at <u>www.blacklace-books.co.uk</u>

Alternatively, send a large SAE with a first-class British stamp to:

Black Lace Guidelines
Virgin Books Ltd
Thames Wharf Studios
Rainville Road
London W6 9HA

# Thanking Vesuvius
## Primula Bond

The idea of swinging in a hammock above the Bay of Naples seemed like utter heaven when Samantha first suggested it. We were sitting in the British Museum at the time, staring at the shrivelled remains of someone who had failed to escape the eruption of Mount Vesuvius in AD 79. Every six months or so we'd meet there for some sisterly bonding, to ponder the exhibits until we felt sufficiently educated. Then we'd repair to the pub so that we could catch up – or rather I could listen to tales of her doomed love life.

'Except that I don't really have a love life at the moment, unlike you, lucky thing.' Samantha sighed, tapping my engagement ring as we waited to cross the road. 'How is the mysterious Geoffrey, by the way?'

I conjured up my imaginary fiancé from the collage of magazine cuttings stuck to my pin board at home. I love my younger sister, but she's too nosy by half. I had to invent Geoffrey to keep her and my other friends off my back.

'He's fine. In the States, actually. Dying to meet you.'

'Which is why you'd be the ideal travelling companion. Respectable, spoken for, always available ... There's an extra space in the villa, you see. You love the sun, or you used to. You're a brilliant cook. There'll be plenty of culture. And you won't be competition when we're out pulling the locals.'

'We?' I paused at the door of the pub.

'Me and Greta. Don't look so horrified.' Sam flicked her golden plaits at me. 'She speaks English really well now. We're best mates.' Now she was blushing.

'For some reason clients always want us on modelling assignments together.'

'You mean you still haven't twigged why identical *Frauleins* in scraps of lace and shaking their booties like the Cheeky Girls is such a winner?' I said, with not a little trace of incredulity at her naivety. It was then I caught sight of my dishevelled reflection in the tarnished pub mirror – long hair falling out of a chaotic top knot, big eyes watering over the emerald-green pashmina protecting my face from the late spring chill. I was not so much cheeky as peaky.

'I suppose we *are* alike –'

'You're their best investment since what's her name, who's always in the society pages. Come on, doll. Why do the pair of you want someone like me coming on your girlie holiday?'

'We don't, really.' Sam bit her lip and pushed her way to the bar to order my favourite Merlot.

'Oh, that's charming.'

'I mean, it's the agency who suggested it. In fact they'll only let us have the time off if we take a kind of –'

'What? Minder?'

Sam giggled. Even her laugh made me feel ungainly and ancient, but protective too. I'd looked after her since our mum died, done everything for her until the talent scouts took over and it was time for me to get a life.

'Chaperone. Apparently we're not considered proper adults, even at the age of twenty. They don't want us misbehaving and ruining our looks for the Gleneagles shoot next month.' She pouted her pillowy mouth. 'You're even to make sure we don't get sunburned.'

The idea of swinging in a hammock over the Bay of

Naples with a pair of nubile honeys in tow would not have been my first suggestion for an ideal holiday – but it didn't stop me from accepting the offer. I even wangled for the holiday to be paid through the agency and, after some toing and froing, cast caution to the chill wind and went for it.

The peachy villa was paradise regained. Hidden in a lush garden on top of a pink cliff overlooking a small, deserted beach, it had cool flagstoned floors with terracotta tubs of huge cacti dotted about the poolside terrace and entrance. Tiny finches darted about the bougainvillea and the whole place hummed with life and heat. And right there was the hammock I'd imagined, slung especially for me between two black pine trees.

The days passed without incident. I relaxed on the terrace while the girls gossiped about the agency and the high dramas that seemed to occur with regularity in that world of fragile egos and beautiful creatures. I read the latest blockbuster novels, dozed in the shade and took photos of the landscape.

We were near the end of our week's sojourn when my girls got restless – as young girls do. I was on the terrace, as usual, dunking almond biscuits into my cappuccino while they sipped at pressed lemon juice. As always, I had flung a kaftan over my bathing suit before joining them for breakfast but, as soon as I got outside, the heat sucked at me. I paced about on the hot stones, desperate to take it off, take everything off, and jump into the pool.

'Carla says it's a heatwave,' murmured Sam, fanning herself with my newspaper. 'And that's some achievement in a place that regularly reaches thirty degrees. If you look towards the mainland, you can see smoke from the forest fires.'

Carla was round the corner of the house, dressed in her smart white maid's uniform. We watched her snapping out sheets to hang on the line. No wet patches under her long brown arms. The heatwave evidently didn't bother her.

'We're safer here, then,' I said, 'unless we take that trip to Pompeii.'

Sam and Greta shook their heads. They were extraordinary. Even their jerky, haughty movements were the same. They had cut their hair before coming on holiday, long white-blonde fringes swept sideways across their narrow faces, but cropped close at the back so that their exposed necks were raw, like stalks.

'We'll suffocate if we stay here. But, please, not Pompeii. Not today.' Greta stood up, twitching a shiny triangle of pink thong across her waxed pubes. I didn't know where to look, because she was topless too, her small round breasts jutting on her ribcage, daring me to stare.

'Bone,' I said.

Greta squinted through the shadows cast by the vine above her head.

'It's all I can see of you, sweetie . . . skin and bone.'

'We want to go down to the beach,' they said.

I swerved away from her and spilled coffee all over my kaftan.

'Whatever,' I sighed. 'Let the agency treat you like cut glass china. You can do what you like.'

I stepped on to the parched grass area and into the sun. I could hear Carla singing in the sizzling air. My hair seemed to be frying on my scalp and my blood drummed in my ears as my body struggled to adjust to the attack of temperature. Sweat dribbled between my breasts, but I liked it. I liked the way the ferocious heat seemed to coax them into fullness, pushing against the material of the kaftan, the heat spreading all over my skin. Already there were little freckles on my arms. I'd been skulking in the hammock most of the time, except when the girls went inside to chatter to Carla, or have a siesta, and that was when I dived into the pool before lying out on the stones beside it like a slowly roasting lizard, alone with my big white body. But right now I was too shy and self-conscious to bare myself in front of anyone.

The pool was calling to me, but I wouldn't fully uncover myself in front of them.

'Take that kaftan off,' said Sam. 'It's absurd to have that on in this heat.'

'I shouldn't,' I said. 'I'm not like you two – all slender and perfect. There's far too much of me.'

'That's so not true.' Greta opened a raffia bag and started pulling out jewel-bright, diaphanous sarongs, as if she were a magician. 'You are beautiful, Laura. You're all woman. One day I will give all this up and eat chocolate so I can look like you again.'

Sam snorted and sat up. 'But I daresay your Geoffrey likes a nice big handful, eh, sis? Come on, don't be shy. Show us! It's the hottest summer they've seen for decades, and you're all covered up in your old kaftan.'

She and Greta danced around me like marionettes, spindly arms and fingers teasing me, enormous blue eyes flashing above their sharp cheekbones, and then the kaftan was off, flung across the grass.

'Now you're ready for the beach. Won't you try a bikini?' Sam surveyed me, hands on her hips. At least she still had her top on. 'I think you'd look rather splendid, and there are lovely little shops in the town.'

'Don't push it,' I warned, crossing my arms uselessly over my stomach. 'I don't want to scare the natives.'

'The natives! Now you're talking. What are we doing

hiding up here like a trio of nuns?' Sam shoved her sunglasses on and started packing up her beach bag. 'Sun. Sea. Sex. Bring it on!'

'Let me tie this sarong for you.' Greta was beside me, pushing my hands away. She reached round me to wrap a length of smoky blue chiffon round my hips, rubbing like a cat against me. When she moved back her dark-red nipples were huge and prominent.

'You were almost the same shape as me, Sammy, before you dieted yourself into oblivion,' I chattered nervously over Greta's shoulder.

'You can't have big tits and child-bearing hips on the catwalk, Laura,' mocked Sam, snatching up the keys to the hired jeep and stalking into the house. 'Even if you have got better legs than me.'

'Fantastic legs. But you shouldn't hide the tits and hips, either,' murmured Greta, bending to pick up her bikini top. She faced me, smiling at my relief as she tied it over those astounding nipples. 'Someone will want to enjoy those.'

Out of the corner of my eye I saw Carla pick my kaftan off the grass and hold it to her face as she watched us go.

There was no shade on the beach, apart from the thatched deck of a little bar at the far end. The air seemed to be solid in the soupy heat, but there was the tiniest breeze coming off the dazzling water. I followed the girls down the rocky slope, laden with towels and mats and bottles and books.

'Where are you going to lie?' I asked anxiously. 'You've got to watch the sun.'

The cove was idyllic, quiet, almost deserted apart from a scattering of sun worshippers. A couple of surfer dudes were wading out of the sea looking like Greek gods. Or Roman gods, I suppose, as we were in Ischia.

One of these sons of Poseidon wore a wetsuit rolled down over a ridged brown torso and carried a diver's tank. The other had on a pair of faded denim shorts and his skin was the colour of golden syrup. He shook his bleached hair off his face like a dog. The water made runnels through the dark hair on their stomachs and down their strong thighs.

Sam nudged Greta and they went into catwalk mode, swinging hips and ankles athletically across the sand, kicking at the water and tilting their chins over their shoulders as they passed. The boys gaped, as any red-blooded male would do, and muttered some kind of greeting.

I realised I'd stopped on the edge of the sand. My tongue was running across my dry lips as I watched the boys watching the girls. My imaginary Geoffrey had a new face now, modelled on those gods, and a new body to match. Those young buttocks, flexing – it was amazing. Those thighs, swaggering like a cowboy's, as if his dick swung too low. Those brown hands, slapping at each other's shoulders as they parted.

The guy in the shorts walked across the beach. Greta and Sam had chosen a spot and were waggling their hands at me. He nodded as he passed them. After shaking his longish hair off his face again, he went up to the bar and unlocked the door.

'Laura! We need the sun cream!' the girls yelled.

The other guy, the diver, had nearly reached me. I hitched my cargo of beach stuff awkwardly in my arms. He was right in front of me, scuffing through the sand, and I tipped my head towards the girls.

'Demanding little madams,' I said, smiling straight at him. 'Gorgeous, though, aren't they?'

He shrugged. Obviously he hadn't understood. He bent to pick up a magazine that I'd dropped and glanced at the model on the cover. The eyelashes fringing his amber eyes were stuck together with salt water, and drops were gathered along his collar bone. He handed me the magazine, but I couldn't take my eyes off his mouth. He had obscenely full lips, like his mate. The kind of lips you could imagine kissing, then nibbling down your neck, over your breasts, sucking on your taut nipples, kissing your stomach, pushing down, down...

'I didn't notice,' he said suddenly, brushing past me to walk up the slope. I could smell his sweat mixed with the hot rubber of his wetsuit. His voice was low, the voice of a much older man, and with an almost perfect English accent.

I let out a kind of shivering laugh of denial, and bustled off towards the girls.

The blond guy started up some music, and the few other people on the beach raised their heads testily.

'Remember your duties,' said Sam, snatching the sun cream off me and kneeling up behind Greta, who had taken her top off again and was staring out to sea. 'Got to keep the sun off.'

'I think it's too hot already,' murmured Greta, closing her eyes. Sam smoothed the cream on to Greta's back with exaggerated movements, nuzzling into her neck and letting her hands trail round to her breasts and stomach. She glanced across the beach. Sure enough the barman was leaning on his counter, tipping beer into his mouth, and I swear he was massaging the front of his shorts.

His diver mate had reached the top of the slope. My stomach lurched as he hoisted up a surfboard, muscles flexing down his sides. Come down, come back down here. He stared at Greta and Sam, then propped the surfboard against his jeep and started to peel his wetsuit over his hips. A line of hair ran down his stomach, leading into his groin. I ached to see what was there;

the proud thing he no doubt possessed quivering out of his wetsuit. I breathed quickly, impatiently. It was safe to look. He'd never imagine I was lusting after him. I was invisible beside the dazzling young girls; a motherly figure in my sarong and my big straw hat.

'Come on, Laura. Your turn.' Greta knocked me to my knees and whipped my hat off. My hair tumbled down, warm coils on my skin. Sam giggled, dancing round us while she undid her top. Greta pushed me on to my front and Sam stole my sarong, running into the sea with it trailing behind her like a wing.

'When did you last have a man inside you?' Greta whispered, sitting astride me and dripping oil on to my spine. 'I see you looking, Laura. You look at everyone.'

I tried to push her off me. I wanted to see the diver naked, but she locked me between her thighs and rocked her neat butt over mine as she pulled my bathing suit down to my waist and stroked the oil up and down so that my skin started tingling in places she hadn't even reached. My thighs were squeezed together and the lips of my pussy were stuck with moisture.

'The last time I was on a beach, actually, a few years ago,' I groaned as her fingertips dug into me. The jeep's rackety engine fired up. So he was leaving. 'I was cute then, like you. Slim, sex on legs, tits that stayed put when I moved.'

'So you looked just like Sam?' Greta flicked my hair off my shoulder and massaged my neck. 'But you're still sexy now. You still have these amazing breasts – so big, so juicy.' I blushed into the towel and let loose with some information that I thought would either shock or amuse young Greta.

'My boyfriend had the biggest dick you've ever seen. Constantly bursting out of his Speedos, he was.' My pussy twitched at the memory. I was definitely wet down there. 'Oh, the heat. It made us so horny.'

'It was Geoffrey?' she asked.

'Oh no. Long before his time. But that's how it was back then. We were always at it, especially on holiday. Grabbed at sex like we were starving.'

Just then Sam called out and Greta slipped off me. Sam was dancing about coquettishly as the barman shook cocktails. Greta went over to them and snaked an arm around Sam's waist.

On the other side of the beach the diver had left his surfboard and wetsuit by the rocks, but his jeep was roaring up the dusty track, scattering stones. I crawled over the hot sand to where Sam had dropped my sarong. Hell, no one was looking. I stood up and stretched. The light danced off the water. I couldn't resist. I flung myself in and washed all that heat and sweat off me until all I could hear was my own heart drumming.

And later, while my girls nibbled shellfish at the bar, I lay down and let the sun sink into me while I dozed off. A young cock remembered, hot and swollen from hours in the sun, nudging between my loose, lazy thighs, waking me, pushing up inside where I was always so ready, now so empty, invading all that moist darkness with solid inches of pumping, thrusting, thrusting...

'How can you bear it out here? You're not even burned. We've been in the shade all day.'

Their shadows were blocking out the still blazing afternoon sun.

'Must be my natural habitat.' I yawned, sitting up. Only the stiffening of my nipples told me that my bathing suit had slipped down. I pulled it up slowly and reluctantly, relishing the kiss of the sun on my breasts.

Both girls had hands on hips in slightly defensive gestures.

'We don't want to go yet,' Sam said, as I moved in slow motion to gather our things. 'Paulo's mate is coming back soon, and we're going to party.'

I couldn't focus. They jumped like stick insects against the glare of sun. My head was thick with sleep and the sweaty dreams of summer sex I'd been drowning in.

'Whatever. But just remember, it's only a couple of days before I hand you back.' I rubbed my eyes. 'They'll roast me alive if you misbehave.'

'So stay with us,' said Greta, rearranging my shoulder straps. 'Have some fun.'

'Oh, honey. I'd cramp your style.'

The other guy's jeep was skidding up in a cloud of dust, eager to get the party started. I made my excuses, and headed instead towards the track and turned to wave. Greta was watching me go while Sam tugged at her. The boy in the hut was nodding his head to some music and rolling a joint. And, above the dust cloud, out over the sea, still that wispy trail of smoke from the forest fires.

'You're going home now?'

The diver was dry now, his hair glossy and black, and he was wearing a ripped black T-shirt. I could see the pulse going in his neck. I realised that the erotic dreams I'd been having on the beach came with this face attached, this body. Hidden under my sarong, I ached for him.

He seemed to be waiting for me to answer, but I was so warm, so weak with imagined pleasure that all I could do was smile weakly at him, shrug casually as if sad to miss the fun, and move on past.

Early next morning it was hotter than ever. I was up, dressed and eager to go. After breakfast there was still no sign of the girls, so I stamped up to Sam's room.

Carla came out, delicately wiping her upper lip. 'They are sick, *signora*,' she said. 'They ate bad fish at the beach.'

She looked flushed, and two buttons of her white uniform were undone to reveal the deep crack of her cleavage.

'Hung-over, more like,' I said. 'Now we'll all be in trouble, and it's almost the last day.' I flung open the door. 'We're going to Pompeii. It'll take a whole day to get there and back.'

Their shuttered bedroom was like a perfumed oven. The villa had several bedrooms, but they'd chosen to share – no doubt sharing the secrets and giggling over the things that amuse young women of their age. The ceiling fan flicked round, stirring expensive musky aromas around the room.

'We can't go,' Sam groaned.

The shutters clattered open. Greta was in Sam's bed, one arm flung across my sister's body and apparently fast asleep.

'Did you stay at the beach too late last night?' I demanded, staying by the window. 'What did you get up to in that shack? And why is Greta in your bed?'

'What are you, my mother?'

Greta lifted her hand to hush Sam's mouth.

My breath was difficult to catch. 'That's what I'm here for, isn't it? To keep an eye on you?'

Sam shakily wiped her forehead. Her hair was drenched with sweat. 'They weren't interested. We had fun, but those blokes are weird. They didn't want to fuck us. They were probably too stoned.'

Greta opened her blue eyes and grinned across at me. 'Perhaps they didn't like me kissing Sam with my tongue. Some men get a hard-on to see that, but –'

'Shut up, Greta, you'll upset her,' growled Sam. 'Laura's not into all that.'

'I'm going to Pompeii,' I snapped. 'I think you should come.'

'You won't rest till you've had your fix of culture, will you?' Sam pouted petulantly and then sank back on to the pillow.

Greta looked at me. 'She is sick, you know, Laura. You go get your fix alone.'

That Oscar Wilde was right. Youth is so wasted on the young.

The coach growled and swayed around the winding coast road. Here on the mainland the sky was smudged grey with smoke from the forest fires. I glanced across the bay to Ischia, where my girls lay nursing their headaches in their stifling room above the deserted beach. My insides tightened as I imagined Greta fondling Sam, straddling her as the sheet slipped off, leaning forwards to kiss her with her tongue.

I wanted to keep watch, to throw a bucket of cold water over them. But I also felt liberated, alone in this air-conditioned coach, away for a few hours from their knowing perfection. The only other people who could stand the heat were an elderly couple and a scruffy group of students.

Pompeii was everything I'd expected. The sizzling, deadly heat was just right to create the doomed atmosphere, as was the noonday sky darkened with the threat of fire. I trailed through the ruined shops and houses, past columns with no roof to support, along the narrow streets where chariots used to race, flapping my guide-book in front of me and wrapping my shoulders with yet another sarong. The heat scrambled my brain. I gave up trying to concentrate on the details and just absorbed the history.

'And this was a bordello,' said the deep voice of a tour guide behind me as I wandered into a warren of tiny chambers. 'These were the whores' rooms. Those shelves were the beds where they pleasured their clients.'

My blood buzzed in my ears. I'd imagined the voice. Sex dominated my mind completely. I blamed the heat. I was being stupid, trying to feel twenty again. I couldn't get Sam and Greta out of my mind. I couldn't stop the ache that had begun yesterday when I yearned to see the diver's emerging young body, made worse by Greta oiling me in the sun and asking me when I last had a man ...

The other sightseers were trailing back to the coach. I leaned against the wall, limp with frustration, and closed my eyes.

'The blonde lady from the beach.'

Then came the smell of sweat and of man, mixed not with rubber this time but fresh laundry. A white shirt sleeve blocked my way out. The sunlight was extinguished, but the heat inside my belly was even greater.

'The diver from the beach,' I gasped aloud, wetting my lips. My body seemed to be licked by fire. 'What are you doing here?'

'I'm a part-time tourist guide. It's my job, among other things.' He laughed, framing me with his other arm. Close up, and fully clothed, he looked older – in his 40s, I'd say; one of those guys who has spent a lifetime outdoors being rangy and rugged. He was close up against me now, the buckle of his trousers jabbing through my flimsy dress. His legs trapped me against the old wall. 'So where are your frisky little bodyguards? Left you alone for once?'

'It's the other way round, actually. I'm supposed to be looking after *them*.' I wanted to kick myself, sounding so prim. 'So ... I don't know what you did to them at the beach last night, but –'

'I didn't do anything to them,' he said, sounding shocked. He shook his head, his eyes gleaming. I could feel the long hard shape of his cock through his trousers pressing up against me, and a shaft of excitement shot up the back of my legs.

'It's you I'd like to have sex with.'

I shook my head so hard it banged against the rough wall, breathy laughter sputtering out of my mouth. I was imagining things, surely, although the thrust of that cock was real all right. I could definitely feel it trying to nuzzle through my skirt, into my bush. I tried to sidle sideways, but my legs wouldn't hold me up.

'So little room in here, don't you think?' I blustered nervously. 'I thought I was in a bakery. Or is it a police station? What are these cells? What did you say this place was?' I slithered along the wall, craning my head this way and that. I was seeing nothing, so aware of his body right up against me, all that maleness pulsing into the cooked air.

'It was called the *lupanare*. The frescoes should give you a clue. Take a good look.'

He pulled me away from the wall and, balancing one hand on my hip, fingers feeling my flesh, he pointed upwards. Very faint, cracked figures, painted in terracotta and black, were etched over the ancient bricks. At first I thought they were dancing, or praying, but no. They were copulating, rutting, humping, in every position under the sun. Here was a tough man gripping a slender girl's thighs while she stretched out gracefully and he fucked her from behind. There was a woman with elegant coiled hair straddling a man's cock as he reclined on cushions.

'It's like a menu, see? All the services you could get for your *dinarii*.' He whispered right into my ear. 'Or perhaps the pictures were just the porno of the day – pictures designed to get them horny.'

There was such a heavy silence in the chamber that I felt as if I were being sucked right into the frescoes. Another pair knelt up and went at it face to face, togas slipping to the floor. A man simply stood, displaying his thumping erection. A woman solemnly lowered her face into a man's groin. Another woman sat on the bed with them, staring directly at me.

'Do you think they were still in here when the lava came?' I was leaning against him now. The etchings were so delicate, yet so businesslike. Imagine giving pleasure for money. God, I could be there, selling myself, climbing on to a great meaty penis and lowering myself down, down on to its rigid shaft . . .

'Were they petrified exactly as it found them, you know, *in flagrante*?'

'Some of them, yes. But what a way to go.' Now both his hands were resting on my hips. I was too turned on to resist as he started to tug my silky dress up my legs. 'Imagine coming to visit your favourite tart after a long day's hard work, paying your fee, fucking her senseless or getting her to suck you off, getting all tangled up and hot on the bed, with not a clue what's happening to the city outside these walls; just lost inside her, pumping your life away.'

He ran his fingers up under my dress and sank them into the soft flesh of my buttocks, lifting me quickly so that I was forced to wrap my legs round him. The sarong slipped off my shoulders and landed on his foot. I could feel my sex lips slicking open, moistening in the lacy knickers as my dress floated round my waist. Now his eyes were on a level with my breasts and we both looked down at them, bulging honey-dark in the half-light.

There were still people about. Footsteps scraping along in the dust outside.

'They wouldn't have stopped, would they, even if

their hearts were clattering with fear?' I said, throwing back my head and arching my throat as my nipples hardened against the tight bodice of my dress. 'They would have gone on and on, saying, "Don't stop until I come; whatever it is can't touch us in here."'

The diver carried me round the corner out of sight and slammed me against the wall.

'That's right. Safe inside the *lupanare*. Everyone fucking like there's no tomorrow.'

He dug his fingers into my butt cheeks, easing them apart, and then his fingers were in the damp crack between them, searching and sliding over my tender flesh. I couldn't tell whether it was sweat or whether I was creaming myself, waiting for the moment. I was alive with excitement now, opening myself wider to swallow his fingers, to grip him, grinding myself against his white shirt, staining it with my juices as I wound my fingers in his hair to smother him between my damp breasts.

He groaned unevenly as his fingers slid in and out of me, releasing my urgent, musky scent, driving me wild with wanting. I slid my hand down his stomach to find it, scrabbled at his belt, grinning at the bestial grunting noises I was making as his teeth easily tore my flimsy dress and nipped sharply at the nipple sparking there.

Suddenly there were soft, questioning voices jostling in the doorway, coming in, coming round the corner, the click of a camera, and then a gasp. A stifled giggle, then another gasp and another click of the camera before the feet shuffled away.

He lifted his head, lips wet with his saliva, and we stared at each other, eyes glittering in the suffocating gloom. I was quivering violently now, with the effort of gripping him and with the ferocious desire to have him, right there in our own hot whore house.

'So now they have all seen us.' He swore under his

breath, his face so close to mine. 'I have to go. I have to join my group.'

'Fuck your group,' I snapped. 'Let them come and see. Let's recreate the energy of the old bordello.' I kissed him hard, pressing my mouth on to his gorgeous lips. He paused, then his tongue snaked hungrily around mine and I let my feet drop to the floor and we staggered backwards into one of the little alcoves which used to be the sumptuous couches of lust.

I barely felt the scratch of rough stone against my back as we fell and he reared over me on his hands and knees, just like one of the hungry men in the etchings. I unzipped his trousers and there was his big penis standing hard and straight and there were my legs, hooking him into me.

He edged across the narrow shelf. How tiny those Pompeiians must have been! I was half raised against the wall, but our bodies were stuck together now and there was the round tip of his cock opening me up, then the long, smooth shaft sliding in. I was so wet now, so smooth compared with the rough stone of our make-shift bed. My arms and legs were wound around him and his hands were squeezing my breasts, pinching my nipples as he bit my neck, pausing to listen for any audience, and then we were rocking wildly together, his cock thrusting and bursting and filling me totally.

Outside there were more voices and some shouting and laughter, but they receded, and then one or two coaches sounded their horns. I laughed, and threw myself back against the stone bed. His full weight was on me, shoving me up against the wall as he did what was natural. His knees were scratched, my shoulder blades were scratched, but then what sounded like some kind of siren wailed up in the city of Naples and a helicopter whirred overhead. My diver started to groan again, and I thought of where we were – the volcano and all its eruptions gathering over us. I laughed to myself as I felt my own underground currents drawing and pulling, gathering into a point, sucking me under, sucking him in, and the commotion outside and the prospect of crowds of tourists pouring in to see the show only drove my excitement on until I felt him shudder. I was too excited to hold back and, grinding myself against him, I came too, wave after wave of glorious ecstasy rippling in and out of both of us until we could catch our breath again.

I could barely walk as we staggered out of the *lupanare* and back through the ruined town to the car park.

'The fires are all along the coast now,' said my diver as we got to my coach. He wrapped my sarong around my neck, fingers lingering on my skin. 'If we don't go now we'll all be trapped.'

The sky was a venomous yellow and there was a scorching and ripping in the air.

'Somehow that doesn't scare me,' I said. 'I'd like to be trapped here with you.'

'I'll meet you on the beach tonight,' he called as he backed towards his own bus. 'If Geoffrey doesn't mind.'

He was pointing at my finger. The girls must have told him I was spoken for, though that hadn't stopped him seducing me in the *lupanare*, had it? I took the false engagement ring off, held it up so that it glinted against the livid sky, then threw it over the wall to be buried in the dust of Pompeii.

'It's a date.' I laughed. As my bus rumbled back towards the coast, I looked up at Mount Vesuvius – and thanked her for the favour she had done me.

# Veselé Velikonoce Fiona Locke

Trust me to find an English guy *sans le vice anglais*. It was so unfair.

The Vltava seethed beneath its bridges and I seethed above, staring down into the chilly, churning water. The rippling reflections of the Gothic statues flanking Charles Bridge were silhouetted against the choppy blur of the pale morning sky. Behind me the endless crush of tourists elbowed their way across the bridge towards the castle.

I could still hear Ian's voice in my head: 'Oh no, don't tell me you're into that naughty schoolgirl thing.'

Tears stung my eyes, but I scrubbed them away. As a matter of fact I *was* into that naughty schoolgirl thing. And a lot of other things I wasn't about to share with him now.

It was the whole point of coming here. Ian had wanted to meet in clichéd, overpriced Paris. But I'd insisted on Prague, promising he'd love it and dropping far too subtle hints about my real motives. I came here often, but I'd never been for Easter. And Easter was the time to be here.

The Czechs have this curious tradition, you see. On Easter Monday the men and boys hunt down the girls in the village and whip them with plaited willow switches called *pomlázka*. It's supposed to keep them healthy and beautiful all year long. And after a girl has been whipped, she ties a red ribbon to the end of the *pomlázka*. Then she is expected to reward her whipper with a gift of brightly painted eggs and *slivovice*, plum brandy. It's a unique compliment – being thought pretty enough to be worth whipping.

I had fantasised about a marauding gang prowling the city streets in search of victims. Their leader would spot me and send his followers after me. They would chase me down a darkened alleyway and corner me. Then they would play with me and pass me around, roughly yanking up my skirt and baring me for the Easter whip. I'd struggle, but there would be too many of them. They'd whip me while I protested and pretended to hate it. My resistance would not go unpunished, of course.

Then I had imagined Ian with his own *pomlázka*, bending me over the railing of Charles Bridge, making me healthy and beautiful while startled tourists looked on with open mouths. Afterwards he could drag me back to the hotel and screw me silly. Or better still: invite the Czech guys along. They could take turns holding me down while they all had their way with me.

But damn him!

It had gone wrong from the start. Prague wasn't his idea of a holiday retreat. The macabre relics and gruesome history were too morbid for him. He thought the people unfriendly and their language barbaric.

Not me. I thrived in the dark wildness of the city, its eerie shades and shadows. And the language! There was something untamed and primitive, almost tribal, in those snarled clusters of consonants. It was rough and raw, just the way I liked my sex.

I'd been such a good girl when I was little. But my expensive boarding school education had made me rebel against all that Victorian correctness. And Petr, my Czech boyfriend at university, had cultivated my disdain for the pretty and polite – and taught me some of his language. He was also the one who had told me about the Easter custom.

Then I met Ian. He was a rare mix of coarseness and culture. Old money lavished on porn. His chiselled features reminded me of Sting and he had the erotic menace of a Hollywood villain – the one you'd choose over the hero.

The night we met he had stood behind me on the balcony at the Knightsbridge Hotel, tracing my spine with his finger, commenting in his West End accent that I wasn't wearing any knickers. I melted as he slid his hand up the inside of my thigh, telling me all the nasty things he was going to do to me when he got me back to his room. His presumption was exhilarating and irresistible. I skipped out on the Christmas party and spent the rest of the night exploring his body and letting him learn about mine. That had been only a few weeks ago.

Now he was here, in my favourite city, in my favourite hotel. It's called U Zlaté Studny, 'at the golden well'. A fabulous sixteenth-century corner house on Karlova, two hundred yards from Charles Bridge. It has painted beamed ceilings and an arched Gothic cellar. Utterly decadent. The kind of place where you could happily spend the whole holiday in bed and forget the tourist attractions. The hotel was the only thing he'd liked yet about Prague. Besides the beer. And we'd left a proper mess for the poor chambermaid every night so far.

I didn't understand. He was happy to do all manner of obscene things with me and to me. But he wouldn't do the one thing I wanted most. Why was the idea of spanking me such a turnoff?

The huge, sad castle of Kafka's nightmares rose from Hradcany on the far bank as I headed back into Staré Město, the Old Town. The familiar buildings didn't cheer me, though. I felt the eyes of the caryatids and gargoyles on me, mocking me. Even the stucco saints decorating the hotel looked scornful as I slunk past, not wanting to run into Ian. I'd stormed out of the breakfast room in a huff after his eye-rolling comment. It's a cardinal rule: you don't laugh at someone's kink. Ever.

I battled my way through the crowds, past the shops selling puppets and postcards and KGB hats. When I saw the asymmetrical spires of the Týn Church in the Old Town Square I began to cheer up. No one was going to ruin my Easter plans. I'd come here to be whipped, and whipped I would be. Ian could get stuffed.

I was tingling with anticipation. I had barely slept the night before. I had chosen my outfit carefully, though I knew I would probably freeze to death in it. My tartan skirt was indecently short, showing off my long legs. The slightest breeze would also show off my red silk knickers. I wasn't wearing a bra beneath my tight white shirt and the chill morning soon made that obvious. I was revelling in 'that naughty schoolgirl thing'.

All weekend the tourists had been buying Easter whips and waving them around as though they knew what to do with them. I waited and waited for Ian to ask me what they were for, but he never did. He probably assumed they were decorative, just some sort of weird folk art.

They make monster ones for display, but the traditional ones are about two or three feet long and made of eight woven switches. The *pomlázka* doesn't look like anything but a whip and I was baffled that Ian was so clueless and uncurious.

I couldn't help eavesdropping as a street vendor explained the custom to an American couple. The woman blanched, but her husband had a twinkle in his eye. I envied her. I thought it was funny that the guidebooks never warned female travellers about it. Trying to lure unsuspecting Westerners for their twisted games ... Kinky buggers.

The square was filling with people, a few carrying *pomlázky*, but no one with the sense of purpose I hoped to see. They were mostly tourists. Still, I smiled coquettishly at every whip-bearer I saw.

Everywhere there were stalls and stands and marquees, with locals selling their wares. The market was bustling with activity and noise. A band was setting up on a small stage in front of the church while horse-drawn carts clip-clopped past on the cobblestones.

There was a blacksmith pounding on an old-fashioned anvil by an open fire as people stood around watching. Some of his creations looked like S&M toys and I flirted with the idea of asking him to make me a pair of shackles.

I stood in front of the Jan Hus monument, appreciating it more without Ian's disdainful comments. Hus is a Czech national hero, a priest who was burned at the stake as a heretic in 1415.

'Grotesque,' was Ian's reaction. 'And the sculpture's too modern to be here, obscuring the baroque buildings.'

I muttered something about the forest and the trees, and decided not to show him the shrine to Jan Palach, who set himself on fire in protest at the Soviet occupation in the 60s. The Czechs are a passionate lot.

I also decided to skip my favourite day trip, to Kutná Hora and the fabulous ossuary at Sedlec. The crypt is festooned with bones and skulls, hanging in bizarre decorative arrangements. I giggled as I imagined what Ian would say about the massive bell-shaped piles of skulls and the Schwarzenberg coat of arms fashioned out of bones. There's even a chandelier that contains every bone in the human body.

Petr had dressed me up as a goth girl and molested me in the graveyard outside. I remembered how he twisted his hand in my back-combed hair, pulling my head back to bite my neck while his other hand crept up inside my black velvet shirt. I squirmed against him as he pinched the hard buds of my nipples. Then he reached down the front of my skirt and into my knickers, teasing me where I was wet and waiting. I wanted him to bend me over a tombstone and violate me right there. But we were rudely interrupted and chased away by a woman who accused us of profaning the sacred ground.

Ah, the good old days, I thought. Ian had seemed so promising.

I meandered round the square, feigning interest in trinkets and baubles. I stared admiringly at a stall full of handmade leather whips and riding crops, an advertisement if there ever was one. I even stopped to watch the hourly performance of the *orloj*, the fifteenth-century astronomical clock, as its mechanical apostles appeared in the window and bowed.

But no one approached me.

I expanded my hunting ground, searching the maze of mediaeval streets and alleyways that fed into the square. No takers. Finally, I returned to the square, frustrated. I sat down at a table in one of the outdoor cafés. A couple of English louts walked by, leering at my short skirt and bare legs. I ignored them.

All around me, nothing but bloody tourists. Where were the locals? They were so good at fleecing the tourists everywhere else. But they were missing a great trick here: all these cute foreign females to whip without fear of retribution. If the girls were offended, the men could merely shrug and say, 'Sorry. Is tradition in our country.'

Bugger.

'*Co se děje, slečno?*'

I jumped at the voice. There was a man standing in the shade just behind me. I sized him up instantly. He was everything I liked about Eastern European guys. He had a dancer's wiry, angular build. He was slightly unshaven, but not scruffy. And there was a hint of danger in his wolfish eyes. I wondered how long he had been standing there, watching me.

He'd asked me what was wrong; my disappointment must be obvious. '*Nic*,' I said, hoping I'd got the word right. 'Nothing's wrong. I'm fine. *Mám se dobře. A vy?*'

He smiled, showing me his sharp little teeth, perfect for nipping delicate bits. '*Dobře. A mluvíte dobře česky!*'

That made me laugh. No, I didn't speak good Czech. But I appreciated the compliment.

'*Děkuji*. Do you speak English? *Mluvíte anglicky?*' I never know which language you're supposed to ask that in.

'Happy Easter,' he said by way of reply. He had a thick, husky accent.

'*Veselé Velikonoce*,' I responded in kind.

He glanced down at the table. 'You are alone?'

Was I ever. I nodded.

Again that sly smile. Oh, he was cocky. He knew bloody well I wanted him to join me. I gestured at the chair across the table. '*Prosím*,' I said grandly.

But instead he sat in the chair next to me and suddenly I felt wanton, flirting blatantly with a stranger in a public square. But I just couldn't bring myself to feel guilty. Besides, the whorish feeling wasn't entirely unpleasant. Or unfamiliar.

He watched me, his dark eyes roaming over my face and body with brazen familiarity. The assessing gaze of one who knows exactly what he likes. I sensed he knew exactly what I liked too. I felt naked under his scrutiny. It kept me off balance and made him unpredictable. I was not in control.

'*Jak se jmenujete?*' he asked.

I hesitated, trying to think of a fake name. But

nothing sprang to mind, so I was forced to be honest. 'Fiona.'

He chuckled. 'You are not sure?'

I had to laugh too. 'No, I'm sure. Fiona.' I looked at him expectantly. 'And you?'

'Václav.'

I loved the way he said it. Vahts-luv. A growl and a purr. They say German is the language of authority, but nothing makes me want to submit quite like Czech. And my companion had a quiet, natural authority. The air of someone accustomed to being obeyed. 'A nice name,' I said, sincere. 'Very ... vampiric.'

His brow furrowed slightly. '*Prosím?*'

A chink in his armour. I shrugged. 'Sorry, I don't know the Czech word for it.'

He thought for a moment and then his eyes sparkled. 'Ah. You mean I am like *vampýr*.'

I looked down at the table, abashed.

He lifted my chin with his hand, looking into my face with perfect audacity.

I pressed my legs together, thrilling at his touch.

'No,' I murmured. 'I meant...' I didn't know what to say. But he clearly wasn't offended.

He laughed. 'No?' he echoed. 'In Czech you mean yes.'

That made me blush even more. It was so easy to slip up on that one. The Czech word for 'yes' is '*ano*', which Czechs often shorten to '*no*'. '*Ne*,' I said quickly. 'I meant *ne*.'

He seemed delighted to have discomfited me and I was never more relieved to see a waiter in my life.

'*Pivo*,' I said. I don't care much for beer, but the Czech Republic has the best beer in the world, so it always has to be tried.

'*Dvě piva*,' Václav interjected, holding up two fingers for my benefit.

I looked out across the square that swarmed with

people, savouring its noises. The blacksmith, still pounding iron into rings and chains. Squealing feedback from a microphone as the band began to warm up. A couple arguing animatedly in some Oriental language a few tables away.

The waiter appeared with our drinks.

I held up my glass. 'Well, cheers,' I said.

Václav clinked his glass against mine. '*Na zdraví!*'

I took a long drink.

'You have had whipping?' he asked suddenly.

I choked, spluttering beer all over myself as I turned scarlet. I had nearly forgotten. 'Um, no,' I murmured. '*Ne.*'

Václav looked thoughtful, then nodded and took another drink.

I did the same, gulping down half my glass.

'You know Easter tradition, yes?'

I decided to downplay my knowledge. 'Kind of. Well, I mean I've heard about it, but ...'

He leaned forward as though imparting a secret. 'You are looking for *pomlázka*,' he said in a low, conspiratorial tone.

I giggled like a shy teenager. Oh yes, I thought. I am looking for man with big *pomlázka*.

'Yes?' he prompted.

I took another drink to buy time. But it was hard to swallow with him studying me so intently. I suddenly wished his English wasn't so good, that we were having the conversation in Czech. Then I could claim I didn't understand. 'Yes,' I admitted. 'I heard about it and I was curious. But no one seems to be doing it.'

He sighed and sat back in his chair, staring at his empty glass. 'Is true. Is not common now. Not in the city.'

'Women hit back now?' I asked with a laugh.

But the waiter returned then and I shook my head when he asked if we wanted more.

Václav told him that we did.

'No, really, I –'

'No is yes,' he reminded me brightly.

'*Ne*,' I said firmly, trying not to smile. '*Děkuji*, but *ne*.'

But Václav turned to the waiter and said something in rapid Czech. The waiter grinned and replied, glancing at me. This definitely wasn't the 'service with a snarl' that Ian had complained about. Václav said something else, but all I caught was the word '*slivovice*' and the waiter was off to fetch it.

I couldn't believe it. 'It's too early,' I protested. 'I shouldn't drink during the day.'

'Is Easter,' he said. 'You must enjoy.'

That's what I'm afraid of, I thought. If you get me drunk I *will* enjoy! I stole a glance at his lap. His legs looked strong and muscular – a lap I could lie over. And his arms could hold me down with little effort. His hands looked rough and callused, the hands of someone used to hard work. Hands that could smack a girl's bottom quite effectively.

After a perfunctory check-in with my conscience I capitulated. Ian hadn't earned fidelity. 'OK.'

Václav beamed. I knew I had just agreed to more than a simple shot of brandy.

The *slivovice* loosened me up and I was nicely buzzed when Václav said, '*Tak. Je čas.*'

I played dumb. 'Time for what?'

He grinned and looked me in the eye. He didn't need to answer. He just gestured for me to follow. I did. He made his way purposefully to a vendor's stall. Several *pomlázky* stood in a bucket of water, soaking. I shuddered at the realisation: these were meant to be *used*.

Václav took his time, turning them around and

inspecting them as though selecting a fine wine. I could feel the heat pulsing in my groin. And suddenly I wanted to chicken out. It was like making it through the long queue to the roller coaster and then wanting to turn back. You know the ride will be spectacular. But climbing aboard is the hardest part.

He picked one and swished it through the air while I stood beside him, flushed and squirming. People were staring. And not just the tourists. I watched as he had a lengthy and serious discussion with the vendor. Both men cast glances in my direction as they talked, making me feel conspicuous in my slutty schoolgirl skirt. Their conversation was beyond my meagre vocabulary, but some of Václav's gestures needed no translation. It was obvious to everyone watching what was being discussed.

I blushed furiously, fidgeting where I stood. It felt like I was back at school, waiting nervously outside the headmaster's study, forced to endure the knowing gaze of passers-by. Only this was much worse.

At last Václav paid for the whip. As they say, be careful what you wish for. I assumed my rakish Bohemian would lure me into an alley and whip me. But that wasn't quite what he intended. Instead, he took me by the wrist and led me towards the centre of the square, just in front of the stage.

'Where are you...?' I started, then realised what he had in mind. 'Oh no, you can't be serious!'

He didn't speak; he just tightened his grip on my arm. I resisted, pulling away so that he practically had to drag me. I felt helpless and overpowered, though I knew there was no real danger. There were about a thousand people watching. Somehow that wasn't much comfort.

At the centre of the square he released me. I wasn't going anywhere. He smiled at me wolfishly, tapping the *pomlázka* against his palm. He said something in Czech, but I didn't understand. My cheeks were burning and I glanced around me at the crowd. The band had stopped playing.

Then he put his right foot up on a box and lifted me effortlessly over his knee, my feet well off the ground. I didn't fight him. It all seemed to happen in slow motion, like a dream I was powerless to control. I grabbed his trouser-leg for balance and he coolly raised my skirt. I whimpered, but there was nothing I could do. Not even when he pulled my knickers down. I was completely exposed. The cool April breeze touched my wetness and I shivered. Despite the chill I felt feverish. It was deathly silent all around us.

I felt his hand on my lower back, holding me in position, and before I could prepare myself there was a burst of fiery pain. I gasped and the *pomlázka* struck again.

Instinctively I kicked and tried to twist away, but my feet had no purchase. He held me down firmly and continued to whip me. I had waited a long time and come a long way for this experience and I didn't want him to stop. But I couldn't resist indulging a little fantasy of non-consent.

'Please,' I said breathlessly. 'No! No!'

He chuckled at that. 'No means yes,' he said archly.

Soft laughter behind me brought me back to the reality of the public display. No one interfered. No doubt they thought it was a performance put on for the tourists.

I encouraged him with exaggerated squeals and mock struggles, though the whipping was genuinely painful. It wasn't at all what I had imagined. It was better.

He pressed me down with more force and the sharp, stinging strokes fell harder and faster. I wrapped my arms around his leg, clutching him tighter with every stroke. I soon forgot all about the audience. Being helpless was intoxicating. I was completely at his mercy.

Then a strange thing happened. I suddenly found myself on the other side of the pain. I still felt the plaited switches lashing against my backside, but it no longer registered as pain. I perceived heat, but that was all. The slow-motion sensation returned and the strokes became languorous and sensual. I moaned and sighed as each bright flash drove the warmth deeper. The pain had become pleasure. I was flying.

I drifted in the bliss, only dimly aware of the pain.

Then someone somewhere was saying my name and I realised it was Václav. The whipping was over. He put me down again and I was too embarrassed to look at him.

But he said my name again and I raised my eyes. He held up the *pomlázka* and I saw that the tips of the switches were shredded. I blushed and reached back to touch my bottom. The pain returned as I felt the heat and imagined the bright red stripes criss-crossing my skin. I wondered what the audience had thought of the show. I couldn't bring myself to face them.

Václav watched with satisfaction as I pulled my knickers up and winced at the contact with my burning flesh. I smoothed my skirt down, still in a daze. Endorphins were bouncing around in my head and it was more intense than the best orgasm I could remember.

'You are OK?' Václav enquired solicitously.

'Uh-huh.'

'Good.'

With that he bent down and took hold of my legs, lifting me over his shoulder. I squealed in token protest, but he put a proprietary hand on my bottom and gave me a little swat. I yelped. Then he carried me away from the stage, fireman-style. The crowd parted for us like the Red Sea and I half expected a round of applause. No one leaped to my rescue; I clearly didn't want rescuing.

He took me down a side street and then into an alley flanked by large, dark buildings. Their shadows loomed above us, shielding us from prying eyes. He set me on my feet.

I was trembling, still high from the experience. My knickers were positively soaked and my sex was throbbing with desperation. I could see from the bulge in his trousers that he was in a similar state. As he looked at me hungrily I felt my mouth begin to water. Everything seemed heightened. Every nerve in my body was alive. The whipping had awakened senses I didn't know I had.

I flashed back to my gang-bang fantasy. Václav had been bold enough to drag me into the square and expose me and whip me, but would he be bold enough to take me here and now, in the alley? I wanted it. I wanted to resist and have him force me. The thought made me weak and the silence between us was becoming excruciating. He was watching me like a predator. Waiting for the kill. The first move would have to be mine.

I took a step back. Back towards the street that led to the square. *Take me.*

He took a step forward, the corners of his mouth turning up slightly. It was obvious he knew what I wanted. He was playing with me.

My breathing was shallow and my heart pounded in my chest. I took another step and made as if to turn, to leave.

In a flash he seized my wrist. I jumped, startled and exhilarated.

'No,' I whispered, deliberately.

Václav turned me slowly until he was behind me. He caught my other wrist and pinned them both together behind my back. Then he pushed me forward, against the wall, pressing himself against my bottom.

'No means yes,' he growled.

I went limp in his arms, closing my eyes as arousal flooded in me, threatening to drown me. My need was as intense as the whipping had been and it was all I could do not to beg him to take me. But he was the one in control, not me. And he would do it his way. I wanted him to.

He raised my skirt again and squeezed my tender bottom. I moaned at the pain. My knickers surrendered to him again as he slipped his hand inside the waistband and yanked. The delicate silk tore easily and a convulsive shiver ran through me. His fingers explored the dewy crease and I writhed against them, urging them inside.

At last I heard his zip as he released himself. I felt his hardness between my cheeks and he took me in one violent thrust that made me cry out. He was still holding my wrists. I was completely defenceless.

I cried out again, louder this time. And again, he knew exactly what I wanted. He covered my mouth with his other hand, pulling me close to him as he pounded into me from behind.

With his hand over my mouth I had the freedom to be as noisy as I wanted. I screamed, relishing the primal release as he ravished me. His thrusts slammed me against the dirty wall again and again. The friction of the bricks against my nipples was pushing me over the edge. I never knew it was possible to feel so liberated and wanton.

Václav had known me from the start. Like the perfect tango partner forcefully leading me through the dance, he knew exactly where I wanted to go. He leaned in close to my ear and whispered with wicked affection, '*Děvka.*' Whore. I melted. My legs were like water as he said nasty things to me in Czech and I trembled at the words I recognised. '*Coura.*' Slut. Oh yes, this was the language for talking dirty.

I struggled just to make him tighten his grip, letting him know I liked it rough. He snarled at me not to fight him and I closed my eyes, abandoning myself to the exquisite torture as he took what he wanted.

I screamed into his hand as I felt my own climax overtake me. But he didn't release me. He kept me prisoner, forcing himself deeper and deeper. He pushed himself up inside me as hard as he could, staying there until I felt the spasms of his climax. His cheek was pressed to mine, scratching me like sandpaper as his orgasm began to ebb.

At last he released me and I had to lean against the wall for support. My wrists ached and my mouth burned from the pressure of his hand. I felt well and truly debauched. For a moment I was afraid to meet his eyes, ashamed of my pleasure.

But he gently pulled my hands away from my face and made me look at him. He was grinning.

I didn't know what to say. It was incomparable. I had the sudden sense that nothing in my life could ever be as good as this.

Nearly a minute passed in a silence that was anything but awkward. We were both short of breath as we adjusted our clothing. The front of my white shirt was stained with grit from the wall. My knickers were ruined. I shook my head in amazement as I took them off and looked at them.

Václav stood watching me. He had retrieved the *pomlázka* from the ground and now he held it towards me, offering. Expectant.

I remembered the rest of the ritual. 'I don't have a

ribbon,' I said coquettishly. 'But you can have these.' I displayed my torn knickers.

He smiled approvingly. Blushing, I tied them to the ragged end of the *pomlázka*.

I couldn't help but wonder what Ian would say when he saw the marks.

# Magic Fingers Sylvia Day

'Does that feel good?' he purred in a voice soaked in sexual intent.

Alison buried her face in the mattress and groaned. Strong, masculine fingers kneaded the length of her spine with blatant skill until the pleasure was almost too much, her body vibrating with sensations that radiated outward from his touch and pooled in her core.

She fought off the overwhelming urge to give in to an orgasm while, against her will, her back arched into his palms.

'You're so responsive,' he murmured. 'The slightest movement of my hands and your body replies.'

Her insides melted at the approval in his tone. She wanted to roll over, to have those hands caress her breasts, pinch her nipples. Lord, how she loved to have her breasts played with and they were heavy now, swollen in anticipation of his attention. Her nipples strained, peaked hard and waiting for the clasp of his fingertips.

'A little harder?' he queried, his deep, rumbling voice promising untold carnal delights. 'A little faster? A little deeper?' His wicked mouth dropped lower. 'Tell me what you need, Alison ... what you want, so I can give it to you.'

She shivered. She wanted to tell him to dip those magic fingers between her legs, rub her, stroke inside her, make her come.

But she couldn't say those things.

Her body didn't care though, and her legs parted anyway, in silent invitation.

His hands slid down and cupped her bare buttocks, kneading them. She groaned. He was killing her. She would die if he didn't take her. Right now.

His lips brushed her ear. 'Time's up,' he whispered.

Her hands clenched into fists and she wanted to cry. Five days of torture. She had to be a masochist.

Alison sat up, not bothering to hold the towel to her full breasts. What did it matter? She wouldn't be seeing him again.

His breath caught in his throat.

She looked up quickly and for an instant she imagined lust hidden in the azure blue of his intense gaze. And then there was nothing but a professional, impersonal smile as he handed her the thick terrycloth robe with the resort's logo embroidered on the front.

She shook her head ruefully as she slid off the massage table and covered herself. Wishful thinking. It went hand in hand with the torrid fantasies she'd been having at night.

'Thank you, James.' She managed a smile, even though her entire body ached with unfulfilled desire. 'It's been a pleasure.' She moved towards the door.

'See you tomorrow, Alison.'

She turned and tried to make her mouth curve again, but couldn't. She drank him in one last time, thirsting for him. He was tall, dark, built like a warrior and with the gentle hands of an angel. Dark, thick brown hair fell over a strong brow, framing beautiful eyes the colour of the ocean just outside the door. He was gorgeous, every inch of him, from the austerely masculine beauty of his face to the sculpted body built for pleasure.

'I won't be seeing you again,' she informed him. 'I'm checking out tomorrow.'

He arched a brow, clearly surprised. 'Oh. I didn't know.' He paused, as if he were waiting for something. The moment stretched out, becoming uncomfortable.

She wanted to touch him, just once, just to see what he felt like, just for the thrill of it. She wanted to bury her face in his throat and smell the scent of his skin. She wanted to lick him, all over.

She wanted. Badly.

'Goodbye,' she choked out miserably as she fled the room.

Alison sat at her lonely table at the outdoor buffet and pushed grilled tilapia and fresh pineapple around her plate with a fork. The meal was delicious, but she couldn't eat. Her gaze lifted and moved leisurely over the multitude of diners, the tempting aroma of delicacies from every continent and some favorite local dishes drifting over her in the tropical breeze.

It was dusk, the deep orange of the sun sinking into the clear blue of the Jamaican water. She looked off the patio to the private beach below. It was empty now, but during the day it was packed with travellers, some of whom she'd convinced to come here.

In appreciation for the amount of traffic her travel agency brought to the resort, the general manager regularly sent her free vouchers. Usually she gave them away during promotions she ran to advertise her business. This year, feeling restless, she'd decided to come to the resort herself, to live a little.

'Isn't James divine?' cooed a throaty feminine voice just beyond her right shoulder. 'I could eat him alive.'

'Definitely,' agreed the voice's companion. 'The best thing about this resort is that yummy masseur. I'd have five appointments a day if they'd let me.'

The throaty voice dropped conspiratorially. 'I slipped him my spare room key today.'

'Carla!' her friend exclaimed in astonishment. 'You didn't!'

'I did,' Carla replied smugly. 'He seemed especially hot for it today. And I'm hot to give it to him.'

Alison sighed miserably and pushed her plate away. She'd first heard about James from a similar conversation a week ago. Then she'd heard the same story replayed over and over again. Breakfast, lunch and dinner, female guests at the resort raved about the to-die-for masseur with the sinful voice and blessed hands. After two days, she'd made an appointment for a massage. And after two minutes with James she'd been drowning in lust. He certainly had a rare gift.

Like an addict, she'd returned to the small hut every day of her holiday for another hour of his sweet torment. She'd kept hoping her desire would ease, but instead it had only grown worse until now she was permanently turned on, her body achingly prepped for sex. Even her vibrator could not ease her need for James, hot and hard, thrusting into her.

She was leaving the next morning and she'd never see him again. She was already experiencing the withdrawal symptoms.

Alison rose from her chair and headed towards the bar.

In her fantasies, she believed she was the only one James talked to in a sexually suggestive manner. She imagined that he was hot for her and her alone. That he waited as eagerly for their appointments as she did, and that he relished the opportunity to touch her bare skin and knead away her troubles.

In reality, she discerned from eavesdropping that James talked to all the female guests as if they were his next sexual conquest. She was nothing special; he treated her no different.

Leaning against the bar, she ordered a Red Stripe with a shot of Appleton. Downing the shot, she took the beer and strolled out to the beach to watch the sun set. Even at night the air was warm, the breeze a light caress. Alison closed her eyes and took a deep breath.

She wasn't the type of woman who had one-night stands, but she'd have one with James. She wondered if it was loneliness that made her so susceptible to indulging in her fantasy of sex with a stranger. She'd spent a week in a foreign country, alone. A quiet person by nature, she wasn't good at making friends and so had hardly spoken a word to anyone in the last seven days. She'd thought it would be relaxing after the never-ending phone calls she dealt with at work.

It wasn't relaxing. It was boring. And lonely.

Finishing her beer, Alison turned and walked back to the hotel. She slid her keycard into the lock and stepped into her room. Being on the second floor, she'd felt safe keeping the windows open. She wrinkled her nose when she saw that the maid had closed the sliding glass door and drawn the blackout curtains. When the door shut behind her, she was plunged into darkness. She moved towards the bed and the light next to it.

'Would I be wrong in thinking you want me to fuck you?'

She stilled in shock as the deeply sexual voice curled around her in the obsidian room. She went from tingling arousal to raging desire in the space of one shuddering breath.

'James?' she whispered. She sensed movement in the darkness, but heard nothing.

'Would I be wrong, Alison?' he asked again.

She swallowed hard, her hands clenching into fists. 'No.'

He sighed. Then she heard movements, sounds of

him disrobing, baring his luscious body. She could scarcely breathe. With shaking hands, she reached for the lamp.

'Don't,' he murmured as if he could see her.

'Why?'

'You'll feel me better if your sense of sight is diminished.'

Her hand fluttered to her throat. *Feel him.* 'I want to admire your body.'

'Next time,' he promised in a rumbling caress of sound.

She sank on to the edge of the bed, her buckling knees no longer supporting her. *Next time.*

He'd take all night making love to her, she knew. He was just that kind of man, potently virile. She heard the tear of a foil packet and the sound of latex stretching. She could barely think, her imagination running away from her.

He came to her unerringly in the darkness, sinking to his knees before her. Laying his head in her lap, his breath left his lungs in a rush as her palms settled on his shoulders. She flexed her fingers, feeling his taut muscles and warm skin. With her fingertips she urged his chin upward. Then she bent forward to bury her face in the curve of his neck as she'd longed to do for days.

'Alison.' Her name floated through the room on a pained whisper. 'Damn you.'

She stilled, her tongue pressed against the salty column of his throat, unsure of what she had done to anger him. At her hesitation, he pulled her to the floor.

With his heated hands on her thighs and endless patience, he pushed her short sundress upward with painful slowness, kneading the skin he exposed.

'What have I done?' she asked breathlessly, her hands fisting into the carpet as he stoked her arousal.

His mouth dropped to her thigh and pressed a hot, open-mouthed kiss there. Her eyes slid closed as she gave up the effort to see him. He lifted her leg and tongued the hollow behind her knee. She shivered.

'You were going to leave,' he growled, his hot breath gusting across the sensitive skin of her inner thigh. 'After five days of torturing me with your body, allowing me to touch you without truly touching you, you were going to leave without having my cock in you.'

Her eyes flew open and she arched upward into his mouth, unbearably aroused by his blunt speech. 'James.'

'I couldn't ask you,' he said in a groan, his mouth moving upward. 'If I was wrong about the signals you were sending, if you complained, I'd be in deep shit.'

Her hands came up and her fingers shifted through his silky hair, massaging his scalp. 'You asked,' she pointed out.

'Because you didn't. And time was running out.' He spread her thighs and tongued her through her damp thong. From deep in his throat came gratifying sounds of pleasure. 'God, I knew you'd be ready for me.' He nuzzled her with his face. With a harsh tug, he tore the skimpy piece of lace away and buried his mouth in her wetness.

Her orgasm wasn't far off. Five days of foreplay and fantasy and repeated sessions with her vibrator had kept her on the edge of a powerful climax. As his tongue entered her with obvious skill, her body tensed expectantly. It was too much – the combination of the anticipation, his pursuit and the culmination of her fantasies all at once.

'I don't do these things,' she gasped. 'I don't have sex with people I don't know.'

In response, his mouth surrounded her clitoris and sucked. Hard.

Her climax hit her with full force, tearing through

her body, shuddering against his mouth, pouring over his tongue.

She was still spasming when he rose and kneeled before her, drawing her legs across his thighs. With his hands on her hips, he lifted her up and pulled her slowly on to his erection. Oversensitised from the power of her orgasm, her body resisted his entry, but he pressed forward inexorably.

To her surprise and delight, he was built beautifully all over. In her fantasies, she'd made him superiorly well endowed. In reality, he was. All of her life, her sex partners had been average in size. James was anything but. She writhed on the floor as he filled her, taking his time, making her feel every inch.

'Does that feel good?' he asked when she moaned long and loud. He flexed his hips and sunk in further.

'You know it does,' she whispered hoarsely.

'Did you dream of this, Alison?' He pumped in and out twice, drugging thrusts that stroked all the right places. 'I did.'

Alison was startled by the admission. Was he telling the truth? Did he do these things, say these things, to other guests?

As he began a slow, steady, expert fucking, she found she didn't care. Not right now. He could have been with the willing Carla. Instead, he'd taken a risk on her.

He paused, keeping her impaled while his strong, well-worked hands slid under her dress, down her torso, and cupped her breasts.

'Yesss,' she hissed with pleasure.

James chuckled. 'Tell me what you need, Alison,' he coaxed. 'Tell me how to please you, tell me what you like.'

His magic fingers plucked at the aching points, twisting them, tugging them. 'I can feel the pulling of your nipples on my cock,' he whispered, flexing inside her in response. 'I knew it would be like this, you're so responsive.'

She arched into his palms, into his penis. 'Only for you.'

He groaned and, holding her tits in his hands, he resumed his thrusting. And deep inside, the heat curled. Hot and heavy, spreading outward until she was inundated with sensation.

James's heavy breathing thrilled her, his convulsive grip on her breasts excited her, his appreciative murmurs pleasured her, and through it all, her fantasies satisfied her. Her pussy clenched – once, twice. She tried to hold it off, tried to make it last.

'Don't,' he grunted, tweaking her nipples. 'I've already waited long enough.' One of his hands reached between their legs, his thumb pressing against where they joined, feeling himself sliding into her. His fingers rested over her clit, rubbing against it with every downward stroke. With a low moan, she came, convulsing around his invading hardness until he joined her, flooding her with burning heat.

'Come on, Alison,' he murmured, as he tucked her closer into his side. 'Let's go for a walk.'

She whimpered, half asleep and afraid to move. Afraid to find out it was all a dream. 'Don't want to,' she grumbled.

'I hope you don't think I'm done. After five days of teasing, I'm just getting started.'

Her head turned towards his, trying vainly to see him, and his firm lips connected with hers. A kiss.

He kissed like he made love, with expert awareness and casual skill. With a tilt of his head, he altered the angle, granting him deeper access for the velvet stroking of his tongue. Alison moaned into his mouth, instantly awake and vibrantly aroused.

Everything was so new to her. She didn't do things like this; she didn't attract men who looked like James.

She pulled back slightly. 'Is there anything you don't do well?' she asked and felt his smile curve against her mouth.

He stood and pulled her up with him. Reaching down, he gathered up her dress and pulled it over her head. 'Did you think about me fucking you, Alison, when I massaged your body?'

'Yes,' she admitted. 'All the time.'

He reached for his shorts and she felt the heavy weight of his erection brush against her leg. When he stood, she wrapped her hands around it.

'How did I take you?' he asked in a choked voice as she stroked him softly, gently.

'Every way.'

He groaned as she tightened her grip.

'But I could always see you.'

His hand at her wrist stilled her movements. 'When we get outside you can see as much of me as you want.'

Her hands brushed along his ribs, admiring his lean strength as he dressed. 'Hurry.'

James straightened and bent forward, his wicked tongue swirling around the shell of her ear before dipping inside. She shivered with longing, ready to feel him inside her again. But he laced his fingers with hers and tugged her towards the door.

They moved with haste through the hotel, staying in the shadows when possible until they reached the private beach.

In the darkness the water was black, rippling with moonlight and soothing as it lapped rhythmically against the shore. All along the coast, the twinkling lights of various resorts competed with the brilliant stars above. It was beautiful, simply breathtaking, and a sight she would have missed if James hadn't come for her.

A fence bisected the beach, separating the resort from the public area beyond. James led her into the warm water, taking her around the barrier. He pulled her away from the place where he was an employee and she was a guest to an area where they were no more than lovers enjoying the magic of the Caribbean.

He turned to her, all moonlit beauty, a Roman statue's physical perfection come to life.

'Why me?' she couldn't help asking.

He shrugged and drew her closer, into his arms. He threw the question back at her. 'Why me?'

Before she could answer, he reached for her breast, palming it, squeezing it, robbing her of thought.

'Alison. Tell me about your fantasies. Everything.'

The gentle waves surged softly around them as she flushed in embarrassment. She wasn't like him. She didn't know how to speak so bluntly and not sound stupid. 'This is a fantasy.' She gestured with her hand to the view around them. 'This night. This place. You.' She brushed her fingertips over his lips. 'Most especially you.'

He sank slowly beneath the waves pulling her with him until they sat in the shallow water and the warmth of the Jamaican ocean washed over their chests. Her dress clung to her breasts, the nipples hard with desire, and he concentrated all his attention on them. Just the way she liked. Men didn't seem to pay as much attention to breasts any more. But James did. Floating, she wrapped her legs around his waist.

'God, I love the way you respond to my touch.' He

tugged her nipples and chuckled when she shivered. 'I could do anything to you, couldn't I? You'd let me do whatever I wanted.'

She moaned, her body on fire.

He lowered his head to her breast, sucking with such force it was almost painful. Gently, he chewed on her nipple through the wet cotton then laved away the sting like a cat with cream.

'Take me to the beach,' she begged. 'Fuck me with your fingers.'

He stood, lifting her easily, and moved on to the beach. 'I bet you don't normally talk like that either, do you?'

Alison turned her head and looked at the resort. Palm trees swayed softly in the evening breeze and the soft strains of reggae floated in the air. It was enchanting. 'Maybe it's this island. But I think it's just you and your magic fingers.'

'Magic fingers,' he murmured, laying her down beyond the surf. 'I like it.' His splayed fingertips moved down from her breasts and tickled her ribcage. He slid down until he lay on his belly in the sand. Urging her thighs apart, he lifted her dripping dress and exposed her to his gaze.

She lay completely exposed while he pleasured her, tasting with his tongue. He was so unabashedly fascinated with the female body and she realised then why he was so successful at making women feel so desirable. It was not the individual woman who appealed to him, but womankind as a whole.

The blunt tip of a finger paused at her opening and she lifted her hips in invitation.

'Breathe in,' he ordered. When she did, her body sucked the finger inside. Stroking, caressing, he studied her intimately. 'I've wanted to do this for days.' Then he pressed against a secret spot inside her and she jerked in stunned amazement. 'There it is,' he purred in satisfaction and stroked her again. She cried out in pleasure.

'Ah, Alison. I want to touch you all over, fuck you everywhere, hear all the sounds you make.'

'Yes,' she pleaded, falling for his magic touch and sex incarnate voice. It was forbidden, sex with a stranger. Just the thought made her want to come all over his hand.

'All those sessions in the hut,' he whispered. 'Hearing you moan, feeling your body flex and arch under my touch, I almost came in my pants every time. No one's ever been able to arouse me without touching me, without even trying.'

Two fingers entered her, stroking deep inside, moving slowly.

'I'm going to drink all this cream when I'm done, Alison. Will you like that?'

She moaned, riding the edge, so close, hovering. He kept her there deliberately, enjoying her tension, her helplessness.

'Will you like it?' he repeated.

He was torturing her. Well, she could torture right back. 'Almost as much as I'll like drinking you.'

With a groan, his fingers plunged faster. She begged and cursed, bucking up against his hands, loving the feel of being filled and pleasured by his magic fingers. She'd known it would feel like this, wanted his touch, deep inside her. Her hands reached up, pinching her nipples. Lost in the beauty of the island and an attentive man, she came against his hand to the sounds of his low-voiced encouragement.

She woke to sunlight on her face. Her body ached all over, her muscles sore and unwilling to move, still languid with pleasure. Looking at the pillow beside her, she saw that James was gone. She sighed in disappointment. She'd wanted to look at him one last time before she left. Wanted one full lingering look at the hard body that was in such amazing shape it rendered the man tireless.

He'd made love to her all night, just as he'd promised. She hadn't thought it possible that a man could remain hard that long or fill her with desire so many times. She hadn't known a man could talk like he did, with a mesmerising voice and devilish words.

She hadn't known it could hurt so bad to say goodbye to a stranger.

It took her an hour to get into the shower and an hour more to get packed. Despite these delays, it was still all too soon that she stood at the checkout desk and looked over her bill. It was much, much less than it should have been and it took her less than an instant to discover why. In the column of totals, the five massages balanced out to zero.

She stared the paper, her hands shaking. James had whispered, only hours ago, that he should have paid her for the privilege of touching her. She'd thought they were just words, sultry seduction. After all, who'd pay to touch her? But he'd been serious.

Dazed, she signed the register and, before she lost her courage, pulled out her business card and laid it on the counter.

'Please see that James, the masseur, receives this. He expressed an interest in travelling.'

The pretty Jamaican girl behind the counter offered a knowing smile and turned to the small cubicles that lined the wall behind her. She slipped the card in the box labelled 'James' – along with the other dozen that rested there.

Alison smiled sadly and slipped on her sunglasses. There were a few moments left before the shuttle came to take her away from paradise. She moved to the bar and ordered a daiquiri, relishing that tartly sweet taste of strawberries as she strolled to the beach. She kicked off her shoes and stepped on to the sand, her gaze moving past the multitude of sunbathers to the public beach beyond.

Was it only last night that she'd stood in this very spot and wished for a little less loneliness?

She bit the tip of her straw and looked at the massage hut. At this very moment James was working. His hands were gliding over another woman's back, his velvety voice was murmuring coaxing words like a lover would.

The sun beat down and festive music played from the speakers hidden in the palm trees. Guests laughed and enjoyed their holiday. Life went on.

Alison finished her drink and left the empty glass on the bar. It was time to go home.

'You look like you need another holiday.'

Alison looked up from her desk and managed a smile. 'Too much work to do.'

Kathy, her assistant, arched a brow. 'I thought a break would do you good, but you look worse off than when you left.'

She felt worse off. She'd been back at work almost a month now, but it would obviously take longer to get back into the swing of things.

'You look like you haven't slept in days.'

She hadn't. Every time she crawled into bed she thought of James, hard at work with his magic fingers, the Jamaican shore just outside while an aroused woman drowned in the pleasure of his touch.

A hundred times over she wished she'd been more bold, more of a vixen. He'd worked so hard on her, pleasuring her body endlessly, asking nothing in return.

She'd loved every moment of it, had thought she would die from the rapture of it. But if she could go back, if she could do it all over again, *she'd* take *him*. She'd pleasure him mindless. She could spend days worshipping his beautiful body.

Impatient fingers snapped in front of her face. 'Hello? Alison?'

Startled, she snapped out of her reverie. 'What?'

'Sleep,' Kathy reiterated. 'You need some sleep.'

'I'm fine. Just a little tense,' she lied, feeling more so after the arousing mental images she'd just sifted through.

'You need a massage,' purred the deeply masculine voice from the doorway.

Kathy swung round quickly, blocking her view. But Alison didn't need to see to know who it was. Her breath caught.

'Hi,' Kathy called with a come-hither lilt to her voice.

'Hi,' he said softly. 'I just leased the space next door. Thought I'd drop by and introduce myself to my new neighbours.'

Kathy stepped forward, hand outstretched. 'Kathy Martin, travel agent extraordinaire.'

He shook her hand. 'James Mitchell, masseur.'

'Wow. I love massages.' Kathy turned, her eyes wide, obviously smitten. 'This is my boss, Alison.'

Alison pushed back from the desk, her heart racing, her palms sweating. She stepped around Kathy and halted, arrested by the sight of him. Dressed in loose, low-slung jeans and a tight black T-shirt, he was luscious and way too hot to handle.

'I can't believe you're here,' she whispered, afraid to move in case she woke up before they had sex.

His mouth curved wickedly as he moved towards her. His aqua gaze raked her blazer and sundress appreciatively. He stopped a mere inch away, close enough to feel the heat from his skin. He reached down and laced his fingers with hers. 'I thought I'd offer my new neighbour a free massage.'

She melted at his first touch, turned on just from the scent of him – a heady combination of sex and desire.

'I'm game!' Kathy pitched in.

James chuckled, the warm, rich sound making her nipples ache. His gaze never left hers. 'Stop by in a couple of hours.'

'A couple of hours?' Kathy repeated, finally catching on to the sexual tension that sweltered around them. 'Wow!'

'That's not my usual,' he murmured. 'Alison's special.'

She stared up into his gorgeous face, stunned.

'Ouch!' he muttered with a frown. 'You pinched me.'

'I wanted to see if you were real,' she confessed. 'You're awfully dreamy.'

He laughed and then bent low, his mouth brushing her ear. 'Would I be wrong in thinking you want me to fuck you? Right now?'

'James!' She shivered.

'Would I be wrong, Alison?' he asked again, his shoulder brushing against her hardened nipple, his tongue swiping her earlobe.

She swallowed hard and clutched his hand. 'Yes.'

He paused and arched a brow. 'Really?'

'*I* want to fuck *you*.' And she wasn't embarrassed to say it.

He grinned with approval. 'Let's go.'

# Rocky Mountain Rendezvous
Kimberly Dean

The sunset was gorgeous. Jenna relaxed into her lounger and shielded her eyes as the sun dipped low in the sky. At such a sharp angle, her sunglasses were practically useless. Still, she couldn't make herself look away. The sky was alive with streaks of oranges, purples and pinks. The remaining yellow rays bounced off the choppy surface of the lake, making it appear as if thousands of diamonds bobbed on the surface. She was tempted to reach out and grab one before they all disappeared.

Which would be soon.

She glanced at her watch for what had to be the hundredth time and sighed. 'Hurry up, Shane.'

Once the sun slipped behind the peaks that surrounded Indigo Lake, the sky would fade and the water would grow dark. If he didn't hurry, he was going to miss the whole thing. You couldn't see a sunset like this in the city. She knew, because the view from the dock was one of her favourites. She'd rented this cabin just so she could share it with him.

So where was he? She was starting to get worried.

*And frustrated.*

She shifted on her lounger, glancing around timidly. She'd driven up here early to take advantage of the afternoon rays and, as always, tanning had made her horny. As inconspicuously as possible, she rubbed the toes of her right foot against her left shin, supposedly fighting an itch. And she was. Only it was higher. Much higher, and rubbing her legs together did nothing to ease her distress.

In vain, she ground her bottom harder against the cheap plastic chair.

Tanning always did this to her. She loved to strip down to a bikini. She adored feeling the sun's rays caress her curves, her dips, and whatever secret creases they could find. This afternoon had been no different. The skimpy cut of her new red bikini had let the sunshine touch her all over. Her skin was warm, oiled, and tanned to a golden brown. Her body radiated heat from the inside out, and a tiny pool of sweat had collected in her navel. She wiped it away. She didn't need it to remind her that she was slick all over.

Whistles from a boat of fishermen nearly an hour ago had left her that way.

You're going to regret it if you don't get here soon, lover boy, she thought. The sunset wasn't the only thing Shane was going to miss. Her body was humming. Much longer and she'd take care of things herself.

She glanced again at the horizon. She hoped he was at least on his way. The winding mountain roads could be difficult to follow after dark – if he wasn't lost already. Indigo Lake was only about an hour-and-a-half drive from Denver, but the turnoff was easy to miss. This was Shane's first visit. Once a person got away from the noise, lights, and traffic, it seemed like a different world.

That was precisely why she liked it so much.

'Well, poop.'

She didn't know what to do. Cell phone reception up here was iffy at best, and she'd already left three messages on his work phone; one to tell him she was leaving, another to tell him she'd made it safely, and a third to ask where he was. Besides, she knew he wasn't still at the office.

He couldn't be that stupid.

She frowned grumpily. His work habits were the reason she'd pushed for this getaway in the first place. Plain and simple, Shane worked too hard. She knew he was in the middle of a big project, but the hours he'd put in on it were ridiculous. She wasn't a high maintenance girlfriend, but she'd warned him he'd better start showing a little more attention. Or else.

Was it really that hard to buy her some flowers, candy, or maybe say ... *get his cute butt up to the lake so they could enjoy a weekend together?*

His cute, tight butt ... 'Mmm,' she murmured.

OK, so maybe she'd give him the benefit of the doubt. Besides, she wasn't in the mood to let anything spoil what had been a wonderful, relaxing day.

She swung her legs off the lounger and stood up. The diamonds had left the lake and it was starting to take on its indigo cast. She pushed her feet into her flip-flops, tied her sarong low on her waist, and grabbed her watered-down glass of lemonade. The wooden dock creaked as she walked back to the shoreline.

She pushed her sunglasses onto the top of her head as she headed across the grass to their rented cabin. Just the sight of it made her happy. The simple, one-roomed, log structure spoke of a simpler time, although she much appreciated the luxuries of electricity and indoor plumbing. She'd found this place when her company had held a business retreat. The main house hosted conferences, but it was these rustic out-of-the-way cabins that kept her coming back. Some had lake access, while others were tucked away in the pine trees that grew thick around the lake. With as warm as the weather had been, she'd chosen this one so she and Shane could take a dip in the lake if they wanted.

Apparently, it was going to have to be a moonlight swim.

Which, come to think of it, could be even more fun.

A devilish smile spread across her face. She couldn't help it. Being outdoors like this filled her with energy and made her feel adventurous. Besides, a little hanky panky in the lake would be the perfect way to deal with the after effects of her tanning session. She could still feel ripples running through her body. Each step she took made her sarong brush against her legs, and her nipples tightened in response. She bit her lower lip. Hanky panky was so much better with two.

The door to the cabin groaned as she opened it and stepped inside. She hesitated, though, when she heard the rumbling of a vehicle. She concentrated on the sound, but it wasn't Shane's BMW; that thing ran like a clock. She glanced across the room to the phone on the bedside table and saw the red light blinking. That was probably him, though. She set her glass down so quickly that lemonade sloshed onto the table. Wouldn't you know it? She'd been out there trashing his good name, and she'd missed his call.

She hurried to the phone, but the noise from the vehicle outside grew louder. She scowled as she accessed the message box. What was it with men and their big trucks? Did they need to compensate that badly? That din was going to scare away all of nature's little bunnies, squirrels and birds.

'Hey, sweetheart. It's me.'

She concentrated on the call, but the noise of the engine became louder and she had to plug her ear to hear.

'Please don't be mad. You know I hate to do this to you.'

Do what? Her eyes narrowed. Oh, he wouldn't dare. The vehicle outside rumbled like a freight train, and she turned her back on it. She needed to hear this.

'I've run into a bit of trouble getting out of here.'

Out of the office? She let out a feral growl. She was going to strangle him with her bare hands.

And maybe she'd practise on the redneck driving that monster truck!

'Zip it, would you?' She flipped back the curtain on the window as the crunch of tyres on gravel became louder. Was he intending to drive right over her cabin?

The light was getting dim, but relief spread through her when she recognised the vehicle. It was Shane – only he was in Shawn's 4X4.

Car trouble. She let out a laugh. Here she'd been ready to string him up and the poor boy had had car trouble.

A silly grin spread across her face. She knew that shouldn't make her happy, but it did. She hung up the phone and hurried out the back door. Shane was just stepping out of the big truck into the shadows beneath a pine tree. The hazy light didn't stop her from seeing the layer of mud on the monstrosity he drove. Her nose curled. For as much as his brother loved that truck, you'd think he'd wash it more often.

'Jenna, I'm sorry,' he called as he slammed the door shut. He rounded the truck, but came to a dead stop when he saw what she was wearing. 'Whoa. Damn. You look –'

She planted her hands on her hips to let him see his fill. His eyes nearly bugged out his head, and she stifled a laugh. Oh, she was going to have some fun with this. 'Better make it good.'

He looked at her dumbly. 'What?'

'I've been waiting for you all afternoon.' Teasingly, she ran her finger down her breastbone into her cleavage. 'You need make it up to me for being so late, mister.'

His gaze zeroed in on her breasts. '*I* need to make it up to you? Didn't you get a message?'

Jenna felt the hum return to her body. He was practically salivating. Still, he stood twenty feet away with his hands stuffed into the pockets of his well-worn jeans. Poor baby. He thought he was in trouble. She decided to turn up the heat.

'I was just listening to it as you pulled up, but it was a little hard to hear.' She quit toying with the string that held her bikini top together and pointed at the 4X4. 'Car trouble, I understand, but did you have to borrow that thing from your brother?'

His head turned slowly towards the truck. He waited a half-beat before turning a mischievous smile on her. A delicious shiver ran through her as he sauntered towards her. When he stood only a breath away, he cocked his head and looked over her lustily. 'I did if I wanted to get up here – and I did.'

Darn it, he'd turned the tables on her. He was the one who was supposed to be squirming. She tilted her head back to look up at him. 'I'm still waiting.'

Boldly he reached out and tweaked her nipple. 'You look sexy, sassy ... and horny as hell.'

Oh, God. That tweak had shot right to her core. She couldn't take it any more. She lunged at him. 'You're right about that.'

'Ooof!' he said on a sharp exhale as he caught her.

She'd jumped right up into his arms, wrapping her arms and legs about him like vines. He was tall. She shimmied up further, loving the friction of his clothes against her nearly naked body, and covered his lips with a kiss. 'Apologise, slow poke – and be creative about it.'

His arms automatically came around her, and his roguish grin widened. 'Will a slow poke do?'

'What do you think?' She brushed her mouth against his again. This time he was ready. The kiss he gave her was so sexy and intimate, her toes curled and her flip-flops smacked against her heels.

Damn, she should have lured him out here sooner. He was different out in the wild – tougher, almost brutish. He was wearing jeans, boots, and a T-shirt – not his normal business suit – and she liked it. A lot. His musky scent blended with the smell of pine in the air, and it made her feel a little untamed. She kissed the side of his neck and found his pulse pounding. 'I was worried, you know. I thought you were in a ditch somewhere or lost on the side of a mountain.'

'Get real. When have you known me to get lost?'

'Duh. Like every other week.'

'Oh . . . uh, yeah. Well, I'm here now.'

'Good thing.' She nuzzled the side of his neck. 'I've been tanning. You know what that does to me.'

His hips shifted against hers. 'I'm getting a good idea.'

He was holding onto her like he didn't ever want to let her go. His hands were stroking up and down her spine, across her bottom, and along her thighs. The skin-on-skin contact made arousal unfurl deep in her belly. She hadn't realised how much she'd needed his touch. 'You'd better hurry,' she whispered.

He went uncharacteristically quiet, but she could feel the hard press of his cock against her mound. Instinctively, she rocked against him. He groaned, and his fingers bit into her bottom.

'Baby, you tempt a man to do things he shouldn't,' he said tightly.

The soft words sent a thrill through her. 'Live dangerously, Kilkenny.'

She expected him to kiss her. To carry her into the cabin. To do something.

Instead, he did nothing. A muscle ticked wildly in his jaw, but it was the only movement he made. 'Are you sure?' he finally asked.

She glanced at his face. The heat in his eyes ... The strength in his touch ... 'Oh, yeah.'

That slow smile returned, and his eyes sparkled. He looked like a hungry wolf just thrown a piece of raw meat. She took a deep breath and felt her nipples brush hard against his chest. The fresh air, the darkness, his moodiness ... It added a new component to her lust, and she felt reckless.

'Find out how much,' she whispered, daring him.

His eyebrows lifted, but he didn't break the contact of their stare. As brash as she'd been, Jenna's nerves still went jittery when his hand slowly moved from her bottom to between her legs. He let out a grunt of frustration when he encountered her sarong. He gathered the material impatiently until he found his way underneath it. Yanking the crotch of her bikini bottoms aside, he sent his fingers searching. Her desire pulsed hot and hard when his callused fingers touched her.

'Damn,' he murmured as he stroked her intimately. Watching her face closely, he pushed into her. 'Slick, soft and welcoming.'

'Oh!' she gasped. He'd started with two thick fingers, but was already working in a third. The pinch made her entire body go on alert.

His eyelids became heavy. He crammed all three fingers deep and let them curl like curious worms. 'You feel incredible.'

So did he.

'Shane,' she groaned. She let her hands cruise over his wide shoulders. 'Take me inside. Now!'

His eyes became clouded, but when he turned towards the cabin, he didn't head to the door. Instead, he pushed her right up against the hewn logs.

'Uh uh. My way,' he said. His gaze swept up and down her heated body. 'We do it right here. Au naturel.'

'What? Wait!' she said, her breath catching. Recklessness was one thing; exhibitionism was another. At least in the water, nobody could see any ... hip action. Night had fallen, but the moon would be up soon. The other cabins weren't that far away. 'Somebody might see.'

'You wanted me to be creative.' He wiggled his eyebrows at her before pulling his fingers abruptly out of her. Those devious fingers started working on her bikini top.

*Whooo. Whooo.*

'There's an owl watching,' she hissed.

He laughed, and two quick tugs sent the twin triangles of fabric flying. Jenna self-consciously clapped her hands over her breasts. It left her with no defences when his hand slid suggestively down her belly to her bottoms. He only bothered with the tie at one side of her hip. The material dropped and swung limply back and forth between her legs. The open access was all he needed.

The moon rose behind him, casting light onto her body, and she shivered. He was looking at her like he could devour her.

'Look at you.' He sighed. 'Drop dead fucking gorgeous.'

He reached for the zipper of his jeans, and she squirmed. This whole back-to-nature thing was a little much, but the naughtiness of it made her hotter than she'd felt under the afternoon sun. She glanced around to see who or what else might be watching, and her excitement peaked.

'Fucking gorgeous,' he whispered again, looking deep into her eyes.

A thrill rushed through her when she felt his broad

tip bump against her. With one smooth thrust, he pushed all the way inside.

'Ohhh,' she groaned.

His jaw went slack, and his body shuddered. He took a moment, buried deep within her, but then pulled back and began thrusting frantically. Her body arched, and she clutched at his shoulders. He was slamming home with every thrust.

'Christ, you feel good,' he panted.

Jenna moaned. He felt better. Each thrust ground her butt against the logs of the cabin, but her sarong protected her delicate skin. The contrast, though, was enough to make her want to yell. So she did.

'Shane!'

He bucked harder, nailing her to the wall. Jenna could hardly stand the pleasure. It felt naughty, exhibitionistic, and so damn good. She clawed at his T-shirt until she found her way underneath it to smooth, hot skin.

'Look at me,' he growled as he kissed her again. He lifted her legs higher around his waist. 'Give it to me, baby. Give it to me.'

She clutched at the strong muscles of his back. They were going at it like two wild animals, and he was enjoying it as much as she. Satisfaction had tightened his face until he looked fierce.

'I'm close,' she gasped, suddenly overwhelmed by the wild emotions bubbling inside her.

He grunted, thrust hard, and lodged himself deep.

She tightened around him, and he smothered her cry with a kiss. He bucked against her one last time, and Jenna felt him spurt inside her. His weight pressed heavily upon her, and she sagged against the cabin, limp and satiated.

It was a long time before she noticed the crickets chirping or the wind whistling through the pine trees around them. The moon had risen higher in the sky, illuminating their lovers' clench to anyone who might chance a look. An echoing *Whooo* told her that Mr Owl had stayed for the whole show. She didn't care.

She'd just had the best fuck of her life.

'That wasn't a slow poke,' she said breathlessly. Emotion suddenly swelled inside her chest. She liked this guy so much. They'd only been dating for three months, but he was smart, successful, and unbelievably hot. His work habits frustrated her, but now that she knew how to get his attention . . . whew!

'Can we go inside now?' she asked, her lips brushing against his ear.

'Is there a bed in there?'

'King-sized.'

'Oh, yeah.' He carefully lifted his weight from her and gathered her into his arms. 'We're going to need that.'

Much later, Jenna watched Shane from that same well-used bed as he tinkered around with the fireplace. It was summer, but at such a high altitude the air cooled off quickly. Besides, the room just didn't seem complete without a fire crackling. She glanced around the cabin. It seemed so simple by today's standards: a bed in one corner with a bathroom off the back, the kitchen near the front door, and a nice big stone fireplace as a centrepiece. The thick, log walls and exposed rafters made the place seem cosy and private.

And privacy was important, considering some of the things they'd done together.

A blush caught her by surprise, and her gaze went right back to Shane. He was having trouble keeping the fire alive and had settled back on his haunches to watch that it didn't go out. Again.

It was his fourth try, and she couldn't help but laugh. 'Need some help?'

He threw her a look over his shoulder. 'Think you can do better, Sassy Pants?'

'Sassy Pants?' she sputtered. She rolled her eyes and flung back the covers.

'My mistake,' he said, his gaze locking onto her body. 'You're not wearing any pants.'

'Smart ass,' she huffed. She marched across the room to him, but was keenly aware of her nakedness. She couldn't help it. He was watching every sway and jiggle of her body.

She watched him right back. The flames in the fire-place had finally caught, and they illuminated him, the light licking against hard muscle and sinew. The pure masculine beauty brought her arousal back with a rush. He was stronger than he'd been. More muscular. She knew that Shawn had been dragging him away from the office to the gym, and the benefits were showing.

It was enough to make a red-blooded woman drool.

She bopped him on the shoulder as she kneeled in front of the fireplace beside him. 'Sassy Pants,' she muttered again. 'That brother of yours is a bad influence.'

He caught her before she could get comfortable and lifted her so she straddled him. The hair on his thighs bristled against the back of hers as she settled onto his lap. His strong arms came around her, and with a sigh, she leaned back against his chest.

'What do you have against Shawn?' he asked, his voice close to her ear.

'Shawn? Nothing.' She ran her hands back and forth across his forearms. This was nice, sitting so intimately in front of the fire. Tonight, they'd gotten back some of the closeness they'd lost in recent weeks. In fact, she felt closer to him than ever. She didn't want to spoil it with talk of his brother.

He cupped her breast and gently fondled her. 'Come on,' he coaxed. 'Tell me the truth. He seems to get you all riled up. It bothers me.'

Not as much as it bothered her. Shawn did get her worked up, but in more ways than she wanted to admit. 'He's a pain,' she said simply.

That prompted a quick laugh out of Shane.

'Well, he is,' Jenna said. She glanced over her shoulder. 'He's always teasing me and playing practical jokes. He can never be serious.'

'Yes, he can. He just likes you. That's how he shows it.'

'By pestering me? What is he? Eight years old?'

Shane's hands caressed her intimately. Her nipple perked up under his attentions and poked into his palm. 'Definitely not eight,' he murmured.

Jenna let her hands run along his thighs. His touch was distracting her, but if he wanted to know her feelings for his brother, she was going to tell him. She was still miffed about a thing or two. 'That singing telegram he sent me at work was not funny.'

'Yes, it was. Admit it,' he said, giving her nipple a firm pinch. His tone changed. 'At least he remembered your birthday.'

Her breath caught at the sting. It only drove home the memory that Shane had forgotten. He'd been in Europe on business. 'Well, maybe it was a little funny,' she said, trying not to dwell on the issue.

'And thoughtful?'

'Don't push it.'

He hugged her more tightly and one hand trailed straight down her belly. His fingers brushed against her patch of dark hair before disappearing between her legs. She arched sensuously when he cupped her. 'He's crazy about you, Jenna. I'd like it if the two of you could get along.'

Her stomach dipped. With the way he was touching her, her thoughts went to a very naughty place.

'It would make me happy,' he said.

She nibbled on her lower lip nervously. He just wasn't going to let the issue go. She didn't want to cause a rift between the two of them, but she had to tell him the truth. 'I think it's a little more involved than that,' she said softly.

His hands hesitated, and he leaned over her shoulder so he could see her face.

She couldn't meet his eyes. 'Shawn wants me,' she finally whispered.

'And?'

*And?*

She looked at him, dumbstruck.

'He'd do anything for you, Jenna. Anything at all.'

Words stuck in her throat. What was he saying? Didn't he understand? His brother wanted her, his girlfriend, in a sexual way.

'Can't you give him a chance? For me?'

Her heart began to pound triple time. Shane understood just fine. It was she that was a little slow on the uptake.

Heat suddenly suffused her. The warmth of the fire was bombarding her, but it wasn't nearly as hot as the chest rubbing against her back or the hand stroking between her legs.

'You and Shawn would be really good together,' Shane said. He nudged her knees wider and static electricity jumped from the rug beneath them.

It seemed to shoot straight to Jenna's core, and she shuddered.

Wide-eyed, she looked at him. She peered into his dark eyes, and realised he was serious. Her thoughts whirled. She'd known the two brothers were close, but she'd never imagined this. What, exactly, were they into? The possibilities made her squirm in his arms, but yet, she didn't try to get away.

The muscles in his arms bunched as he adjusted her on his lap. Her thoughts were too chaotic to understand until he lined her up with his ready cock. She sank down and a sigh of pleasure left her lips. Oh, he was incorrigible.

'Just think about it,' he said as he began to rock their bodies together in a slow, sultry motion. 'For me.'

How could she think of anything else? She closed her eyes tightly, but that didn't stop her thoughts from running straight to the forbidden. Shawn did want her. She'd caught him looking at her many times, and he was a hottie in his own right. When he wasn't irritating her to death, she'd looked back – but she'd never let that on to Shane. She was a one-man woman, and she hadn't wanted to hurt him. Besides, looking was all she'd ever done.

But here he was, telling her she could do more. He wanted her to do a lot more.

Her fingers bit into his thighs. With each slow stroke, her thoughts bounced from one brother to the other. It made her feel wanton. Sexy. Desirable.

And totally out of control.

She tried to bounce more quickly on Shane's lap, but he wouldn't let her. Using his strength over hers, he turned and settled her lengthwise onto the fur rug in front of the fireplace. 'Stretch out for me, baby. On your belly.'

Jenna let out a slow purr. She'd never been so stimulated in her life – physically, mentally, or emotionally. Not missing a stroke, he put her on her knees and she unfolded. She went down slowly until she was prone with her legs spread wide. His hand slid under her to tilt her hips back at just the right angle before he lowered his weight onto her.

'Mmm,' she murmured. She stared into the fire dreamily. Two sexy brothers. One hot night.

'Good?' he asked, his hips moving leisurely as he pumped in and out of her.

It was better than good, especially with the naughty things he'd said to her. It made everything seem more scandalous. Debauched. Illicit.

And maybe a little enticing?

Her fingers curled into the soft fur. It tickled her at all the right places. She closed her eyes and let herself sink into the feeling. 'Perfect.'

He was in no hurry. Together, their bodies undulated slowly. The fire crackled as the summer breeze blew outside. In the distance, Jenna heard her owl hoot.

'Who are you thinking about right now?' he whispered into her ear.

She didn't even think of lying. 'Shawn.' She sighed.

He pushed deep and ground against her. 'Good girl,' he said gruffly.

He dropped a kiss onto her temple, and her low moan filled the cabin. When the orgasm started, it was hot and pure. Where it ended and the next one began, she never knew. She came hard, and she came long.

And both Shane and Shawn were right there with her.

Sunlight woke Jenna the next morning. She groaned as she rolled away from the east-facing window. She'd forgotten to pull the shade.

Shane tucked her against him as she snuggled into his chest. 'Too early?' he asked, brushing her hair over her shoulder.

'Too bright.'

She shifted even closer, burying her face against his

neck to blot out the sun's rays. Instinctively, she wrapped her arm about his chest and her leg around his waist. She came fully awake when she felt him bump up against her.

'Too sore?' His voice rumbled through her.

She groaned. She was, but she wasn't going to let that stop her. She let her tongue dart out to touch the pulse at his neck. When he shuddered, she pushed him onto his back and kissed her way up his jawline.

What a wonderful way to start the day. The fresh country air made her feel free, strong, and sexy. Her hand slid down his chest. She'd just found his cock when her stomach grumbled.

Beneath her, Shane let out a laugh. 'Ah, sweetheart. You need sustenance if we're going to keep this up for the next two days.'

Next two days? Lord help her.

She rolled off of him and pushed her tangled hair over her shoulder. 'There's food in the kitchen. I'll make something.'

'No, no,' he said, catching her by the shoulder and pressing her back against the mattress. 'You've been doing things for me all night. I'll run down to the bakery in town.'

Jenna sagged against the pillows. Something chocolate and gooey sounded perfect. With the way they were going, she'd burn off the calories before lunch. 'Wait,' she said, a thought occurring to her. 'Do you even know where the bakery is?'

'What? Oh yeah, I saw it on the drive up.' He threw her a cocky grin. 'I was hungry, but then I got here and someone distracted me.'

He kissed her before climbing off the bed to search for his jeans. He looked out the window as he pulled them on. 'God, what a sunrise,' he said, surprising her.

'We should go out for a hike later. Know any good trails?'

'Name your level. Wussy beginner or super stud mountaineer?'

'I think you know the answer to that.'

She rolled her head on the pillow towards him and smiled. It made her feel good that he wanted more out of her than just sex. She wanted to do everything with him: hike, bike, swim, and even talk. 'Did you get to see any of the sunset last night?'

He threw her a wink. 'It was nearly as gorgeous as you.'

She blushed.

'Try to get some more sleep,' he said as he grabbed his keys. He dropped a quick kiss on her brow. 'I'll be back as soon as I can.'

'Mmm,' she said, already scrunching up her pillow. 'Drop some bread crumbs or something. If you get lost, I'm too tired to come find you.'

He gave her bottom a quick tap. 'Sassy pants.'

She grinned and watched him walk out the door, but noticed something on the floor behind him. She laughed when she realised what it was. He wouldn't get far without his wallet.

She pushed back the covers and walked over to pick it up. The well-worn leather flipped open when she lifted it, and his picture stared up from his driver's licence. She couldn't contain her curiosity. 6'2". 210 pounds. Brown eyes. Brown hair. Shawn Kilkenny.

Jenna froze. She looked again, but the name didn't change.

Shawn Kilkenny. *Shawn.*

Her brain stumbled, but then took off at a lightning pace. She spun around towards the fireplace. Oh, no. It couldn't be – but her nerves began to sing that it was.

That devil!

The phone caught her attention, and she lunged for it. Her hands shook so badly, though, it took her forever to get the message to play again.

'Hey, sweetheart. It's me.'

Her entire body jerked when she heard Shane's voice. It was different from the one she'd heard all night. Not much, but different enough to make her insides start to shake. Oh, God. How could she not have realised?

'Please don't be mad. You know I hate to do this to you. I've run into a bit of trouble getting out of here.' Shane's voice sounded distracted – as if making the call wasn't one of his priorities. 'One of our contractors just informed us that he's not going to meet his deadline. That means I have to make a bunch of calls and reschedule everything. Believe me, sweetheart, I'm just as upset about this as you are.'

Oh, really? Somehow Jenna doubted that.

The message continued. 'I know you'll understand, though. You're always so good about that. And hey, I just talked with Shawn. He was thinking about going fishing this weekend, so I told him where you are. He said he'd drop by and keep you company. Maybe you two could cook some s'mores or something.'

*Cook some s'mores?* Jenna let out a snort. He really was clueless, wasn't he? She slammed down the phone, unable to listen any longer. Her mind was abuzz. So she was 'always so good' about being stood up, was she? He hadn't even been listening to her!

A truck door slammed outside, and she twirled around. Suddenly, she found it hard to breathe. And him!

Shawn's little practical joke had gone way too far. She blushed when she remembered all the things they'd done together. And her naughty thoughts as they'd made love in front of the fireplace. She gasped. He hadn't been talking about a three-way. He'd just wanted her to be thinking about him.

The deviant!

But it had worked ... she hadn't been able to get him out of her head.

Her sense of indignation wavered. It was outrageous, but he'd pulled this stunt just to be with her. She was well aware that he'd been bird-dogging her ever since she and Shane had first hooked up. This wasn't a momentary fascination on his part.

It wasn't on hers, either. If she were honest with herself, she had to admit she wanted to be with him, too. If she'd met him first, she would have been all over him. He made her laugh, the sex was incredible, and he'd always been more attentive than Shane.

She was a one-man woman, but that didn't mean her man couldn't change.

She heard his footsteps start to come her way. She crossed her arms over her chest as she waited, but a smile pressed at her lips. Oh, this was going to be more fun than anything. She was ready and waiting when he opened the door. 'Hello, *Shawn*.'

He froze, one hand on the door handle. When he realised she was standing there buck naked, he quickly closed the door behind him. 'Easy now,' he said anxiously. 'Don't blow a cork. I never meant for this to happen. I got here and you just assumed ... hell, you're the one who jumped me.'

'You could have stopped me.'

'Are you insane?' The look on his face turned pleading. 'Oh, come on, Jenna. I'm mad about you. You've got to know that.'

'I do.'

'Just let me –' His head snapped back. 'What?'

'Oh, don't mistake me. You're going to pay, buddy boy. You're going to spend the rest of the weekend doing some very creative apologising.'

The worry on his face was swiftly replaced with a wicked grin. 'Anything you want, baby. Just say the word.'

'I want you.' She crooked her finger at him and smiled saucily. 'Get over here, you evil twin.'

# The Andromeda Pose
Maria Lloyd

I followed a man home once, like they do in detective novels or spy movies.

I was on holiday all alone in Paris one weekend in late summer, on an impulsive escape from London. It was *hot* and Paris was decimated for 'le Midi'. I was alone, and indeed wanted to be so, sitting at a café watching the passers-by, immersing myself in the sights and smells of a different city. When I finally grew bored I paid my bill and walked down to the Musée Rodin. I love the gardens there, and the large sculptures set out among the greenery. Some are life-size nudes of marble or bronze. I spent some time ambling along, admiring my favourites.

Then I saw him. My mystery man.

He was dressed quite formally, like he had just left the office and had popped in on his way home. He looked vaguely familiar. When I showed signs of half recognising him he gave me a half-smile in salutation. He wore his blond hair close cropped, and his blue eyes were hooded against the strong summer sunlight which slanted across the gardens. But what struck me most about him were his hands. They were large, for he was a tall and muscular man; yet he held them with a delicacy that belied their strength, loose fingered, like a practitioner of t'ai chi.

He admired the statues as he strolled around the gardens a few paces ahead of me. When he reached the torso of a Greek goddess he surprised me by leaving the path to invade the shrubbery around the statue just so that he could reach out to stroke, quickly and deftly, the stone flanks and rounded bottom of that perfect naked woman. I felt amusement, surprise, and a melting as though he had touched *me* there ... which gave me a jolt of pleasure.

I watched the slope of his broad back, his neck, his arms, and his groin, as hungry for his form as he was for the statue, while the background traffic of Paris hummed above birdsong and roses scented the summer evening.

Then he resumed his stroll as though nothing untoward had happened.

I pretended to examine the headless Hercules, keeping tabs on my mystery man in the periphery of my vision as we continued our tour. I was dismayed when he suddenly checked his platinum watch, as though recollecting an appointment, and decided to move towards the gates with a steady, rolling stride.

As I watched him move with his lithe easy grace I decided on impulse to follow him, if only for a few blocks or as far as the metro, so that I could continue to watch him a little while longer.

Even though his living flesh was not quite as beautiful as the bronze and marble gods, he exuded something – a charisma, a lure – which I had not felt in a long time and it dragged me along like a moth locating the right pheromones which would lead to its mate.

I tried to be discreet about it: my sandals made soft footfalls on the baking boulevards and my summer skirt swished as I quickened my pace to keep my quarry in sight. There were still many people on the streets so I could follow and blend quite easily as my mystery man turned this way and that, crossed a road or two, with that brisk yet graceful gait of his, as he headed away from the eighth arrondissement. He knew where he was going and I wondered what his final destination would be. A drink with his lover, a meal with his wife? Did he have a wife?

Still I followed him, until I felt I was quite lost. The area became more exclusive. Attractive wide avenues planted with trees were flanked by the high brick walls, heavy grilled doors, which guarded large Victorian houses and their spacious gardens from prying eyes. From what I saw they were all beautifully maintained, though some looked like they had once been part of a terrace but now survived alone – the remnants of the Franco-Prussian, First, Second World War? – and a few more modern houses had been built between them. I wondered what they were like inside.

I was dismayed when my mystery man paused beside one heavy door, took out a credit card key and swiped through the sophisticated security gadget mounted on the brick wall. The door swung open smoothly.

For a moment he stopped to look back up the street and I froze guiltily – the only pedestrian, the obvious lost tourist. He merely gave me a ghost of a smile, a dancing light of challenge in those blue eyes. Then he turned and went through the door.

I cursed my bad luck. My sleuthing had come to nothing, and I had found my quarry so very attractive. An impulse made me rush forward to check if the door had indeed swung closed after him. I gave an experimental push and it gave way. Either by accident or design, the door had not been secured properly.

My heart thudding, I crept through the door and it swung completely shut behind me before my head had time to operate and realise I had committed trespass.

I was on a wide gravel path, luckily screened from the large gabled house by some coppiced chestnut trees.

On either side were smooth lawns bordered by bloom-ing roses and other shrubbery. At certain points along the lawns stood garden sculptures. Many were similar to those at the Musée Rodin – beautiful naked bodies and torsos, marble or bronze, in the Greek style.

I could not see my mystery man – he must have hurried straight up to the house – and I was anxious to get out of sight before he happened to glance through a window and discover me. I took the path that headed towards the densest part of the garden, which led around to the rear of the house, checking for signs of CCTV cameras while I wondered what to do. I was soon in the shade of camellia, magnolia, and rhododendron bushes. Glossy umbrellas of leaves supported huge pink blossoms that shed petals over my hair and the baked earth of the path. I breathed in a vestige of damp earth from the deeper shadows as I walked towards another sculpture of a *kouros* – one of those beautiful statues of youths that ancient Greeks had placed in temples to Apollo. It was so exquisite, I wondered if it were genu-ine. I stroked the cool smoothness of the marble rever-ently, even though I half expected to touch living flesh, so real it looked here in the shadows. My palms trav-elled over its wonderful chest, its neat genitalia and tight buttocks. Always, in museums I had longed to touch such sculptures, but one was never meant to touch the exhibits. Now I caressed to my heart's con-tent, almost forgetting my predicament. The marble base upon which it stood was rippled with ivy and there was an offering of a lily at its feet which smacked of pagan rites. How decadent yet touching. It reminded me of a Saki story.

I tore myself away to pursue the path towards the rear of the house. It seemed safe to stay on this path close to the high garden wall, which was thick with wisteria, clematis and, in sunnier patches, peach trees trained on to trellis. Bees droned lazily between the blooms, sticky with yellow pollen, and a gorgeous pale-blue butterfly flitted across the path. The birdsong among the shrubbery sometimes grew into shrill territorial warning as I approached.

I grew hot and sticky with tension. I wished my heart would stop thudding and my breath would slow so I could enjoy the exquisite peace of the place, cloistered away from the city outside.

Soon I came upon another lifelike statue, this time neatly tended in its own little clearing. It was a marble woman, beautiful and naked, crouching as though in the act of bathing. Hellenistic curls trailed down her perfect back, across her voluptuous hips. Her exquisite face gazed down the lawn towards the rear of the house. Even as I darted forward to experimentally caress her small breasts, her pear-shaped bottom with the palms of my hands, I realised with dismay that I could be visible from the back windows of the house. I hurried on across the clearing towards a path flanked by high yew hedges, where I was screened safely once more.

I stroked the soft dark greenery gratefully (so warm and yielding in contrast to the marble) and carried on down the path. Soon I came to a T-junction, then another. I swung right each time and realised I was entering a small garden maze. By now I was quite blasé about the risks I ran in getting lost here. This place had enchanted me and I wanted to see and enjoy as much as I could before I was discovered, or had to try to climb my way out.

After a while I reached a little square clearing that exhibited yet another sculpture, and a wrought-iron bench to sit upon. I sat down to rest and admire the sculpture. This was a more modern piece and carved from oak. It depicted a naked man and woman, almost wrestling with passion – the man about to enter, the woman gripping his biceps for support as she arched back ... a look of bliss, abandon, on both faces, like lovers who have waited in a drought of despair for the chance to meld in this way once more ...

I was moved by its realistic immediacy. It was so human and tender it was beyond pornographic. I had only ever known such crazy passion for real once in my life and the sculpture reminded me of how alive it made you feel to yield to the moment in such a way ...

Eventually I realised that the summer sun was beginning to fade and the evening was approaching. It would be more dangerous to find my way back to my hotel after dark. I had to figure a way out. I roused myself to walk around the sculpture one last time, stroke the smooth flanks, the raised phallus, the perfect breasts ...

'Beautiful, are they not?'

I jumped, turned. It was, of course, my mystery man. He had changed into espadrilles, a pair of old jeans, a tight striped T-shirt and looked divine for it. He held a hurricane lamp in one hand and a half-smoked Galois in the other. Early moths tried to beat against the glowing glass walls of the lamp, and he lazily waved the Galois in their direction so the tobacco fumes would ward them off.

'Pardon, Monsieur?' I asked, wide eyed.

He gave a little laugh. 'Come now, you are English are you not?'

I shrugged. 'Is it that obvious?'

He raised the lamp and really looked me up and down. Took in my leather open-toed sandals, my long bare legs, the linen skirt, the silk tunic now dampened with sweat, my leather handbag bulging with sunglasses, maps, leaflets and the usual paraphernalia of a tourist. I shifted a little, guilty under his scrutiny, before swinging my long hair back over my shoulders as I straightened up in a gesture of bravado. I was conscious that my auburn hair had collected little sticky leaves and tiny falling petals on my nature ramble. Not very dignified.

'To me you are the epitome of an English rose.' He gave a slight bow in mock gallantry.

'So you are a connoisseur of living flesh as much as of wood and stone?'

'Of course. Whenever I get the chance.'

There was an awkward pause. I supposed I should apologise for trespassing and make haste to leave, but some sense of rebellion, defiance, pricked me. He seemed so casual and amused, like I was a naughty schoolgirl and this happened to him all the time; women followed him through city streets like the moths lured to his hurricane lamp. He seemed only mildly curious about me.

While I was madly curious about him.

'Do you live here alone?' I asked.

'I do.'

'This place is amazing. You ought to open it for the public.'

'Where would be the fun in that?'

He was laughing at me, at my bravado and pompous prissiness. I could not help but smile back.

'I guess it's more fun for private parties,' I conceded.

'You have no idea.' He took one last drag from the Galois, and the glow gave his face a satyr-like sensuality as he screwed his eyes up against the smoke, pouted his lips to exhale. Then he dropped the cigarette stub and ground it into the path. Such vandalism surprised me. I resisted the temptation to pick it up – and again caught him watching me with a mocking smile.

'Since you are here, would you like a tour of the rest of my sculpture maze?'

I felt a leap of excitement. 'That would be very

interesting, thank you.' I paused doubtfully. 'If you would like me to pay –'

'Pay?' His voice was amused, quizzical.

'For the privilege.'

'I see. It could be very expensive.'

'I have money.'

'A rich English rose.' He chuckled. 'We'll see. This way.'

He led me down another hedge-lined path which wound this way and that. Sometimes our hands brushed, and I felt overwhelmed by that earlier attraction I had experienced. He smelled of musk and citrus, of espresso coffee and tobacco – all familiar, and yet not quite, to my English sensibilities.

Soon we paused to admire another sculpture. This one showed the man and woman in the midst of making love, the woman mounted on top, supported at the wrists by the grip of the man, arched like a high-wire act in the frenzy of her own pleasure. It was cast in gorgeous fluid bronze.

'Do you like them?' he asked, raising the lamp to look more closely at my face as I stood, rapt in absorbing the sculpture.

'Very much,' I said at length, as I walked around the sculpture and smoothed the metal limbs. 'And to be able to touch ... It's quite a thrill,' I admitted. I lapped up the experience – to enjoy my holiday pastime of admiring works of art in such an intimate way that I was lost in the beauty of the form, the shadows. The added luxury that my fingertips could retrace the artist's contours ... when I glanced at him again I noticed he was watching me in the same hungry fashion that I absorbed the sculptures – like I was a thing of beauty to savour. The observation made me shiver with surprise and longing.

He smiled. 'Come, I want to show you the centre of the maze.'

I followed him for some time, as the hot Paris night began to glow, and the night-time rustlings of the garden blotted out the distant city traffic, so that it seemed we were somewhere more exotic – Morocco, perhaps – an oasis in a desert land, sequestered and private. The tension of being alone with a strange man was replaced by a strange intimacy as we enjoyed the garden, each other's closeness, and progress along the path in silence.

When we finally reached the centre of the maze I was surprised to see no sculpture. Instead there was a small summer house, festooned with honeysuckle and briar rose. At its centre was a large oblong of marble, an empty pedestal. The pedestal was strewn thickly with beautiful waxy white lilies. On a stone bench that lined the summer house were placed many votive candles and incense sticks to give the feel of a pagan grotto, awaiting the invocation of a god or goddess.

I approached the pedestal. It was then I noticed the shackles, bronze and covered in verdigris, chained to a large hoop at the base, which were laid upon the lilies.

I turned to laugh and raise an eyebrow. 'So this is a place of pagan sacrifice? How Dennis Wheatley of you.'

He laughed a rich throaty laugh that sounded the way high-roast coffee tasted. 'I'm sorry you are disappointed. This usually houses the pinnacle of my collection – a statue of Andromeda, which unfortunately has been returned to the sculptor for cleaning and repairs. Do you know the legend of Andromeda?'

'I think so. Her mother Cassiopeia boasted of her beauty, and in revenge the Nereids persuaded Neptune to send a sea monster that could only be placated by the sacrifice of Andromeda. She was left chained to a rock – but she was rescued from the dragon by Perseus, who married her.'

'That's right.' He turned to me with a winning smile. 'Now, the payment you mentioned earlier. I wonder if you would agree to be my Andromeda for tonight?'

'What?'

'It would not be for long, and it is a warm night. You see my dinner guests will be expecting the tour I just gave you and I would hate to disappoint them.'

I stared at him in astonishment. 'You expect me to strip naked and stand on that pedestal while you file strangers past me?'

'Please. They'll think you're some professional model. And you can change pose, I would not wish to cause you any discomfort. Come, are you not even a little honoured, to be invited to be Andromeda, the most beautiful of women, the one thing of living beauty in my sculpture garden?'

He leaned forwards then, to brush a strand of hair away from my cheek in a sudden tender movement. I closed my eyes, wanted him to embrace me ... but he paused, and when I opened my eyes he merely watched my expression hungrily, waiting for an answer.

I trembled in frustration and excitement.

'If I refuse?' I asked faintly.

He shrugged. 'Well, with the deepest regret I think I may have to call the police. Trespass is a serious offence in this area. The very rich are not welcoming of over-curious tourists – what if you made off with their treasures?' I laughed at the absurdity of it and he laughed too, but I could sense the steel in his eyes. He would make trouble for me, no doubt, if he followed through.

'Which seems more pleasant,' he cooed coaxingly, 'a couple of hours in a busy station, a police cell ... or an hour chained to my beautiful marble plinth?'

'Chained?'

'Oh yes. For authenticity.'

My heart skipped a beat. I looked at the pedestal. It was a beautiful setting. All the prima-donna, exhibitionist, secret harem fantasies inside me were begging to do it.

As I stood by this charismatic man, infused with desire, I wanted to see it through. See what endgame he had planned.

'Very well,' I said. 'To help you out. For an hour or two. Then you will release me from my debt for the trespass and the tour?'

'Absolutely.' He smiled, took a brass key from his jeans pocket. 'Please undress and we'll hide your clothes and things in that thicket.'

I stared at the key. 'How long have you had this planned?'

'Since I first saw you admire my statue of Aphrodite from the house. A goddess worshipping another goddess. But come, won't it be a thrill? To be on the receiving end for once, the adored? Please, you have already said yes. Undress.'

I opened my mouth to object but found that I grinned back instead. Of course he was right. It was a wonderful opportunity if only I allowed myself to surrender to the magic of this evening, this garden ...

It was no hardship to strip off, and let the warm scented breeze stroke my bare skin. It was no hardship either to let his blue eyes stroke the contours of my naked breasts, my flat stomach, my tight buttocks, my bare feet ...

'Beautiful, as I thought,' he said. Quickly he stowed my folded clothes, my bag and sandals away. 'Now I will help you on to the pedestal.'

I was surprised when he scooped me up easily and set me down gently on the plinth. His jeans and T-shirt were rough against my nakedness, the heat and feel of him overpowering. Then he released me just as quickly and climbed up beside me. Our feet crushed ankle deep into the strewn lilies, slightly releasing their scent.

He pulled up the shackles attached to the chain, used the key to open them. The wide bands fitted easily around my ankles and braced them slightly apart – a stance so familiar in Greek statues. Then he placed the other fetters around my wrists. The thick chain balanced heavily between manacles and shackles and the loop in the base of the pedestal.

'If you get tired, you can kneel or sit,' he said. I nodded, feeling the weight of the chain keeping me steady in my stance. The way I was manacled meant my upper arms squeezed my breasts slightly together and my fettered hands brushed against my sex.

'I'm quite comfortable at present,' I said in my prissy English way as he jumped down to admire the effect.

His eyes glittered in admiration and he smiled. 'You look exquisite,' he said simply. 'Now I must go and prepare for my guests. Au revoir.'

It seemed a dream to stand there while I watched him take the lamp and walk back down the maze. Now I was alone in the garden, illuminated by candlelight. The brass fetters that imprisoned me made me a part of the garden. They were smooth on the inside, pitted and weathered on the outside. I rubbed against the heavy chain experimentally, tried a different pose. The weight was cooling against my sweat-slicked skin, erotic. The lilies were soft and smooth against the soles of my feet, my ankles. It felt decadent to tread upon such an abundance of hothouse blooms. I watched the moths flit by, the candle flames flicker, and entered a serene trance-like state. All I needed to do was stand here, in the warmth of a dark-blue night, until Monsieur Mystery Man came to release me. How simple could an evening's relaxation on holiday be? It was a fitting payment for the enjoyment I had experienced in his sculpture garden.

I'm not sure how long I stood there before he returned with his guests. This time he was dressed in crisp white shirt and dinner jacket. He again held the hurricane lamp and this time was smoking a cheroot. He was flanked by three other men, also in dinner jackets, and three younger women, immaculate as only Parisiennes can be, in diamonds and little black dresses.

His blue eyes were soft and spoke volumes to me. I gazed at him and smiled, even as the others exclaimed and walked around me.

'Marvellous, Henri,' one man exclaimed. The man came close to the pedestal, and to my surprise reached out to stroke my calf. 'Where do you get them from? You are such a clever collector.'

'That is my secret,' Henri replied with a smile, 'but I am afraid that photography for private use is all that is allowed with this Andromeda.'

I was reeling from the implications of his speech when one of the women, a black-haired beauty in vamp make-up, reached out to test the shackles around my ankles, and stroked the plane of my feet. 'Can't we play?' She pouted. 'She looks so beautiful.'

'I'm afraid not, Cherie.' Henri put his arms around her and pecked her cheek, guiding her away. 'It is not in the terms of the agreement. She is for me alone.'

So I stood there, glowering at him for making me a pawn in his usual after-dinner games, while the beautiful dinner guests took their digicams out of jacket pockets and evening purses, and took pictures of my silent naked form. They strained to get close enough to angle in on my sex, my breasts from different positions and compared the results. I did indeed feel like a statue in a museum, ogled, admired and catalogued with a certain avid, impersonal, but possessive scrutiny.

I deliberately froze my face into a mask of defiance, perhaps like the expression Andromeda wore when waiting for her monster ... Henri had not told me so many photographic souvenirs would remain of my 'little favour' for him. To add insult to injury, he took out his own digicam and revelled in taking images of me from every angle. I tried to flash him a warning that enough was enough.

'If Andromeda could just squat for a short while...' he said, smiling cheekily at my discomfiture.

I frowned, while everyone cooed and exclaimed that this was such a good idea.

Well, I was getting a bit stiff. And I could not help return the amused glint in his blue eyes. He was protecting me well enough from their avarice. A true collector, proud of his latest prize.

So I squatted down for more photo opportunities, close-ups of my breasts and my shadowy parted sex. Sometimes when Henri was not looking I felt surreptitious fingertips reach from behind to brush against my breast, between my buttocks. It was just the treatment I had given stone sculptures myself in the past, after all. Then Henri noticed this, or decided it was enough, and announced it was time to shepherd his guests away.

'Come, we have some excellent coffee waiting for us back at the house,' he called. 'I'll return for Andromeda later.'

He was the last to leave the clearing. He turned and blew me a kiss, with such a charming and sheepish look of apology and gratitude that I had to laugh and blow a kiss back. My annoyance faded and I found myself liking him even more.

Alone again, I found that I was trembling. I felt hot, sticky, aroused, flushed with stage fright and desire intermingled. Henri had treated me like his piece of living sculpture in every sense and I had thoroughly enjoyed it.

A long time passed. I sat cross-legged, squeezing my breasts between my forearms, letting my sex be cooled by the breeze, and wondered if Henri's guests had claimed all his attention. Perhaps he had forgotten me. But then I saw the glow-worm that was the hurricane lamp returning down the dark maze path, and Henri reappeared.

This time he wore silk pyjamas of Antwerp blue.

'Glad you remembered me before going to bed,' I said, rising smoothly from my sitting position.

'Of course. I'm saving you for my bed.'

'I think I have more than adequately paid my debt to you,' I retorted, even as my breath quickened, 'so don't get any ideas.'

He placed the hurricane lamp on the stone bench before he swung up on to the pedestal beside me. I trembled as his hands traced a long swathe across my shoulders and down my flanks, brushing against breasts and buttocks. His touch was warm and dry and I leaned towards it like flowers lean towards the sun.

'I've wanted you since I first saw you caress my statue of Aphrodite,' he murmured. 'I dare you to say that you do not want me.'

I could not have if I had tried. I felt his silk-clad body press against me, and as this big blond man with his intense blue eyes began stroking and soothing me, tantalising me as I trembled in my chains, I could only gasp, 'Yes, yes I want you. I've wanted you since I saw you at the Musée Rodin, and watched the way you stroked that statue ...'

'Like this?' he whispered in my ear, as his hand possessively cupped my bottom.

'Yes,' I whispered back, melting to the tenderness of his touch.

He picked me up and gently laid me on my back upon the strewn lilies. Their waxy petals were a silken mattress over the marble and I sank into their caress just as Henri sank into me, raising my manacled hands above my head so he could feast more easily on my jutting breasts, licking and softly sucking my salt skin. His kiss tasted of burgundy wine, Roquefort cheese and strong coffee as I suckled his searching tongue hungrily. My shackled legs grew rigid and gripped his. We mirrored his sculptures of love-making in our passion and consummation as I cried out into the night.

A night owl cried out from somewhere in reply and we both laughed.

Henri took the brass key from his dressing gown pocket and began to unchain me.

'My guests have all gone home,' he whispered, 'and I have food and wine and many more delightful treasures inside my house ... if you'd care to stay the night.'

'I think Andromeda owes her Perseus that much,' I replied, as he picked me up and carried me, naked, back through the maze.

# The Snake Thing Jan Bolton

Nature turns up the volume in the tropics. Twisting orchids unfurl fecund with pollen; mangoes and papaya hang heavy with sweet sap and legless creatures slither and slide over the rich earth and into the teeming undergrowth to hide from humans. In the sweltering heat of midday, skinks and undulating millipedes head for the shade and doze in the mulch. Everything in the Australian rainforest beats with a pulse of magnified rude health and grows to a size that is guaranteed to inspire awe and wonder in someone who has grown up in an English suburb. Giant seeds and plants with leaves the size of rowing boats fan out over the forest floor. Fruits and flowers burst joyous and loud into life, and in the senses. No miserly little berries that poke their heads out once a season to allow a starving robin a snack; here the fleshy and succulent fruits of an ancient mysterious landscape flaunt themselves year round at the hungry hornbill and the ravenous kookaburra. Too much choice, but here we are, they announce, dazzling orange and yellow, bountiful, juicy and abundant with nectar. Birds screech and caw with delight, and into their bellies they go.

The steaming humidity of Queensland was having a marked effect on my psyche. I was becoming increasingly fascinated with the biodiversity and size of everything around me. At dusk, huge bats swooped low, screeching over the main avenues of Cairns, diving into the tops of the plane trees that lined the wide streets and hanging on the branches. At night, long-snouted, nocturnal mammals scurried over rooftops looking for tasty scraps, and at dawn the chorus of birdlife was an altogether richer and fruitier sound than that heard in my parents' Suffolk garden. The humidity enveloped my skin and my senses, and, apart from those moments spent wrapped in a thick dry towel after my morning and evening shower, I was always slightly damp with a glistening sheen of perspiration. As daily exposure to the sun prompted a gradual bronzing of my limbs and chest, I began to look tanned and glossy. I adjusted easily to the climate for one who has spent almost all her life in the Northern Hemisphere.

I'd been in Queensland for about a month. My travelling companion, Rachel, had come to the end of her holiday and had returned to Britain, leaving me to explore the rainforest and the Great Barrier Reef alone for the final leg of the journey. I'd seen my first barracuda, and eaten my first barramundi, but I'd yet to experience the exotic holiday affair that I had craved since arriving in Australia. In the evenings I wandered around the town, dipping into the internet cafés and taking advantage of the ice-cold cheap beer served up in the many bars. It was a young person's town. There were backpack hostels everywhere and the air was alive with the sexual excitement of scores of pleasure-seeking young tourists looking forward to the thrill of flirting – and the drink-fuelled encounters that would be notched up in the parks and on the waterfront after the clubs had chucked out in the early hours. During the daytime, those who needed to sleep off the excesses of the previous night could doze in the shade around the hostel pools, or lounge on their beds mesmerised by the ceiling fans.

Yet, despite my increasing sexual frustration, I hadn't

joined this shag-happy throng. It should have been the easiest thing in the world to pick up a buff Aussie bloke in a neon-lit, music-filled drinking venue, but I was far too fussy for my own good. Rachel had laughed at me when, on our last night together, I said I was more easily seduced by intelligent conversation than brawny good looks.

'Why on earth did you come to Australia, then – as opposed to New York or Paris?' she said, laughing, as we sank cocktails on the verandah of a Byron Bay bar. 'At least you should head to Melbourne,' she said, when I had bemoaned my lack of lovers. 'That's where the intellectuals are. You're heading into occa territory going up to Queensland.'

'Yeah, but it's tropical and glorious,' I said, 'and I want to swim with the fishes and look at the coral. There's not much of that in Melbourne. It was even raining there yesterday, can you believe it?'

Rachel was not as bursting with contradictions as me. Her sexual tastes stretched little further than hipster surfers in baggy shorts who carried waterproof bongs stuffed with Nimbin weed. A few tunes on the guitar and a couple of hours spent toying with each other's hair extensions and it was off into the moonlight for Rachel and her bronzed dreadlocked suitors. I gave up counting how many tattooed and pierced conquests she notched up during the two weeks we spent in Byron. I needed more than a few puffs of weed and a shot of wheatgrass juice to get me in the mood – and I'd never really been one for work-shy beach bums with vague pipe dreams; I liked my men a little more active and determined than that.

I guess I hadn't really been putting out the right signals to attract anyone, though. Strutting about on a dance floor and showing off wasn't really my style; I always left that part of a night out to those more obviously comfortable with displaying their availability. I preferred to play the game of seduction in the daytime. I loved to feel the sun on my back and on my skin as it warmed me to my core and heated the blood that was set to racing by thoughts of the rugged outdoor types that were synonymous with this part of the world. I wanted a man who was at home in the wilds – a bushcraft specialist or jungle expert used to spending long periods alone, immersed in nature and living on his wits, but full of survival techniques and ways to get through the long hours spent going walkabout. So far I had met rugby fanatics, diving instructors and tour guides, but they were all too puffed up with self-importance for my tastes, and I was no good at competing with the more outgoing women who gathered around them, boosting their already sizable egos. I wanted sex, but I didn't want to display my desires in the company of other backpackers.

It was during the last week of my holiday, in the least likely circumstances, that I was to find a happy compromise, although quite how far I went that day in the cane fields still has the ability to shock me as I sit here now, back in England, trying not to let myself get too worked up when I think about those three guys: Geoff, Aaron and Chuck.

I decided I needed a change from spending every day sailing or mucking about in the water. I'd done so much snorkelling I could write a book on it, so one day I caught a bus to the small zoo that was situated about 15 kilometres inland. I was dressed in a short khaki skirt and a white cotton shirt that emphasised my tanned breasts and skimmed my midriff. Three months spent travelling in India and the Far East had given my already olive skin a rich colour, and I'd reached that level of tan where, even in 30-degree heat, I could get away with one coating of factor 15 on the arms. I wore platform espadrilles whose laces criss-crossed my slender calves and my hair was tied into a messy bundle on the top of my head, effecting a tousled appearance that I hoped connoted sexiness. Although I didn't really expect that I would find love among the lizards, there was always the chance I would meet someone en route.

The near-empty bus rumbled past endless sugar cane fields before we arrived at the cheerfully painted building that promised 'all things scaly and slithering'. I hadn't yet spotted anyone I wanted to speak to, so I contented myself with drinking in the natural surroundings. As well as having a koala sanctuary, the zoo specialised in reptiles, which delighted me. There was an active involvement in the creatures' welfare at this zoo, and an opportunity for visitors to cuddle koalas and handle giant specimens of python and other non-venomous constrictors. A board advertised a two o' clock display by 'the snake man', and visitors could ask questions and have their photo taken with one or two of the more docile residents.

I've always loved snakes. The couple of times I've had the opportunity to hold one, I have always been an enthusiastic volunteer. I love the sensation of their wonderfully cool, scaly bodies wrapping themselves around me. The pairing of women and snakes does something to my imagination, as I think of high priestesses in ancient civilisations enacting curious sexual rites, mesmerising their acolytes with wild erotic dancing. Today, I would have to be content with two minutes of contact with Susie the python, but that didn't seem so bad. I could always drift off into mythological reverie later on. For now, I wandered into the dark and humid reptile houses, smiling at crazy-looking, bug-eyed turquoise tree frogs and trying to discern what was a sleeping amphibious giant and what was part of a tree, as the cicadas and crickets filled the room with their exotic trilling noise.

Two o'clock came and a small crowd had gathered around the snake pit. The only other women in the audience were older, mumsy types who looked as if they had been brought there under duress by kids eager to get a look at the lethal taipans and copperheads, perhaps with the promise of a live kill of some small rodents thrown in.

Then, Geoff, the 'snake man', walked into the display area carrying two wriggling burlap sacks held at arm's length. Dressed in the zoo uniform of sage-green pants, and a light, khaki-coloured short-sleeved shirt, he had more than a little military look about him, apart from his shoulder-length mop of thick black hair. He was built for wrestling testy reptiles to the ground. His tanned arms flexed, his biceps bulged and my stomach flipped over with lust as he tipped his lethal charges into the dust with a casual confidence that spoke of many years' experience. He was my bushman, all right, in looks, dress and attitude.

He went through a brief lecture, delivering the facts about his slithering companions with a relish that played to the audience's desire to know the full extent of their powers. And, as each species was mentioned, a writhing serpent of that variety was tumbled out of the sack and kept at bay with a forked stick that prevented it from making off into the crowd. I was transfixed – the heat was at its full power and the movements of the reptiles, combined with my increasingly weak disposition at the sight of this specimen of Antipodean manliness, was making me display obvious signals of arousal. I kept finding myself licking my lips, playing with my hair and touching the sides of my body as I stood in provocative poses. I hadn't intended to distract him, but what I was doing was, I suppose, with hindsight, somewhat risky given the lethal nature of his job.

Although no one else could see my crude attempts at flirtation, as I was stood at the front of the crowd facing the pit, Geoff couldn't fail to notice me. The fact that his attention was diverted – albeit for a couple of seconds – in this dangerous company, gave me a thrill that appealed to my secret wicked side. I love to see men at work, doing manly things; I have to admit that the idea of distracting an important, masculine man from his job turns me on more than anything I can imagine.

He'd begun the display with a cheery, confident delivery, but after about ten minutes he started to look irritated, at least until the more dangerous, venomous creatures were back in their sacks. Then it was time for Susie the python to come out. When it was my turn to hold her, Geoff cut me a look that was as deadly as a snake's as he allowed the huge graceful reptile to slide up my body so its head darted out to explore the people standing behind me.

I was beaming with delight, throwing my head back in rapture as the strange, cool feel of the heavy beast eased around my neck and chest. My time with Susie was up all too soon, and Geoff handed her to his female colleague, who went on to introduce her to a group of teenaged boys. I felt a hand on my shoulder and whipped around.

'You wanna learn a couple of things about snake handling, young lady,' snapped Geoff, his hands on his hips and his chin jutted upwards in a combative gesture. 'Do you think it's funny or clever to distract a bloke when he's responsible for controlling a venomous monster from doing what comes naturally?'

I was tempted to make a clever quip but one look at his reddening, angry face made me change my mind.

'Ah, no, it's not clever,' I quietly conceded. 'I don't know what came over me ... blame it on the heat, I guess.'

'You're in Australia. It's hot every bloody day here. Most women are able to control themselves.'

I looked at the ground, then looked up at him as he towered above me by a good six inches. To be so close to him was making it worse. He'd worked up a good sweat during the display and was exuding a strong, musky scent that was making me hotter than ever. For all his irritation, his eyes were fixed on my breasts and his gaze kept darting to my legs and back to my eyes in what was an undisguised gesture of lustful appreciation. I found the courage to apologise to him properly, flashing a winning smile at him that calmed him down. At my telling him I was English, something seemed to fall into place for him, and he said, 'Oh, so that explains it,' although I never got to know why.

'I'm heading off to the cane fields in about twenty minutes,' he dropped in casually, as he walked back to the office. 'Want to see where I catch and release some of the snakes in the wild?'

'Wow, I'd love to,' I enthused. 'It would be a real thrill.'

'Then I'll meet you round back, where the zoo's trucks are,' he said, pointing to the back of the frog house. 'You might want to cool yourself down a bit with a drink from the café or something. Can't go around in that state for too long!' he joked.

I flushed with embarrassment. I had behaved appallingly immaturely but I wasn't going to turn down the chance of seeing the snakes in the wild – something that would be a first for me. I turned and watched him swagger back to the office, his tight, meaty butt encased in his khakis, and I bit my lips in unconscious longing.

I retreated to the ladies' and threw some cold water

over my face and neck and ran the cold tap over the
pulse points in my wrists. I would do well to calm myself
down; throwing myself at someone like Geoff would be
an unknown quantity. It was broad daylight, there was
no drink to loosen the inhibitions, and he might well be
the type who was offended or freaked out by such a
display of wanton neediness. Sometimes, female desire
was a scary thing for a bloke; you couldn't predict which
way the dice would roll if they regarded your behaviour
as too sluttish. I promised myself to play it cool.

I climbed into Geoff's truck after getting myself an
ice cream, noticing he had a cardboard box in the back
ready to release some baby tree snakes into their natural environment. We chatted about how he caught
them, about the time he was bitten – just the once –
and the general state of ecological awareness in Australia. He had a degree in zoology and was studying to
take it further into becoming an expert in venom and
antidotes.

I looked out the window as he gave me an
impromptu lecture on the breeding habits of the whip-
snake. Mile after mile of cane fields lined a long straight
road that continued into infinity. There were no dwell-
ings – just toolsheds and rough huts for shelter from
the sun. Sitting in the truck with my feet on the dash
pushed my skirt further up my thighs. The unfinished
business between us hung heavy and tense. The heat
had caused the seam of my knickers to press between
my legs and it was easy to make small movements that
enhanced the touch. Greg was snatching eyefuls of my
legs as we bumped along the track and I knew that
something was going to happen; I could feel the pent-
up energy radiating off his skin and the atmosphere
was unspeakably awkward with barely concealed lust.
Australian men may have traditional values instilled
into them but the weather does something to their

sexuality – they can't keep their eyes off women or their hands off their cocks, no matter how professional they are.

'Does it get boring sometimes, just the snakes and the road and the zoo?' I asked, provocatively licking my ice cream, unprepared for the boldness of his reply.

'Well, I can always pass the time thinking about sex,' he said suddenly. 'Don't get a lot of it out here.'

I spluttered and coughed as a nervous reaction, unsure of what I was supposed to say, caught in the dilemma of trying to make small talk about the landscape or play along with his opening gambit at upping the stakes. It was in so many similar circumstances that I'd played the nice girl and had made my excuses to leave. Here, in the truck, it was not possible to flee my desires. Here I was with a full-blown rough and ready Australian male and I would never forgive myself if I wimped out and started talking about lizards or something.

'Oh, surely there must be loads of women who find you attractive,' I said. 'You look like you know what you're doing.'

'It's the snake thing . . . it puts women off,' he replied, his gaze flicking from my breasts to my legs.

'It doesn't put me off,' I ventured, getting more confident with my insinuations.

'I could see that earlier! Well, that's quite unusual in a woman. I like that. In fact, there's a lot of things I like . . . you know, sexually speaking.'

I was rooted to the seat, breathless to hear just what it was he liked. To be in control, I'd bet. He was that type.

'I like pulling down women's knickers, bending them over my truck and making them go wild for my cock. Giving them what they want for as long as they want. How does that sound?'

I couldn't believe how up front he was. No man had ever spoken to me in this way before, and I was getting weak with arousal but still too shy to play along with his dirty talk. All I could manage was to bite my lips and smile and say, 'Wow, that sounds pretty good.'

'That's what you want, isn't it?' he asked, more as a statement than a question.

I nodded.

'Well there's no need to be so bloody quiet about it, then,' he roared. 'What's happened to the wild woman at the snake pit? Cat got your tongue?'

'I guess I'm not used to men talking to me like this,' I said. 'I want what you said, you know, but I can't bring myself to say it.'

'Want the man to take the lead, eh?'

'That's right, even if I seem really shy.'

'Listen, you little English tease ... I'm going to have to have you. Look how hard you've got me,' he said, squeezing his crotch. 'Can't work up a bloke like that and then cry off. Not round these parts, you'd be asking for trouble.'

'Trouble? What kind of trouble?'

'Whadd'ya think? Fellas round here like their beer cold and their women ready. They don't take too kindly to know-it-all Europeans with their fancy ways, leading them on and then wanting wining and dining and all that. Bloke just wants to get his end away, and you've been doing a mighty fine job of getting me stiff enough to give you a right good fucking.'

I was shocked by how he had changed his personality as soon as he was out of the confines of the zoo. He'd turned from the professional zoo-keeper to a lecherous horny stud. My mouth was parched and I was shaking with desire and excitement.

'Go on,' he said, full of confidence, 'show me what you got, then.'

I slowly pulled the hem of my skirt up, beginning to feel incredibly naughty for what I was doing – displaying myself like a cheap tart for a truck-driving sex maniac.

'What's it like in there, babe?' he asked. 'Is it wet? Do you know how much you're turning me on?'

I swallowed hard and nodded. 'Well, if you're as turned on as me then it's a lot,' I managed. 'I don't know what I'm doing here, really. It's not something I've done before.'

'Aw, shut up trying to justify yourself,' he said, with typical Aussie brashness. 'You're as game for it as I am, and stop pretending it's all a mistake. We both know what's going to happen, sooner or later.'

And that's when the blow-out happened. The steering wheel spun sharply anti-clockwise. Geoff swerved the truck around a pothole and we ended up in a ditch.

'Aw, fuck it! Not another tyre. Happens all the time round here. And wouldn't you know I used the spare last week. Been meaning to replace it. Just didn't get around to it.'

'So we're stranded out here with no spare?' I said shakily, more worried that he was going to switch off the sexiness and be all practical and that would be the end of my encounter with the snake man.

'No worries,' he said casually. 'Got some mates with a pick-up about ten miles away. They'll be here in a few minutes, soon as I make the call. Better just get that knackered wheel off for 'em, though.'

After checking that none of the snakes had been jolted out of their box, he grabbed my knee for a second before leaping out of the truck, swinging a wheel jack out from under the driver's seat. As I heard him ringing his mates for some help I cursed my bad luck. I was only a few minutes from getting my desires fulfilled when fate had played a cruel hand. Little did I know extra waiting was going to give me more than I'd bargained for. I jumped out of the truck too, keen to feel the sun on my legs and have a look around.

Blame it on the heat, but as Geoff lay under the truck, pumping the wheel jack, his body stuck out from the waist down and a pair of meaty khaki-clad legs and a generous package were mine to ogle. As he slid out from under the truck, his trousers bunched up around his groin and accentuated what was already a promising treat. And he made no bones about getting a good look up my skirt from his position, either. By this time I was faint and frantic with arousal. He brushed the sweat off his brow and looked at me longingly. As he scrambled to his feet and grabbed his tool bag from the back of the truck, I continued to make conversation about the landscape, about Aboriginal survival techniques and life at the zoo. Very British of me, I suppose.

I watched him wield the tyre iron and noticed the sinews and tendons twitching in his arms as he worked the tools. I tentatively reached out a hand and ran it along his arm, licking my lips and making sure that he wouldn't forget what had been promised as we'd started our journey.

He stood up and grabbed me, his hands on my buttocks and his lips on my neck. He was not about to waste time; he slid a finger under my skirt and into my knickers, where it was humid and damp. He ground himself against me and whispered in my ear, 'You're going to get such a fucking.'

There was a clatter of dust and metal and a pick-up truck came hurtling towards us with two men in the cab. They pulled up to a sharp halt, immediately leaped from the cab and walked over to us. They were both wearing overalls with their names emblazoned in a logo on their chests.

'All right, snake fella. You got yourself in trouble

again?' said the taller of the two. 'I told you to get the heavy tyres last time this happened, Geoff. Waste of money using those town treads out here.'

Then, the inevitable, as they clocked eyes on me.

'Who you got riding pillion, mate?' said Aaron, a big blond-haired dude who made no effort to hide the lust in his eyes. 'You've done all right for yourself.'

All three men laughed and looked at me. I was feeling more self-conscious by the second, but I was getting used to the direct way that Australian men conducted conversation.

'You look thirsty, love,' said the taller guy, Chuck. He walked to his cab and retrieved a bottle of water from their in-cab cooler. He unscrewed the cap and passed me this very welcome refreshment. My nipples were sticking out stiffly against my shirt and I was suddenly thinking the unthinkable, but I didn't get much chance to flirt as Geoff was already launching into a description of exactly what had happened.

'So, this one's a right little goer from London,' he said. 'Tried to put me off while I was doing the display earlier. Thought I'd take her out for a ride into the wilds and show her what happens to dirty sheilas who try to pull a fast one on boys from round here.'

The other two men chuckled and looked me over. They were slapping each other on the shoulder and I saw some gestures take place between them that left little doubt in my mind that they fancied getting a piece of the action. They were not bad looking; in fact the three of them were all very well built and fit, without any particular distinguishing features – just regular working blokes.

Geoff continued, 'So what say we sling this wheel on and take a break up in the ridge there.'

The blond guy – Aaron – was instantly in agreement. 'Got a few cans in the eskie, mate. Reckon we might make a party of it, that's if the little lady here don't mind.'

'Oh, she won't mind,' said Geoff. 'She's more than ready for a little light refreshment, aren't you, love?'

I nodded and wriggled around for a bit, unsure what exactly I should do to let them know that the idea of a foursome was not completely out of the question, although, of course, it was out of my experience.

Aaron and Chuck, the taller one, slapped the replacement wheel on Geoff's truck without fuss and towed it out of the ditch. The exertion caused a lot of grunting and masculine display and they stripped their overalls down to their waists so the two of them were bare-chested. In a moment of girlish enthusiasm I grabbed my camera and got them to pose with a couple of tyres from their rig, like a gay calendar shoot of a couple of rough trade grease monkeys. We had fun, mucking about taking saucy shots, and I liked the attention they were giving me, even if it was highly dubious and politically incorrect. Aaron liked photography and made me pose, tits out, on the back of his truck as Geoff and Chuck gave the thumbs up and raised their cans of beer. It was a real lad's dream and I have to say I got a massive kick out of doing the page-three-girl bit.

We'd drunk a few beers by this time, and the fooling around started to turn into something more serious. Geoff and Chuck stood in front of me as Aaron grabbed me from behind. It was time to deliver what I'd insinuated. Aaron held me in an arm-lock so I was pulled back, my bum squashed onto his groin. I wriggled and giggled and twisted around but was held firm. The feel of my smooth bare legs against his dusty work trousers was delicious. And the hard ridge of cock in his jeans was pressing right into the thin material of my skirt. I couldn't help but sway against it. I was aroused beyond measure from the earlier showing off, and not being able to touch myself during this whole scenario was torture.

Geoff came towards me, brushing that thick lustrous black hair from his face and preparing himself for his treat. He touched my breasts and I looked him in the eyes; his pupils had dilated and he had the expression of a hungry man about to feast. His hands dived into my shirt and he once again exposed my breasts to the other guys.

'What beauties,' he said, rubbing his rough hands all over me. 'I've got something that's gonna give you the surprise of a lifetime.' And he wasn't joking. When he unzipped himself and got it out, I thought he had stuffed one of his snakes down there, it was so fat and long. Stroked to full erection it was enormous – and meant only for one thing: giving a dirty tease like me the shagging of her life.

'Do you think . . .' I began.

'We don't do much of that, darling,' said Chuck. 'We don't want to think, we just like to fuck and get our dicks sucked.' There was hearty laughter all round.

'No, let me finish,' I continued. 'I really need someone to, well, will one of you just touch me,' I pleaded. 'Between my legs, please. Just a little touch.'

They whooped and laughed again. Their dicks looked as if they were bursting in their jeans but they had no compunction about speaking their thoughts plain and dirty as anything.

'If I touch her, mate, I'm gonna go off in my pants, I tell ya,' said Chuck. 'It always does me up, touching a woman between the legs. The minute I put my hand down there, it'll be all over. It happened to me once before. I'd picked up this girl who was hitch-hiking and she was really up for some fun, you know. And I was dying to get at her. I just wanted to get her knickers off. But they were so silky I started rubbing her and got carried away with the feel of her young pussy in that satin and she was creaming into them and pushing at my fingers to go into her. Christ, it was beautiful. Anyway, I kept this up too long, and in trying to give her a climax I gave myself one, shooting off before I was ready. She was not happy. She wanted a right good seeing-to as well. Dirty little thing she was.'

'Yeah, you've never been one for holding back,' said Aaron. He was the quietest one of the three, but I could tell that he was no less aroused because of it.

Geoff came at me once more and looked me square in the eyes as he cupped my breasts in his huge hands. 'I need her now, guys. I got to get at her,' he said urgently. 'We can't do this standing up.'

So I was marched into the undergrowth, Aaron still holding my arms firmly, guiding me past the huge stalks of cane with their massive leaves, and away from the highway. As we walked through into the thicker area to one of the toolsheds, I kept snatching glances of the men's crotches, wondering what was going to happen afterwards. How long would I be kept there? Chuck had grabbed an old blanket from their vehicle and looked as casual as if he was strolling in his garden on a Sunday afternoon, with a four-pack of beers swinging from his hand.

He laid the blanket down in one of the narrow gulleys between the cane palms. It was going to be some picnic – but there was nothing to stick in my mouth bar three hard lengths of Aussie finest and a couple of tins of VB. I can't say I wasn't scared; the three of them seemed insatiable. Chuck flipped his belt undone and pushed his overalls and jeans down just far enough to get leverage. His strong stalk waggled at me and he had the fixed expression of a man on a mission. He pushed me down without preamble and, before I had a chance to think about technique or what

I wanted, he was inside me. I was so slippery and ready that he actually cried out in surprise.

'Fuck me, she's soaking!' he shouted. Aaron was handling himself slowly but firmly and grabbing for a feel of my tits as Chuck was fucking me. I loved to see these three men, fully clothed apart from their bare cocks, taking it on the run with a woman they knew would appreciate their rough and ready technique. All my aspirations of wanting intellectual conversation had gone out of the window in the space of one afternoon in the cane fields.

Aaron's cock was playing over my lips, and the natural reaction was to open up to suck him. It was so fat and meaty that I was crying out in the ecstatic pleasure of it all. What luck, to find three guys at once and each of them endowed to porn-star proportions. Not so much the length, but the thickness of their cocks was amazing, especially Geoff, who was standing over us, slowly stroking himself.

Chuck started to go at it, fucking me in earnest and telling me how much I liked it, how much he liked it, and how I was going to be screwed into next week. I knew he wouldn't last long as he kept stopping, desperate to control himself. When he felt he was about to last no longer, he showed immense strength of will and pulled out, puffing and blowing and pinching the head of his cock to stem the build-up. Then Aaron was in my mouth like a shot. He manoeuvred himself into a straddling position and began pumping himself into my face. He was handling his big, full balls with his other hand, rubbing himself obscenely between the legs and getting ready to let go.

'I can't help it,' he cried. 'I'm going to let it go all over you.' And he grabbed roughly at my breasts, and let his semen fly out all over my face and chest. Then Chuck squeezed at my breasts, mashing them against his penis and thrusting back and forth. I knew what was happening – the two mechanics were allowed to have their fun, as long as Geoff got the privilege of the grand finale, being the top dog and the one who would finish off by actually fucking me. Chuck and Aaron got their breath back and cracked open a couple of beers before standing up to walk back to their truck.

'Go on, mate,' said Chuck. 'Fill your boots, buddy. We're off.'

And they disappeared quickly into the undergrowth. I could hear the sounds of the ribald laughter as I prepared for nine inches of heaven and, hopefully, the orgasm that I'd craved so urgently. Geoff's hands were suddenly everywhere. He rubbed at my clit until I thought I would faint with arousal. I heard myself begging for his cock. My sex lips had swollen to their maximum size and I ached with the need to be filled again. It was the most exquisite torture, and Geoff was making the most of it.

He finally eased it into me with a grunt, and I lay back in the rapture of being given all this attention, crying out with the joy of being so thoroughly filled. Then he went at me with a force I'd never known the like of before. He was like a beast, focused totally on getting what he needed. There was no way I could have escaped, even if I'd been mad enough to want to. He was sweating and smelled strongly of male pheromones and the earth. He sat up once or twice to look me over and tease me.

'You want it?' he asked. 'You want my cock?'

I was transfixed by its size and threw myself wildly into the heat of the moment.

'I have to have it,' I cried. 'Please fuck me hard.'

He smiled at this – my first obscenity.

'Again,' he said.

'Fuck me hard, I want your cock in me.'

At this he began to rotate his thumb across my clit, making me say it over and over until I changed my cry to 'I'm going to come, oh Lord, I'm going to come all over your cock.'

I felt the molten heat of my orgasm rush through my legs and into my sex with an explosion of release. I was coming with his cock in me, and that set him off. He didn't so much fuck me as pulverise me with it. Maybe his orgasm was more intense because of the size of him; maybe he was just a dirty bastard, but at that moment I was prepared to be fucked by that man until I was not fit to crawl.

After a few moments regaining our composure, Geoff was back to his usual, workaday self, dusting himself down as if nothing had happened. I was in a state of shock and it was only after a few minutes, when Geoff spoke to me, that I remembered the reason why we had come out into the cane fields in the first place.

'So, girlie ... let's sort out that snake thing,' he said.

I was tempted to suggest that we already had, but I don't think he'd have got the joke.

# Sex? Alison Tyler

In high school, all the boys cared about was sex. And in high school, all I cared about was getting out of high school. I heard the rumours, certainly, the gossip flowing through the halls of who had done what to whom: Sherry in the back seat of a Chrysler with Jordan; Caren beneath the old wooden bleachers with David. *Sex*, the kids all whispered. *Sex. Sex. Sex.*

But although I was curious, I was determined not to join their ranks. I had no desire to become the latest after-school special the others were talking about. If I developed any sort of reputation, it was as a girl who knew where she was going. 'Most likely to achieve' they called it. In truth, I was completely lost.

So I went to Paris.

I was an unprepared eighteen-year-old with a piss-poor sense of direction who had never travelled alone. But that didn't stop me. I'd been saving for the trip for four years, had worked every odd job imaginable in order to sock away enough money – not just for a European vacation but for a proper one. I wanted to stay in a nice place, not a hostel. Wanted to buy pretty clothes, not souvenir trinkets. Wanted to discover what I sensed was a whole world of possibilities that nobody had ever bothered to share with me.

And by 'possibilities', of course, I meant men.

I had two missions on my post-graduation vacation. One was to eradicate my high-school self, to flambé the image of that self in order to rise from the charred ashes like a phoenix – the other was to find the Seine, which some would consider a far easier task, but one that was made considerably more difficult by my pathetic sense of direction. Give me a map, and I'll invariably turn it upside down. Aim me on the proper course, and I'll always take the first wrong turn. As my family likes to frequently point out, there is no metal in my head.

Almost immediately, Paris made me fashionable in ways I never had been in school. Sure, I'd thought I was cool as a defiant teen, favouring a standard uniform of ripped Levis and tight primary-coloured concert T-shirts. But now those rebel-rebel outfits were left behind in favour of a much more chic fashion statement. I didn't want people to look at me and think 'American'. I wanted people to look at me and think 'ooh, la, la'.

And by 'people', of course, I meant men.

By my third day in the city of lights, I had outfitted myself with a whole new wardrobe. With the clothing came a fresh determination to find the famous river, no matter how long it took me. On this afternoon, I was clad in slithery purple cowboy boots, a navy-blue cigarette skirt, and a pale-green top with a frill of antique lace at the collar. My soft auburn curls fell to my shoulders, and my eyes were shielded by classic shades. I walked with my head up and back straight, unlike my normal insolent slouch through the halls of Paly High. Yet I realised that while I might look ferocious and in control, I actually had no idea where I was. The ancient winding streets all appeared identical to me, and the tiny quaint cafés could have been cloned.

Didn't bother me, though. As I hadn't a schedule – 8:40 History, 9:35 Chem Lab, 10:30 Español – there was no place I needed to be. Optimistically, I took a sharp left, expecting to encounter sunlight glittering on silver water, and came instead into contact with a trio of tall young men, all dressed in the bright-blue zippered jumpsuits that denoted workers. One was dark-haired and dark-eyed, and he gave me a sly smile as I walked towards him. I felt extremely aware of my newly purchased Parisian lingerie, the black lace panties and pale-pink bra beneath my chic attire. The man kept his eyes on me as I strode forward, and I didn't immediately notice that other workers had suddenly appeared on the sidewalk, steadily pouring from beneath an old stone archway.

In moments, I was surrounded by a sea of blue jumpsuits. I tried to pay attention to how many men there were, but lost count after seven. The men stopped chatting, and then came in tight, as if collectively wanting a closer look. I felt my heart start to race as they swarmed around me on the sidewalk – eight, nine, ten – not touching me, but so close I could feel their heat. Flushed, I tried to continue walking through their crowd, but was slowed by the sheer multitude of masculinity.

One peeked down at my boots and whistled, admiring my legs. Another motioned for me to lift my tortoiseshell shades so that he could see my eyes. A blond with a boyish face started to speak to me in rapid-fire French, and when I shook my head and whispered 'American', the tone of my voice pleading, he switched quickly to broken English.

'Ah, American,' he said, as if agreeing with me. 'Then you come with us. We have coffees over here –'

'Yes.' They all nodded, as if on script. 'Drink with us.'

So I went. I was eighteen, ready for adventure, and captivated by how captivated they were by me. Several of the older men immediately stood at the bar and talked among themselves, ignoring the juvenile nonsense going on behind them. The rest crowded around several tables, with the three who had seen me first snagging the choicest spots. The dark-haired one sat right next to me, moving his woven wicker-backed chair in close, as if to offer me protection.

After we ordered our coffees, the four of us spoke as only people with a strong language barrier can speak.

'Roller coasters?' the blond one asked.

I nodded. 'Yes. I like roller coasters.'

'Pink Floyd?' another asked.

I grinned now. 'Yeah, I like Pink Floyd.'

And then the dark-haired one, the handsome one, said, 'Sex?'

He waited for exactly the right moment, when the waiter arrived carrying a tray filled with little white porcelain cups of coffee, and there was a hustle of fighting for the container of brown-and-white irregular-shaped sugar cubes and jostling for elbow position on the tiny round table. I looked directly at the dark-haired man, certain I'd misheard, but he only smiled, his eyes locked on mine, and wouldn't look away.

'Sylvain,' he said, pointing to himself. And the rest hurried to introduce themselves, clearly appalled by their rudeness. I heard their names, Jean-Paul, Michele, François, but I focused on remembering just the one: Sylvain. Then they waited for me to introduce myself.

'Kelly,' I said, somewhat sadly – why hadn't my mother named me something exotic-sounding like Desireé, or Antonia, or Natalie? – but they liked it.

'Very American,' one said, appreciatively.

'Kelli,' repeated another, accenting my name in a different way, focusing on the 'li' and giving me my wish. Suddenly, my name *did* sound exotic. I relaxed against the back of my chair and lifted my dainty coffee cup, accepting the feeling of being at the centre of attention. Maybe it went with my new wardrobe and my new name: Kel*li*.

After introductions, they continued to quiz me.

'Bruce Springsteen?'

'River rafting?'

'Sex?' Sylvain asked again, and this time he put one strong hand on my leg under the table. His warm fingers caressed my black-stockinged knee, and I looked at him, startled as those fingertips began to slowly inch up my leg until they disappeared beneath the hem of my navy-blue skirt. He was feeling me up, right here, in the midst of his coworkers – and, even more surprisingly, I was letting him.

'Yes,' I said to Bruce Springsteen.

The fingers moved higher. I suddenly found it difficult to think. Sylvain's hand was warm even through my stockings, and I sucked in my breath as his fingertips finally crested the top of my garters and found the naked skin that awaited him. He slowly caressed my thigh with the rough pads of his fingers, and I closed my eyes for a moment in a failed attempt to refocus my thoughts. The other men seemed completely unaware of what was going on under the table. I had to work to keep it that way.

'No,' I said to Colorado river rafting.

Those probing fingers began to slowly trace circles along my nude inner thigh, inching closer and closer to the very centre of my body. He was going to touch my panty-clad pussy. He was going to run his fingers along the seam of my panties, and that sensation was going to send sparks of lust throughout my body. A shudder worked through me, and I looked at Sylvain, shocked, my voice totally gone.

*Sex*, I heard echoed in my head. *Sex. Sex. Sex?*

His fingertips barely brushed over my beautiful new black lace panties, which were desperately wet now in the centre, and then he pressed harder, drenching the tips of his fingers in my satiny juices. I shifted my hips on the small café seat, and I spread my legs wider beneath the round table top, giving him greater access.

What was the blond saying now? Reagan? Did I like Reagan? I was a kid when Reagan was in office. What *was* he saying?

Sylvain's fingers began to make slow and steady circles up and over my clit. I could feel his touch throughout my entire body. He seemed to know precisely what I needed, as if understanding the way to get a woman off – in public – undetected.

My heart raced in my chest, and it took every bit of strength I possessed not to collapse against the seat, not to push the table over with my leg and let him have me. He smiled in an encouraging manner, obviously wanting me to keep up the 'everything's normal' charade, while he continued to stroke me beneath the table.

'The Red Sox,' one of the men said, and I shook my head.

'Giants,' I murmured. 'San Francisco.'

I realised in a flash that Sylvain was going to make me come, and I put one hand on his under the table, trying in vain to push him away, but he shook his head, motioning for me to release him, and ever so slowly I let go of his hand. In moments, those magical spirals had speeded up, and I felt the undeniable flood of liquid sex juices signalling my impending orgasm. My whole body trembled, and the blond quickly asked me if I was cold, if I'd like another drink to warm me up.

I shook my head *no* and nodded *yes* at the same time, beyond bewildered as Sylvain stopped touching me just short of bringing me to climax. I was on the verge of begging, but I didn't have the words. Not in French, anyway. I stared as he brought his hand casually up to his face and inhaled my scent, his coffee-brown eyes never leaving mine. He breathed in deeply and then smiled.

I thought of the boys I'd been with in school. The

jokesters. The jocks. The ones who would ask me out on a date and then spend the evening tongue-tied, unable to handle the job of being a man. In my few years of dating experience, I'd never once been in a situation like this. Was this what sex was really about? Being felt up under a table while surrounded by a group of total strangers.

As I worked to control my breathing, Sylvain's hand went back under my skirt again, and this time his fingertips slid beneath the barrier of my panties. I felt my cheeks turn a fresh shade of scarlet, but I didn't say a word.

He tilted his head slightly at me now, then lifted his coffee with his free hand and gave me a smile that was so fucking sexy I almost demanded that he take me right there. In the middle of the café. Forget his friends. Forget the men at the bar who thought they were above all this. Forget everything and everyone.

*Sex*, I thought. *Sex, sex, sex.*

He could push the coffee cups off the table, bend me over it, take me from behind. My panties would come down over my garters. My skirt could easily be pushed up to my hips, the soft blue material lifting past the curve of my ass to give him better access. What did he have under that cobalt-blue boilersuit? Was he wearing boxers or briefs or nothing at all?

When he looked into my eyes, he smiled even broader, as if reading every one of my dirty fantasies.

'New York City?' one of his coworkers asked me as Sylvain gently began to finger-fuck my pussy, first with only one finger, then with two. He overlapped his fingers inside me, and the feeling was so intense I thought I might start to cry.

'The subway?' another queried.

*Sex*, I thought, as Sylvain's long fingers probed deeper within my body. I tried to say that I'd ridden the subway. I tried to describe what New York looked like on a cold winter morning. But all I could do was come, in a rush, as Sylvain's fingers thrust into me again and again.

And then, suddenly, he withdrew, and I sat there, staring at the man with the deep-brown eyes who was now lighting a cigarette with sex-dampened fingers instead of looking back at me. I took a deep breath and tried to rejoin the conversation. 'Do you work back there?' I asked, my voice shaking.

'We work at the mint,' one of the best English speakers explained, pointing through the plate glass windows to the building where I'd first seen them.

'You make money?'

'We make the lunch,' he explained to me, smiling. 'We work in the kitchen. Come back tomorrow. Have lunch with us.'

The others nodded quickly, telling me the menu, trying to win me over, and I agreed, knowing that they had no way to find me if I changed my mind. Couldn't track me to my hotel on the tiny rue de Saint Pierre. Couldn't search me out if I didn't want them to. But when I walked out of the café, I looked over my shoulder, and Sylvain was looking right back at me. And in his deep-brown eyes I saw the question one more time: *Sex?*

*Yes*, I mouthed and nodded. *Oui*.

The following morning, I chose my outfit carefully, dressing in a thin white tank top and a pair of navy-blue stretchy pants. I slid on my purple cowboy boots again, and I spent a long time in front of the mirror teasing my hair into tantalising twists and perfect spirals that hung past my shoulders. I wore huge silver hoop earrings that were for sale at all the tiny shops near the Seine – at least I thought they were near the

Seine – I hadn't actually found the famous river yet. But I found the mint. Like some perverted Gretel, I had memorised the way home to the hotel and the way back again.

The men were waiting for me, and they set out a lunch spread on a long wooden table that rivalled any of Paris's five-star restaurants. Yet I had no appetite once I saw Sylvain. He eyed me with the look of a predator, taking his time, waiting, pouring me wine which, he explained, was usually reserved for upper management.

'You like Paris?' one of the men asked me.

'Oh, yes.' I nodded, looking at Sylvain.

'The Eiffel Tower? Notre Dame? The Seine?'

'I haven't seen the Seine yet,' I confessed, and Sylvain came close and pressed his lips to my ear. 'Tonight,' he said, 'I'll take you.'

I glanced up at him, realising that nobody seemed surprised when he put his hands firmly on my shoulders, when he touched me with the motion of ownership.

'I'll take you,' he promised again. Did he mean he'd take me to the Seine? Or did he just want to take me? I had no problem with either thought.

The men seemed to realise that I had made a choice, that out of their blue-clad throng I could pick only one. Sylvain sat close at my side, and he ran his fingertips through my thick auburn hair, pushing it out of my eyes. My hand shook and white wine spilled on to the table. Would he make me come again, the way he had the day before?

'There's a party,' one of the other men said. 'Tonight. A birthday party –'

'You'll come,' another said quickly, and the rest nodded.

'Much more fun. No work. No –' the man gestured at his blue boilersuit '– no uniforms.'

I stammered, 'I'm bad with directions,' but Sylvain was right there, ready for me.

'We'll walk together,' he said. 'At eight, I'll meet you.' And I wrote down the address of my hotel and handed it over, realising that he knew English as well as the blond who had become the spokesman for the rest.

The rest of the meal was a blur, and the rest of the afternoon a nightmare. Waiting for eight o'clock to arrive made me feel as jittery as I had before any high school dance. But I had known how those dates would end – a bit of petting in the back seat of the car. Nothing more. This was something new.

Sex. Sex. *Sex?*

I thought of Sherry in the back of the Chrysler. I thought of Caren beneath the bleachers with David. Suddenly, I understood the appeal of being the news on everyone's lips.

Sylvain arrived on time, wearing a black button-down shirt and inky-blue jeans. In his casual outfit, he looked far more like a rock star than a cook, but it was his hands that I most cared about. He caught me glancing at them, and then he grinned as he looked me over. I had on a dress – a real dress. Not one from a thriftstore, safety-pinned together to fit my slim body, but a form-fitting floral sundress with spaghetti straps. To cover my shoulders, I'd chosen a pale-pink wrap the colour of cotton candy and the consistency of spun gossamer. Sylvain immediately put his arm around my waist and led me down the tiny street towards the boulevard Saint Germain.

'We'll go to the party,' he said, 'but first, we'll go to the river.'

I knew that I should have been paying attention to the route he took. I wanted to be able to find the Seine on my own. But the landmarks blurred before me. I saw nothing but his eyes when he looked at me, felt nothing but his firm body next to mine. His hand slid up and down along my waist, and every few steps, he'd stop and turn me so that we were face to face. He kissed me against the wall of an old building with a bright-blue plaque that read 1787. He kissed me again, pushed up against a silver Citröen DS, and his hands pushed up at the skirt of my dress, so that he could feel the bare skin of my naked thighs beneath.

We walked slowly, and he told me about cooking, and how he had been in kitchens all his life. He didn't have aspirations to work in a restaurant. He liked the low-key lifestyle that went with cooking at the mint.

I told him that I started college in the fall, and that I was undeclared.

'Which means what exactly?'

'I don't know what I want to do.'

'But you know what you want,' he said, and it wasn't a question.

Oh, yes, I knew what I wanted. *Sex. Sex. Sex?*

We reached the river in minutes, and I was embarrassed at how close I'd been for these past few days. Part of my problem had been an unwillingness to ask for directions. As I didn't speak French, the thought of stopping a stranger was impossibly mortifying. Sylvain led me down the stone steps to the very edge of the river, and we walked until we found an empty bench along one of the walls. From this point, we were almost directly across the river from Notre Dame. Tour boats glided past us, all lit up, people dining on deck.

'Are you pleased?' Sylvain asked me.

'Pleased?'

'Does it meet your expectations?' He motioned to the river.

I smiled at him, answering a different question entirely. 'Yes, of course,' I told him, thinking of the pawing boys in the backs of their daddies' cars, then remembering my prom, during which my date drank so much he had to be driven home by a friend, while I was left to sit solo or dance by myself. I thought about sex. In school, *sex* was a four-letter word. Super-charged. Negative. Now, everything had changed.

'The party,' I said suddenly.

'Do you want to go?'

I shook my head.

'Me neither.'

Another boat went by us and, this time, some moron from America yelled out, 'Kiss her!'

Sylvain didn't hesitate. He cradled my head in his hands and kissed me hard. My body thrummed. *Sex. Sex? Sex!*

Slowly, he pulled me so that I was on his lap, straddling him, facing him. Carefully, he pushed my dress up in front, and then undid the fly of his jeans. We were going to have sex here. I realised it with a sudden jolt of awareness. Right on the river bank. In the glow of the yellow-gold street lamps from the boulevard overhead. We were going to do what I'd waited my whole high school career to do.

His fingertips found the wetness awaiting him, and he slid my panties easily to the side. I brought one hand between our bodies and found his hard-on, gripping it with my fist. The look in his eyes changed as I started to play a part in our action. His dark eyes burned into mine as I used my hand to slide up and down his shaft. And then I parted my legs even wider and slowly, so slowly, slid the head of his cock inside me.

To any passer-by, we looked like a couple in a sexy embrace, me astride him, his arms around my back. The poofy skirt of my dress hid the fact that his jeans were open, and that we were connected at the core. Gently, I rocked back and forth, pulling away from him, then slipping back down. I moved my body in a way I never had before, with a sexy confidence that had eluded me all my life. I moved without thinking, without planning, letting the situation dictate the choreography.

We were entirely silent the whole time, focused, intent. Sylvain used one hand between our bodies, to sweetly stroke my clit through the silky fabric of another pair of new panties, and I bit on to my bottom lip and shuddered all over. I wouldn't close my eyes, though. I wanted to see; to see him, to see the ancient stone wall behind him, a puzzle-work of interconnected rocks. I wanted the entirety of the experience to stay with me forever: the sound of the tour boats, the click-clack of women's heels up on the street above, the lapping of the water behind us, the rushing of my blood.

This is what I'd seen when I first rounded that corner and came face to face with the men from the mint. The possibilities. The future. And although I'd thought I had wanted to see the river, *this* is what I'd been looking for on my first trip abroad. And here I was, a girl with the worst sense of direction of all time, somehow finding the route, finding a path that took me exactly where I needed to go.

Sylvain bent his head to kiss into the hollow of my neck. He licked me there, then nibbled his way along my bare collarbones, pulling aside my wrap to reveal my naked skin.

I sighed and arched my body on his, throwing my head back, finally closing my eyes. My soft hair tickled the skin on my back, rippled down over my shoulders as Sylvain thrust forcefully inside me. I thought of him touching me in that tiny café and, as if he knew exactly what I was visualising, he continued stroking my clit at just the right speed as I was rocked back and forth.

The tour boats glided by behind us, and I started to come, gripping on to him, burying my face against his shoulder, my whole body trembling as if from an unexpected chill. But I wasn't cold at all. I was heated from within. I opened my eyes and turned my head, seeing starlight on the water.

Afterwards, Sylvain wanted to walk me back to the hotel, but I grinned and told him no. 'I'll find my way,' I said, and I did, taking the proper turns, winding up right back at the door to my hotel.

Yet the following morning I realised that I still had no idea where the river was. Just around a corner? Just beyond those buildings? I'd have to go out again.

And explore.

# Cowboy World
Mathilde Madden

Hannah crossed her fingers under the table as Daniel gave her his most put-upon expression. 'Babe,' he said plaintively, 'we must have walked miles through this bloody place. We've been to Dinosaur World, Medieval World and Oriental World. We've even been to Nursery Rhyme World; couldn't we just give Cowboy World a miss?'

Hannah bit her lip. There was no way on earth she was missing Cowboy World. She had only come to this odd little seaside pleasure park to see Cowboy World again. In fact, she had only come to the south coast to see Cowboy World again. 'Please,' she said, in deliberately persuasive tones, 'it's only just over that bridge down there, and we've already paid to get in now. We might as well make the most of it.'

Daniel was noisily slurping Coke through the thick straw. 'Yeah, well,' he said, lifting his head and squinting at her, 'the fact we've paid a tenner each to look at a bunch of fibreglass rabbits is no argument in your favour. Babe, my feet hurt, my head hurts. I just want to go back to the B and B, relax for an hour or two, and then spend the last evening of my holiday sampling once again the bizarre nightlife of the English seaside resort. Come on, Hannah, be reasonable. It's my holiday too.' And he forced this last point home by dipping his head and slurping extra loudly as he drained the dregs of his fizzy pop.

Hannah's face started to crumple against her will. 'But you've got to go,' she said rather pathetically.

'Babe, I haven't "got to" anything. I've come here haven't I? It's the last day of our holiday – the sun is finally sort of shining – and I really wanted to go to the beach. Come to that, what I really, really wanted was to go to Greece – not this rain-soaked, miserable one-single-solitary-sunny-day-out-of-ten piss hole.'

Close to tears, Hannah was full-on pouting now. 'I like it here. And the weather's been OK, mostly.' In fact she was only one tiny shred of human dignity away from stamping her little feet. 'Now, come on. I am not getting as near as this to Cowboy World and not seeing it again. I just have to go.' And she got up flouncily and headed down the sloping café lawns.

Behind her she heard Daniel shout something along the lines of 'Do you have some kind of cowboy fetish or something?' And, although she didn't look round, she knew it was loud enough for the nice respectable families sitting outside the café to have heard too. She hoped Daniel was suitably embarrassed.

By the time Hannah had breathlessly crossed the little bridge, with its cheerfully painted arch that informed her she was entering Cowboy World, Daniel had caught up with her and was now kicking up gravel sulkily at her heels. 'All it's going to be is a load of fibreglass cowboys.'

'Maybe.'

'OK, if you're lucky, perhaps a fibreglass Indian.'

Hannah sighed, praying he wasn't going to ruin everything with his resistant moodiness. 'There's a gift shop. Or at least there used to be,' she attempted.

'Woo-hoo.'

And Daniel was right. Hannah couldn't argue with

the fact that Cowboy World was, indeed, little more than a bunch of fibreglass cowboys. Even with the slightly magical air that the afternoon sun was lending, fake cowboys were still fake cowboys. There was, however, a tiny gift shop called 'General Stores', where Hannah tried to cheer up sulky Daniel with the purchase of a cowboy hat, which, she promised him, made him look just like that sexy one off *Big Brother*. And there was also a dingy 'Sheriff's Office', in which sat the name-badge-identified 'Pete': the most bored-looking security guard Hannah had ever seen.

And there was something else. The something Hannah had come to see; not model cowboys, or her boyfriend looking really rather cute in a cowboy hat, or bored Pete, but a something that was actually little more than a wooden shed. A wooden shed, sitting there at the end of a dusty 'High Street' lined with fake saloons and endless fibreglass models. A wooden shed also known as 'The Jailhouse'.

After what Hannah deemed to be a respectable amount of sampling of the various delights Cowboy World had to offer, she led Daniel to the jailhouse.

It was exactly as she remembered from a previous visit – such a long time ago.

Quiet, tucked away a little from the screaming kids climbing up and down the fibreglass model horses.

Dark, lit only by the shafts of sunlight that worked their way through two greasy barred windows set high up on the dusty walls, and the light from a handful of candle-shaped electric lights.

And ominous, the distant sounds of laughing and screaming and general theme park fun somehow muffled by the four very realistic prison cells.

And to think, she had been scared that it wouldn't live up to the memory; worried that she had fantasised about this place so much that the reality would seem mundane. But it wasn't. Not at all. It was absolutely perfect.

The individual cells – two on each side of the room, with a rough sort of corridor in the middle – were constructed of bare open bars, making them more like large cages. The bars were real – clanging metal – nothing fake about them. And the doors of the cells fastened on the outside with sturdy-looking bolts. This was the factor that really made Hannah's mouth dry and her knickers wet. The cells were totally real. If someone locked you in one, you were trapped. A real prisoner until someone let you out again.

After Hannah had stared and stared for several minutes, she remembered Daniel, standing in the doorway. He looked around the jailhouse, and then at Hannah and the expression on her face, and he smiled.

At dinner – their last dinner – back in the cheapo B & B Hannah was, yet again, trying to cajole Daniel into making all her adolescent dreams come true.

'Please, Dan, look, it's open until midnight. We'll go in late – not long before closing – and head for Cowboy World. It's the furthest point from the entrance anyway, so no one will even be there that late.'

Daniel had just got out of the shower. His hair was dripping on the cheap carpeting. He looked at her. He didn't say anything but his expression was sort of promising.

'Please, Dan. Please. It's our last night here and I really need to get this out of my system.'

'Well,' said Dan, 'say I did agree – not that I'm going to – what would I get in return?'

'Oh, sweetie! Don't think for a minute that there isn't anything in this for you.'

Daniel raised his eyebrows. He was standing in front

of Hannah, who was sitting on the edge of the bed, and – post shower – he was only wearing a little towel wrapped around his waist. One of Hannah's favourite looks. A little drop of water fell from his fringe and hit her knee. With a grin, Hannah reached out and loosened Daniel's towel, just a little, but enough that it only teetered on his hips for a second before falling away on to the floor.

Daniel's erection was right there then, right in front of her face, smelling shower sweet, but with just a tiny hint of muskiness underneath.

Taking Daniel's damp buttocks in both hands, Hannah tugged him a little nearer, then stuck out her tongue and licked the tip of his cock, very lightly. Then she pulled away and tipped her head back to look up at him.

'Well?' she said.

'Well, what?'

'Yes?' She leaned forwards and gave Daniel's cock a long luxurious lick from bottom to top, then pulled away again. 'Or no?'

Daniel pursed his lips. 'Can I just review those options again?'

Hannah laughed. 'OK,' she said. 'Yes?' Another long lick. 'Or no?'

'Hmm,' said Daniel, 'can I just –'

'No, you can't,' Hannah interrupted quickly.

'OK, well in that case I guess I don't really have much of a choice.'

'Guess not,' said Hannah.

And before Daniel had even finished his answer Hannah had dived forwards, swallowing his warm needy cock, and bubbling over inside with happiness.

A little while later, and with a soaring heart and knocking knees, Hannah opened the special zip compartment of her case and pulled out her special items, packed a week ago in a spirit of excited optimism: one extravagantly frilly floor-length cream skirt and one pair of heeled lace-up boots. Just the type of things a lady in the Wild West might wear. In fact, just the type of thing a poor wrongfully imprisoned young lady might be wearing the day she got thrown into the jailhouse.

She slid into the skirt, enjoying the feel of the rough silk against her smooth legs. She wetted her lips with her tongue – this was going to be too perfect.

Heading through the park's overly ornate gates that evening, Hannah felt very much the Wild West dame in her skirt and shoes, and she had persuaded Daniel to wear his tightest jeans and a proper shirt with buttons. He was carrying the cowboy hat she had bought him rather than wear it though, because, he said, he didn't want to look like some kind of nutter. But Hannah knew he was going to put it on for her once they were inside the jailhouse and he was playing her nasty cowboy captor.

It was much colder than it had been during the afternoon. A whippy sea breeze toyed with Hannah's frothy skirts and she shivered a bit in her skimpy outfit.

It was already past eleven and Cowboy World was as quiet as Hannah had predicted. No one was to be seen except a different, but just as bored-looking, security guard in the sheriff's office. (Hannah didn't get close enough to see the name badge this time.) Daniel nudged Hannah nervously when he saw him and flashed her a worried expression.

Hannah shrugged and said, 'Don't worry. He looks like he's asleep.'

Luckily this line seemed to convince Daniel, who smiled then and dutifully followed Hannah and her swishy skirts to the jailhouse.

Switching from loving couple to jailer and prisoner didn't seem anything like as hard as Hannah had thought it might be. Once they were in the jailhouse, Daniel took a step back and slapped on his hat, tilting the brim down so it almost covered one eye. Then he sniffed and sneered nastily, grabbing a firm hold of Hannah's bare upper arm.

'OK then, missy,' he said, 'we've had just about enough of your misbehaviour round here. Let's see if a night in the jailhouse doesn't help cool you off a little.'

Instantly, Hannah's knees went so weak she was actually glad of Daniel's bruising grip on her arm. 'Oh,' she said with genuine surprise, 'oh no, don't. I didn't –'

'Shut up,' Daniel snarled, yanking open the door of one of the cells. 'And there's no point in you making all that noise. They'll be no one around to listen to your whining in a minute anyway.'

With that he tossed Hannah inside the cell – so hard that she landed awkwardly on the wooden bed – slammed and bolted the door and walked away.

'No, please. Don't leave me here,' Hannah screamed after him, hammering her fists on the heartless metal bars of her prison, glad she knew the park was deserted.

And nothing, nobody replied.

By the weak light of the faux candles in the jailhouse Hannah examined her cell. She tried the door and found it very solid indeed. She ran her hands along the hard metal bars, enjoying the feel of the cold unyielding material that was imprisoning her, positively relishing the way it was so definitely inescapable. She tried, but there was no way she could reach the bolt on the outside of the door. And rattling the door itself was ridiculously futile.

The cell contained nothing but a bare wooden bed and a concrete floor. Hannah sat down on the edge of the bed and swallowed hard. Now she really was a prisoner. A prisoner in a cell she had always fantasised about.

After a little while the lights in the jailhouse went out. The park must be closing for the evening. Trapped in the dark, Hannah felt her breathing get even faster. She wanted to touch herself already; to snake a hand under her pretty frilly skirt and find out just how wet she was. She gritted her teeth though, and resolved to wait for Daniel's return, which seemed to be taking a long time.

And then he appeared. Suddenly, in the doorway, all tilted hat and wide-spread legs. He was holding a torch, which he pointed right at her, the harsh beam making her shy away and screw up her eyes.

'Having fun?' he drawled.

Hannah didn't say anything. She couldn't think of anything to say except to ask him – beg him – to come right over to her cell and fuck her. And she really didn't want to say that; at least not yet.

The threatening figure in the doorway strode into the jailhouse and opened the door of the cell adjoining Hannah's. This cell shared one barred wall with the one she was locked inside.

'Cell inspection,' said the jailer slowly. 'Need to make sure you don't try anything. Put your hands through the bars here.' And he indicated that Hannah should stick her hands through the barred wall into the cell where he stood.

'I won't try anything,' Hannah said softly.

'Now, bitch.'

With a meek noise of compliance Hannah did as she was told and the jailer smilingly produced a length of scratchy rope, which he used to bind her wrists together, effectively trapping her hands on the other side of the bars.

'Good,' he said when he was done tying her, 'now, time for your inspection.'

The jailer walked back around to the door of Hannah's cell and drew back the sturdy bolt. Hannah felt the atmosphere tangibly change as he walked into the cell with her, and she twisted helplessly against her bound wrists to try to face him. But his hands were on her hips in moments and he turned her back to face the bars.

Hannah shivered. She could barely see anything now, just the dark shapes of the furniture in the adjoining cell. He kept her waiting for a few moments before she felt the cool air where she was wet, as he lifted her skirts. But she didn't get what she was expecting and craving – him thrusting into her hard and urgent. Instead she just got a hand.

The jailer stroked her gently and pressed his mouth so close to her ear she felt the hairs on the back of her neck stand on end. 'You're very wet,' he said, shaping his breath into words rather than really speaking.

His body was tightly pressed against her, forcing her hard against the metal bars. 'Yes,' she said softly, squirming a little in his hands. His hand was gliding close to her clit. She didn't know whether she wanted him to touch it or not. It was almost as if she was so turned on that just a graze on her clit right now would make her come. And she wanted to come, she really did, and yet somehow she didn't. Not yet.

'Such a bad girl. No wonder they had to lock you up.'

And she could hear the smirk in his voice as he said that, and that was enough for her to anticipate what was coming.

Pulling his hand away from her, leaving her gasping and tugging hopelessly against her tightly roped wrists to regain his luxurious touch, he bunched up her frilly skirts in both hands and tucked them into her waist-band. Leaving her jutting arse suddenly bare and exposed.

'That looks nice,' he said, 'but I expect you're cold, though. Bound to be: you've let yourself get so wet.'

'Mmm.' Hannah sighed. She was feeling cold – not to mention helpless and humiliated – but didn't really want to say so, because she knew that would be playing into his hands – quite literally.

'Thought so. I expect you'd like me to warm you up.'

There was a pause then. A breathing space in the game. Hannah realised she was holding her breath. She was tied up and turned on in a shabby seaside theme park. It was the middle of the night and it felt like the end of the world. It was so surreal and yet hyper-real. Hannah exhaled.

And then he slapped her arse, hard.

The sudden shock made her grunt as she was driven by the force of it into the barred wall she was tied to. Even though she had been expecting it, even though she felt it turning her on even more as blood rushed to her groin, she felt indignant. It hurt. It hurt a lot. She didn't know if she could cope with a series of smacks like that.

Already, she desperately wanted to rub her sore flesh, both to soothe it and to feel how much it was burning. And she found she was struggling to free her wrists and do just that, even though she knew the rope was tight and fast. But she struggled nonetheless, succeed-ing only in creating sore red marks on each wrist.

He slapped her again. And although she could tell by the force of the blow that it was just as hard as the first one, it didn't seem to hurt so much. Her bottom still throbbed and she still felt like the stuffing had been knocked out of her, but she also felt something else – very distinct pleasure. Endorphins, said a little voice at the back of her brain. And then he whacked her again. And again.

Until the sting-sting-sting eventually became a slow and pleasurable burn.

He stopped after a dozen or so slaps and paused, leaving her waiting in the cool dark, wondering whether her punishment was over or whether he was just catching his breath before starting up again.

And the answer came with the soft sounds of a belt being unfastened and denim pooling on the grimy concrete floor. And she knew things had moved up a level. He pressed close against her from behind. She felt his erection then, as it grazed her bare buttocks, as hard and smooth as the metal bars, but hot with blood and arousal. And she felt him sigh a little as he pressed close, and sagged at the knees. And that was when she knew it was a matter of seconds.

He was inside her so fast then, warm and smooth and complete, through her and into her, stretching and straightening his legs to get deeper. He was pounding so hard that she felt like she was almost being driven through the bars. Unyielding coldness in front of her and unyielding hotness behind her; she saw stars.

And then she heard a little click, and looked over to see the glow of a cigarette lighter across the room. A face lit up. From nowhere a plume of blueish smoke appeared.

They weren't alone in the jailhouse.

She couldn't even try to guess when he had entered the dark little shack, but she could see him now as she squinted into the dark. A figure, illuminated only by the tiniest light of the glowing red end of his cigarette, was propped in the corner; with his tilted hat and the cloud of smoke now surrounding him, he looked like some kind of iconic image from a film.

She knew instantly who it was. It could only be

Daniel, the boyfriend who was supposed to be the one fucking her in the park jailhouse, the boyfriend who quite definitely wasn't the man behind her right now.

She hadn't noticed the switch straight away, what with the dark and the excitement and the torch light in the eyes. Oh, she had suspected something for a while. But it was only in that moment that she knew for sure that the person fucking her – the person who had spanked her so expertly – was a stranger.

And she realised she didn't care.

Daniel eased himself out of his corner and walked slowly across the creaking wooden floor, pausing briefly to throw his cigarette end out into the night. With a gentle smile he walked into the cell next to Hannah's and reached through the bars to place a finger under her chin.

Behind her the jailer kept right on fucking her, ignoring everything else around him. He was slamming in and out even harder and faster now, but she barely seemed to notice any more, she was so focused on Daniel. And, as she gazed at him, he lifted her chin and pressed his face close against the bars so he could kiss her, squashing his mouth into the gap between the metal uprights. She moaned as their lips met and she was pinned between both men – her cowboys – held from all sides by hard flesh and hard metal.

Daniel dropped his trousers, soft and quick, just like the jailer had done, and his own eager erection sprang out. He fumbled with the rope that held Hannah's hands and yanked it free, holding her right wrist tightly and forcing her fingers to close around his cock. He was already dripping with precome and she worked him fast, making him writhe and reach out to steady himself against the jail cell bars.

And, not wasting another second, Hannah found her clit with her free left hand.

Easily she slipped into the frantic rhythm the jailer was setting behind her, working her clitoris and Daniel's hot hard cock to the tune of her own fucking. Daniel kissed her mouth a little more and then danced his lips away to lick and tease her neck through the bars, until she squirmed and gasped. Behind her she felt the jailer begin to buck and spasm, jerking inside her as he came. She gasped. Then Daniel froze on her neck and she felt his penis twitch and flick in her hand as he came too.

And then they both seemed to fall away from her. Both the cowboys relaxed, their legs buckling. Hannah twisted her fingers against herself one more time and she came too, crumpling like damp paper, sliding to the floor with nothing to hold her up any more.

Around lunchtime the next day Hannah was slumped in the passenger seat of Daniel's little Fiesta, drifting in and out of sleep on the long journey home. Daniel was staring out at the road ahead. He hadn't noticed Hannah was awake.

For a while Hannah just watched the big blue signs count down the junctions as home drifted nearer and nearer.

'Next year you can choose,' she said dreamily as they passed junction 21.

Daniel jolted out of motorway-driver mode and smiled at her. 'If you like.'

'We can go to Greece if you want.'

'Oh, I don't know about that,' said Daniel, 'I think you might be right about the hidden treasures on offer at the English seaside.'

A little later that same afternoon, Pete, one of the security guards in Cowboy World looked up in surprise as his colleague Frank walked in, over an hour before change of shift. Frank had a rather large, rather odd grin on his face and was wearing one of the cowboy hats that they sold in the gift shop.

'Hi,' said Frank, with a wicked smile.

Pete squinted at him. 'What are you looking so pleased about?'

Frank grinned again. 'Wouldn't you like to know?'

Pete raised his eyebrows and then turned back to his newspaper.

Frank stood in the doorway, waiting and grinning.

Then Pete said, 'That girl I saw yesterday, the one that was so interested in the jailhouse, she came back, didn't she?'

Frank's expression changed a little. 'Yeah.'

'There certainly is something about that jailhouse. They keep saying it's dangerous, that someone could get themselves really locked in, but they never seem to go through with changing it, which is a good thing if you ask me, because the kinky girls really seem to love it.'

Frank's grin seemed to slowly melt off his face.

Pete stood up. 'Used to get them once in a while when I was on the evening shift too. Dirty, bad little things, all hot with the idea of being locked up in there, at the mercy of some nasty cowboy.'

Frank opened his mouth, and then closed it again.

'Anyway,' said Pete, as he gathered his belongings ready to leave, 'just one word of advice – in case you get lucky again this season – the switch to turn off the CCTV recording in the jailhouse is just here.'

And he pointed to one of the buttons on the security desk, before pushing his way past Frank, shoving a VHS cassette into his hands as he left.

# The Swimming Pool
Caroline Martin

The sudden lurch of the aircraft, accompanied by crackly instructions from the pilot to fasten our seatbelts until we were through the turbulence, jolted me from my sleep and back into panicked consciousness. I stared, stricken, out of the window and watched the wing dip into an endless sky. I closed my eyes and exhaled slowly and deliberately in an attempt to force my body into a state of serenity.

'You've missed dinner,' my friend Kate told me. 'It was a real treat too. Chicken in an unidentifiable sauce, soggy veg, a dry bread roll and a dollop of something masquerading as a crème brûlée.' She rolled her eyes and passed me a couple of miniatures and a plastic glass. 'Here. Thought you'd need a G and T to calm you down when you woke up.'

'Oh, you wonderful creature,' I gushed, unscrewing the bottles and pouring their contents into the glass.

'I have to say, you certainly seemed to be having nice dreams. You were smiling and kept giggling and towards the end you shouted out, "Oh, yes, like that, yes!" She thrashed her head from side to side, with an ecstatic look on her face.

'I did not!' I protested, trying not to laugh at her ridiculous display.

'Well, all right, not the last bit. But you were grinning from ear to ear and did have a couple of chuckles. Thinking of a certain gorgeous Scotsman by any chance?' She knocked back half her glass of gin and looked at me expectantly.

I smiled at the recollection of my recent encounter with a muscular, sandy-haired Scot. Less than 24 hours ago we had met – and then got rather well acquainted – at a party hosted by a mutual friend. I didn't know his name, exactly where he was from, how old he was or what he did for a living. Beyond his physicality I knew nothing about him, just as he knew nothing about me. And there was the thrill of it: locking eyes with a stranger, the silent agreement, urgent fumbling, the discovery of new flesh, new scent, the sensation of new hands exploring my body, loss of inhibitions. And afterwards, a kiss on the cheek, a shy 'goodbye', maybe even a 'thank you', my feverish body still humming and tingling. And then gone.

'It's going to get you in trouble one day,' Kate said, suddenly serious.

'What is?'

'Your penchant for shagging strangers.'

I giggled and took another slug of my G and T.

'I mean it,' she said. 'It could be really dangerous, you know.'

'He was a friend of George's and we were at George's house.' I tutted. 'What was going to happen?'

She sighed, exasperated. 'I'm not just talking about last night, I'm talking generally. They could be anyone. One of them could turn out to be a right nutter.'

'You make it sound like there's been a few hundred,' I protested.

She arched a golden eyebrow.

'Hey, don't be mean.' I paused to sip my rapidly disappearing drink before venturing, 'Anyone would think you're jealous.'

It was her turn to laugh. 'Worried, yes. Curious even.

Jealous, no, not at all. I've got my James.' She smiled dreamily.

'Well, as a happy singleton, I'm free to do as I please.' I frowned, suddenly concerned about my friend's attitude towards me. 'I don't sleep with just anyone, you know,' I said quietly.

She gave my arm a squeeze and smiled. 'I know you don't, darling. Just be careful though, that's all I'm saying.'

The plane wavered violently again, causing our bottles and glasses to slide across our pull-down tables. I failed to contain a strained squeak – it erupted from my mouth before I could stop it – and I gripped my armrests tightly until my knuckles faded to white.

'For God's sake . . .' Kate laughed and pushed the call button above our heads. A smiling air steward miraculously appeared. 'Two more G and Ts, please,' Kate said. Then, glancing at me she added, 'In fact, let's make those doubles.'

An hour and a half and several gins later, Kate and I tipsily dragged our suitcases from Chania airport and slung them into the baggage hold of our transfer coach. High-spirited but exhausted, we nodded off instantly and were awoken twenty minutes later when we arrived at our apartments. Within minutes we had checked in and collapsed into our beds.

For the next few days Kate and I hung out at the local beach. We drenched ourselves in oil and lay impatiently under the sun, enjoying the sensation of its fiery tongue licking every inch of our heat-starved bodies. We read trashy novels, listened to cheesy compilation CDs and studied our fellow beach-dwellers with a keen interest. Our nights were spent sipping margaritas and flirting with olive-skinned locals but Kate's words about my sexual habits were still at the forefront of my mind so, at the end of each evening, it was Kate's arm I looped my own through as I made my way home to bed.

On our fourth day, Kate's skin began to blister. I stroked cooling aloe vera over the irritation but it failed to soothe her chest and arms, which raged with prickly heat. She scratched her flesh in a savage effort to ease the persistent itching but her clawing simply exacerbated the condition.

'It's no good.' She sighed. 'I need to stay in the shade today.'

I frowned and stroked her hair. 'Well, let's hire a car and visit somewhere,' I suggested.

She shook her head. 'I've just had too much sun. I'd rather stay here. I'll put the air-con on and chill out with a book, then, hopefully, I'll be fine later. You go to the beach.'

I protested but Kate was insistent that her 'contamination' shouldn't spoil my holiday, so in the end we compromised and I agreed to sunbathe around our apartment's pool so that I could pop back and keep an eye on her. I stepped into my swimwear, tied a sarong around my waist and, after casting a concerned look at Kate, who waved more cheerfully than I'm sure she felt, headed out of our apartment.

The pool was busy and I was only just in time to secure one of the few remaining sun loungers. Once settled I opened my book and absorbed myself in the preposterous tale of a supermarket checkout girl who somehow met and married a rock god before becoming a Hollywood starlet in her own right. I wasn't quite sure what had possessed me to buy such a novel but it was easy reading and I found myself enjoying its escapist romanticism despite my cynical nature.

The heat was intense and beads of sweat began to form on my skin. I rested my book against my chest, pages splayed open, careful to avoid losing my place, and ran the back of my hand over my sizzling forehead.

A cold shower of water sprayed my legs and feet as someone jumped into the pool in front of me. My body jolted upright at the suddenness of the unexpected shower, unbalancing my book which slid from my body and slammed shut as it impacted with the ground. I frowned and turned to look in the direction of the pool.

And that was when I saw her.

A stunning golden-haired woman, perhaps 30 years old, grabbed a lilo, which floated beside her. Her toned tanned arms hoisted it from the water and flung it on to the concrete surrounding the edge of the pool. As she swam to the nearest edge I propped myself up on my elbows, rapt in the sight of her.

With effortless grace, she eased herself out of the pool and made her way to the shower. She gasped as icy crystals burst from the shower head, her body flinching and momentarily swerving away from the spray. She laughed lightly before diving under the water again, this time remaining under the powerful jet. Her nipples visibly hardened under the sodden clingy fabric of her swimsuit; they stood erect, poking through the cloth as though eager to escape the chilly water and seek solace once more in the sun. She raised her lithe arms to her head and smoothed her hair as the water gushed over her scalp and face and then cascaded over her shoulders. Her smooth bronze skin shone with the slick combination of water and sun lotion. She looked like a goddess.

My gaze followed her movements as she returned to her sunbed by the poolside. Dripping fat, liquid splodges on the ground, she snatched up her towel then hesitated. She did not wrap it around her as I thought she would but flung it on to her lounger, hooked her thumbs beneath her straps and peeled her swimsuit down. I held my breath as she lowered the fabric over her chest. Full, firm, lusciously round breasts bounced free from their confines. Her nipples which I had just witnessed stiffen under the shower, relaxed a little as they basked under the hot sun, but they were still the longest nipples I had ever seen. I imagined what it would be like to suck them, to feel them harden and extend into my mouth, to rub them with my fingertips, pinching and squeezing the juicy buds until they were rock. I felt my own nipples tighten inside my bikini top and became aware of a growing dampness between my legs.

'You must be careful.'

I jumped guiltily and then turned towards the direction of the voice. Janis, the barman, was collecting glasses. He came to stand in front of me, obscuring my view of the woman.

'You are very pink here.' He touched my cheek gently with the back of his hand. 'And here too,' he continued, grazing his fingertips across my collarbone. 'You are burning.'

Flustered, I shook my head. 'I'm OK.'

He frowned. 'You are very red. It is very hot under the sun at this time of day. It can be dangerous.' He bent down and reached to the side of my sunbed, from where he extracted an empty water bottle. I glanced over his broad tanned shoulder. The woman was now lying on her front, motionless except for an irregular tapping motion of her right foot as she joined the rhythm of whatever music was playing in her headphones.

I sighed.

'Sorry,' Janis said. 'You want me to leave the bottle here?'

'No, no, it's fine. Perhaps you're right. I'll sit in the shade for a little while.'

He nodded. 'Yes, you should cool down.'

I wandered to the shady bar area, closely followed by Janis carrying a precarious tower of glasses and empty bottles.

'Just another water, please.' I perched on a bar stool and placed a couple of coins on the bar.

'So,' he said, setting down my drink and scooping the money into the till, 'are you enjoying yourself here?'

I nodded as I sucked some liquid through a straw. 'Very much.'

'It is very beautiful here, yes? Lots of beautiful things to look at?'

I thought of the woman in the shower and fought the temptation to glance back at her now to see what she was doing. 'Oh, yes, the mountains are wonderful,' I said quickly, taking another sip of my water. 'And the sea's so clear.'

He grinned. 'But you don't need the beach when you can stay here.' He opened his arms in an expansive gesture, sweeping the pool and bar area. 'Everything you need is here, yes?'

I grinned back. 'It certainly is.'

Our conversation was interrupted by several heads bobbing over the edge of the bar.

'Can we have some ice cream?' a group of boys chorused.

Janis smiled and guided the children to the freezer at the other end of the bar. 'Now, what you would like?'

I turned towards the blonde woman who was still lying on her front and sighed again as I remembered the way she had looked as she had emerged from the water; the way her body had responded so brazenly to the changes in temperature as she flung herself into the icy shower and then dried herself under the sun. The way I had felt such a powerful desire as I watched her.

My thoughts were broken by the presence of a man

who, despite an empty bar area, came and stood right beside me, so close that his thigh nudged mine as he stood waiting to catch Janis's eye. I had watched him dive into the pool earlier. Or, rather, I had looked up from my summer reading just in time to see his tight buttocks encased in skimpy black Speedos. I could see now that the sight of him from the front was even more breathtaking. His trunks clung unapologetically to his crotch. The size and fullness of his balls were clearly visible; they hung heavily, barely contained, it seemed, by the fabric of the trunks which stretched to contain their weight. His cock too was on display, its length and form showcased by the flimsy damp material. I stared at its bulging crudeness; it looked obscene. Many women, I imagine, would have looked away disgusted but I felt an aching need between my legs and shifted uncomfortably on my stool.

Janis returned and signalled that he had run out of cold beers. He hurriedly offered to fetch more from the storeroom and the man nodded appreciatively and leaned forwards, resting his hands on the bar. He was bulky; tall and broad with a thick neck and square jaw. His dark hair was cut short although the presence of stubble suggested that he had not shaved for two or three days. All in all, he was attractive, although his facial features and general physique failed to hold my attention for very long. After a preliminary scan my eyes were drawn once more to his bulging Lycra-clad package.

I just had to touch that cock.

Without pausing for a moment to consider what I was doing, I shifted to the edge of my stool and reached out my hand. I placed my open palm flat to the front of his Speedos and pressed gently but firmly. His body instantly jolted upright and he turned to look at me, parting his lips slightly as though to speak. For a moment I was anxious, concerned that he was about to reject my attention, but I left my hand hovering in front of his crotch and he quickly closed his mouth again. I stood up and, without speaking, eased into a position which would conceal my action without alerting suspicion. I pressed him again, harder this time. He groaned softly and closed his eyes as I began to rub in circular motions across the front of his crotch. I increased my rhythm, feeling his bulge swell until I could not stand it any longer. I gripped his shaft through the fabric and squeezed along his length. With my other hand I cupped his balls, alternating soft caresses with firm squeezes. The head now poked over the top of his trunks, a shimmering wet bead visible on the tip. I peered over his shoulder and scanned the pool area; no one was looking in our direction and we remained alone at the bar.

I pushed the front of his trunks down, releasing his straining cock which eagerly sprang free. His eyes flew open in alarm and he took a step back.

'It's OK, no one's looking.' My voice sounded husky, urgent. I couldn't bear the possibility that this would be the end of our encounter.

I looked down at the muscled column of flesh. Now fully erect it lay stretched and taut against his belly. I reached for the tip, circling the tiny slit with my thumb, smearing his juices over and around the head. He closed his eyes again and clenched his jaw. Enveloping the length of him, I slid my hand up and down his hardness, squeezing him and twisting my wrist a little as I gripped him tightly. I peered over his shoulder once more, amazed that no one had noticed our activity. My gaze settled again on the blonde woman from the shower who was shifting position. I gasped as she sat upright, exposing those delicious raspberry-pink nipples once more. Then I gasped again as my bikini knickers were yanked aside and a determined finger dipped straight into my wetness. I tugged his cock more forcefully, pumping him hard as he rubbed my clitoris and pushed one then two fingers inside me.

All the time, I watched the woman who had begun to apply sun cream to her front. I could smell my own arousal as I watched her massage the lotion into her breasts, paying particular attention to her sensitive buds. The cock in my hand began to twitch and I could feel the tension in the man's thighs and arse as he tried to resist the urge to thrust. I squeezed his full balls with my left hand while the right pulled at him roughly. His breath ripped out of him in short sharp bursts. As his fingers found my swollen nub again, I closed my eyes and imagined that his finger was her erect nipple, rubbing and agitating my wet clit and sliding inside me.

Within seconds, I felt a sudden hot heady rush as a powerful orgasm surged through my body. While my pelvic muscles contracted violently with each wave of pleasure, I strained against my body's natural instinct to jerk and buck. Flinging my hips back I slammed my buttocks into the bar, accidentally releasing my grip on the man. His expression was pained but before I had time to grasp it again he had grabbed himself with the same fingers that were slick with my juices. It was the most exquisite sight.

'That's right,' I murmured as he tightened his grip on himself, 'I want to see you work your cock.'

'Oh, fuck.' His eyes were shut tight and he moaned as he began to stroke himself. Despite the previous frenzied activity when my hand had been wrapped around his shaft, pumping him until he looked ready to burst, he began tentatively with long, steady strokes.

'Do it faster,' I quietly ordered him.

He grunted and increased his strokes.

'Yes,' I breathed, 'do it really hard.'

With both hands on himself, rubbing and pulling, he began in earnest to fuck his own hand.

Unbelievably aroused, I reached for his balls, which were pulled up high and tight, desperate for release, cupping and squeezing them. At once I felt his entire body stiffen.

'Fuck,' he growled. 'Oh, God, I'm going to . . .'

Leaning forwards slightly he gripped the edge of the bar with one hand and grimaced as his cock went into spasm.

We both stood wordlessly for a few seconds, hot and breathless. He rearranged his Speedos and I checked myself to ensure my own modesty, although it was probably too late to be worrying about that. The man and I both looked up at the same time and met each other's gaze. He smiled, awkwardly at first and then rather arrogantly.

A dark-haired woman approached us and jabbed him in the shoulder. 'What have you been doing all this time?'

He shrugged and mumbled something.

She sighed overdramatically and reached between us, picking up a couple of bottles from the bar. 'It's a wonder our beers aren't warm now,' she complained. 'They've been sitting on here for five minutes and that's all it takes in this heat.'

Five minutes?

The man and I looked up immediately, scanning the bar for Janis who was nowhere in sight.

'Men!' She tutted, grinning at me. 'What can you do with them?' Bottles of beer in hand, she nudged the man's arm and steered him back to their sun loungers.

When I returned to our apartment shortly afterwards, Kate was sitting on her bed watching a Greek soap opera.

'This is great,' she said without looking up. 'The man with the moustache is married to the blonde who's pregnant with the other man with the moustache's baby. And her dad's just left her mum for another woman who, unbeknown to him, has just been killed in a tragic moped accident. And I got all that without subtitles.' She shook her head in wonderment. 'Amazing.'

I laughed. 'You don't look so red now. Still itchy?'

She shrugged. 'A bit.'

I stood at the foot of her bed. 'It's boiling today,' I said, somewhat redundantly.

Kate smiled and nodded. She looked at the book in my hand and pointed to my bookmark. 'You didn't get very far. Too busy to read?'

'What do you mean?' I carried my damp towel on to the balcony where I concentrated on draping it across the area with far more precision than was necessary.

'Well...' Kate stood behind me, hands on hips. 'There's always so much to do around the pool, isn't there?' she said sweetly. 'So many new people to meet.' She stretched luxuriously and smiled, then leaned forwards and rested on the balcony wall. 'You know, it was so nice out here at lunchtime.'

'I thought you were staying in all day? Why didn't you come down to the pool?'

She shook her head. 'It was shady up here then; lovely and cool. Not nearly as hot as down there. It looked positively scorching from where I was sitting.' She grinned mischievously and tilted her head slightly, a signal for me to take in the view.

I went to stand beside her and stared speechless at the sight before me.

'The pool, the bar ... what a fantastic vantage point we have from here,' she said. 'I didn't know we overlooked all that, did you?'

'No.' My voice caught in my throat as I continued to stare at the bar area.

'Tell you what,' she said brightly, 'I'll get us some wine from the fridge and then you can tell me all about it.'

Kate and I talked into the early hours and drank three bottles of wine between us before we finally drifted into sleep. She quizzed me about Speedo-man, demanding every last detail. But although she was fascinated and shrieked with delight at my lurid confessions, I couldn't help but remember her disapproving words of a few days before. She, like my other friends, teased me about my sexual voracity and expressed concerns, yet was also keen to hear about my encounters. They seemed to take a vicarious pleasure in my sinful tales, as though it made their own safe lives in their safe relationships suddenly wild and exotic. I took their jibes with good humour but wished they could accept my choices without fuss. So, I refused to be brainwashed into searching for my Mr Darcy. So what? What was I missing out on? Monotonous weekends of takeaways, *Football Focus* and the missionary position?

I wanted passion. When I felt a body against mine, I wanted to feel raw emotion – ragged lust and the purest desire. I wanted to take and be taken and be shaken to my very core. I wanted to lose every inch of my being in that moment; to feel so in tune with my body, my mind and my lover that the experience was almost spiritual; to feel sensual explosions that take days to recover from.

All women want this, don't they? The only difference between my friends and me is that, unlike me, they don't believe they can actually have it.

I woke up just after nine feeling distinctly hungover and dragged my dehydrated body into the shower.

Feeling ravenous I hunted in the kitchen cupboards only to find nothing remotely palatable. Kate was still softly snoring so I wrapped my sarong around my hips, pulled on a vest and stepped into my sandals, then made my way out of the apartment complex and on to the narrow road beyond. I had heard our next door neighbours talking on their balcony about a wonderful bakery a few minutes walk away, so I decided to set off to find it and bring back some brunch for Kate and me.

A few minutes walk away became half an hour of my being lost. As I continued to turn down winding streets lined with tiny white houses I desperately tried to get my bearings, but it was hopeless. I had underestimated how hot it would be and had not worn a hat – my head throbbed in the heat and I could feel the back of my neck burning as half an hour stretched into an hour.

Just as I felt ready to drop to my knees and weep, I spotted a man coming out of one of the houses.

'Um ... *kalimera*.' My voice was weak. 'I'm, um, looking for the ... erm ... the bakery,' I said, waving my hands wildly in the hope that my gesticulating would somehow indicate bread. 'The, um, *boulangerie*?' I said feebly.

He smiled and said in perfect English, 'Just around the corner.'

I thanked him profusely before stumbling around the bend, feeling dizzy and slightly sick. Within seconds I was standing in front of the pastry Mecca I had set out to find almost two hours before. And then I fainted.

'Are you OK?' The voice was soothing and full of concern.

I tried to focus and my vision gradually became sharper. Staring down at me – a vision of compassionate concern – was the woman from the swimming pool.

I struggled to sit up and she handed me a glass of

water. Beside her stood an elderly man wearing a white apron – the baker, I presumed – who looked just as anxious.

'Sorry,' I mumbled between thirsty gulps of water. 'How long was I out for?'

The woman looked at her watch. 'Oh, er –' she looked thoughtful '– about four seconds,' she said, smiling.

I laughed and the man gently helped me to my feet. The coolness of the shop and the water had made me feel considerably better already.

'I think you're staying at the same apartments as me,' the woman said.

'That's right,' I said without hesitation. I felt myself blush slightly and added, 'I think I saw you by the pool yesterday.'

She smiled and nodded. 'Well, what about if I escort you back, just in case you pass out again?' She lifted up a couple of bags. 'I've bought plenty and I'm prepared to share.'

We walked at an easy pace, pausing every few minutes so that she could check that I was OK. We chatted comfortably with each other about what we did back home and what we thought about the island. She was on holiday alone after her partner split up with her three days before the flight.

'Well, he sounds pretty stupid to me,' I said as our apartments came into sight.

She giggled. 'Thanks for the support. Actually though, he's a she.'

I felt my cheeks burn but a fluttering in my belly suggested that embarrassment was not the only emotion I felt.

We arrived at the block of apartments that adjoined Kate's and mine.

'Well, we're here but it looks like the maid is too,' she said, pointing to a trolley full of towels and toilet rolls outside her door. She smiled apologetically. 'I don't think I'll be such a great hostess with someone cleaning around our feet.'

I tried hard to conceal my disappointment. 'It doesn't matter.' I shrugged.

She looked thoughtful. 'Well, there's plenty here for your friend too. We could go to yours and just all share it out?'

'Fine,' I said, making every effort to sound nonchalant, and we set off for my apartment.

The apartment was empty when we entered. I picked up a scrawled note that Kate had left on my bed.

'Rash better. Gone to pool,' I read aloud.

We stood for a moment, suddenly awkward. The conversation that had flowed so freely earlier now deserted us.

'I could go back?' she said at last.

'No,' I blurted.

She raised an eyebrow flirtatiously and I felt my stomach dip and twirl.

'Well,' I said hastily, 'if you want to . . .'

'If I want to what?' She smiled mischievously, enjoying my obvious discomfort.

'If you want to go back, then you should go back,' I babbled, 'although if you wanted to stay, then obviously . . .'

Before I had a chance to register, she took hold of my hand. Excitement and fear were a toxic concoction and I struggled to catch my breath as she pressed her lips against mine. I marvelled at their warm softness. As she pushed harder against me I cradled the back of her head, weaving my fingers into her silky hair. She grazed her teeth across my lips, catching my bottom lip, and I moaned as she gently tugged at my tingling flesh. Her tongue eased my lips apart and I sucked on it, pulling her deeper into my mouth. She moved her head away and looked directly into my eyes, stroking my left cheek with the gentlest caress I had ever experienced. The sensation made my skin prickle and I was overwhelmed by the way it aroused my whole body – with the slightest touch this beautiful woman had ignited my entire being. Her green eyes shone as I mirrored her actions, stroking her with what I hoped was a touch as delicate and sensual as hers. She closed her eyes and leaned into me, sighing against my ear.

'You smell lovely,' she whispered, nudging against my neck.

Excitement gripped my chest and I seized her head and pushed her closer to my hot skin. She licked and sucked and nibbled at my taut flesh and I gasped and moaned in shocked delight at the agonising pleasure her actions caused. She increased the pressure of her tongue, sliding it wetly down my neck and along my collarbone, expertly stimulating erogenous zones I didn't know I had. Despite the fact that they had not been touched, my nipples swelled and tightened, standing erect and pushing almost painfully against my skimpy vest top. I bit my bottom lip in an attempt to stifle my moans.

Still with the lightest touch, she slid her fingers beneath my straps and pulled them agonisingly slowly down my arms. I held my breath as she revealed my breasts and felt my legs weaken as she licked each of my nipples in turn, teasing them into ever-stiffer peaks. I watched her lapping at my breasts, amazed by the response she was creating in me. She closed her lips around one of my hard nipples, sucking hungrily.

I tentatively reached for her, curious to touch her body and see how she responded. I carefully lifted her T-shirt until it rested high on her chest. I took in the sight of her bare breasts and murmured my approval before tenderly cupping each one. While she continued to lick and tease my nipples, I squeezed her gently, enjoying the fullness in my hands. I had never touched another woman in this way and the beauty of her body, the sensual passion of the encounter and the wetness that seeped into my knickers thrilled me.

I grazed her prominent nipples with the tips of my thumbs, enjoying their rough texture and was surprised and delighted by how much larger they became at my touch, how they stiffened and puckered as I rubbed and teased them. Curiosity and arousal got the better of me, defeating any concerns I may have had about not knowing how to please a woman, and I caught each long nipple between forefingers and thumbs and rubbed them harder. I felt unbearably aroused by the sight and sensation of feeling them under my skin, while she continued to work my own into a lustful frenzy. As I pulled them hard, she cried out and bit one of my nipples with such force that I arched my back and experienced a light-headed sensation, immediately followed by a molten spasm in my crotch.

I was amazed by my body's intense response and welcomed her mouth as she moved to kiss me again and pressed her body closely to mine. Although satisfied by my unexpected climax, I wanted more than ever to touch her. As we kissed, I let my hands skim down her back – I desperately wanted her to experience the pleasures I had just felt.

A loud knocking at the door startled us and we leaped apart like guilty teenagers.

'Erm, it sounds like you're quite busy...' It was Kate's voice. 'But I've forgotten my key and I really need to come in. So, if you and the lucky man could just make yourselves respectable...'

The woman and I collapsed into giggles and re-arranged our clothing.

'I can hide on the balcony?' she whispered.

I laughed. 'No need. It'll be worth it to see the look on her face.'

I opened the door and Kate raced in.

'I'm so desperate for the loo,' she wailed, pushing past me and heading to the bathroom.

'Why didn't you use the one by the pool?' I asked.

'Roaches.'

When she emerged, she noticed the woman standing in the kitchen for the first time. She raised her eyebrows in surprise, then forced her features into a casual expression. 'Hi,' she said warmly.

'Hi – and bye,' said the woman. 'I'm just leaving.' She signalled to the carrier bags and then looked at me and winked. 'Enjoy the buns.'

Grinning, I walked to the door with her.

'Perhaps I'll see you later?' she said.

I nodded and waved as she walked towards her apartment. Closing the door, I smiled at the surreal situation.

'You might well smile!' Kate bellowed. 'Oh my God!'

'It's not a big deal,' I said, blushing.

Kate looked wide-eyed and headed towards the fridge. 'I think,' she said, taking out a bottle of wine, 'you and I need to have a little chat.'

# Ice Cold in Verbier Angel Blake

They could hear the rink before they turned the corner on to the main drag, the scrape of blade on ice, the excited cries, the blare of the PA all muffled by the snow piled high in drifts around them. Tim had told a sceptical Alana they'd be running a shift system, and couldn't help feeling smug as they were given their wristbands and told to wait after reaching the head of the queue.

It was warm in the changing room, and Tim's glasses had steamed up after the icy cold outside. He took them off, wiped them dry with his sweatshirt, then peered nervously around. He was relieved not to recognise any of the faces. He hadn't been skating for years, having embarrassed himself too often as a gawky teen breathlessly careering down the middle of the rink, and was none too sure of his ability tonight; but he didn't want to sit at home with his parents, especially not while Alana was out having fun.

As he hobbled in the hard skates towards the entrance to the rink, already starting to sweat under the layers his mother had fussed over, he saw her. It was partly her clothes that stood out: the furs wrapped around her, the sheer stockings hugging her long legs. She had her own skates too, small and stylish in comparison with the clunkiness of the rental boots; and she was beautiful, there was no question of that, the doll-like delicateness of her pale face, her lips a shocking carmine slash, setting her apart even from the other pampered faces on display, her shiny brown hair pulled back into a tight ponytail. But it was something else about her, something in her poise as she turned to laugh with her companion, something impeccable, hard and untouchable in her that drew Tim's attention most.

He almost fell when someone barged past him, their mulled wine breath clouding a muttered *'pardon'* as the first in a string of boisterous revellers made their way on to the rink, and he had to hold on to the rail to regain his balance. He hadn't realised he'd been staring, but the commotion had made the girl turn and look in his direction. He felt himself go hotly red as her eyes met his, and he lowered his gaze, staring at his boots as they moved from the soggy rubber on to the ice, but couldn't resist one last glance back before he wobbled off. To his horror she was still looking at him, her crimson lip curling into a cold smile.

He turned swiftly back to face the rink, scanning the crowd for Alana. It didn't take long to spot her. She was in her element, gliding lithely through the slower skaters, and Tim felt a pang of jealousy when he saw the admiring glances she received from some of the other men. He edged on to the rink, digging the blades of his skates into the ice, and pushed off.

Apart from a marked tendency to spin round to the left, which left him facing backwards, gasping, and having to step awkwardly to the side, he soon got the hang of it, and was pushing off more boldly, swinging his arms to build up momentum, until he was at the edge of his control, slightly scared but feeling the adrenalin course through him as he weaved through the crowd. Alana was talking to a man now, their arms linked as they danced on the ice, his sister's effortless skill almost a taunt to him, making him push himself, going faster, flushed now and overheating, his glasses misting from the exertion.

But as he watched her he saw another familiar figure

pass. The girl in the furs seemed to be in a group, including another woman and two men, all, apart from the pale girl he'd first seen, tanned and dressed in the kind of understated luxury that made Tim acutely aware of the shabbiness of his own clothes. But the other girl was nothing compared to the one in furs, and Tim couldn't take his eyes off her as she moved serenely around the edge of the rink.

His attention distracted, he only vaguely heard the cry of *'Schnell!'* before the wind was knocked out of him and he was on his back, still sliding along on the ice. He'd gone into someone, that much he knew, but all he was aware of was a guttural voice saying something that sounded like German swear words, and fuzzy shapes moving around above him.

His glasses had been knocked off, and he looked around him desperately, trying to catch a flash of light off the lenses before they were crushed. The ice sparkled treacherously. Already a small crowd was gathering around them, hands reaching down for the burly figure lying a few metres away, and then he saw them, miraculously intact, near the edge of the rink.

He slid his body over to them, blinking back the cold coming off the ice and ignoring the irritated French and German mutterings behind him, then reached out to grab the glasses. But just as his gloved fingers curled around the frame, a boot he half recognised skidded to a halt in front of him, the tip just running over the outstretched hand and making him sit up and cry out in a choked gasp with the sharp, sudden pain.

He looked up, squinting and shocked. His vision was blurred, but the pain tightened his focus, and what he saw was etched clearly on his mind. The girl in furs, her boot still crushing his hand, faced the edge of the rink and held open the lower half of her coat, to show him a long expanse of creamy white thigh, with a dark patch of fur at its centre.

'Timmy fell over!' Alana squealed delightedly as they got back to the chalet. His parents looked up from the table.

'Shut up!' He shoved her in the back, his voice still trembling from the effort of holding back the tears of pain and humiliation. 'And don't call me Timmy, OK?'

She turned and shoved him back, then looked at their parents. 'Until he can keep his balance, I'll call my kid brother what I want.'

She was only a year and a half older than him, and the line rankled. To his shame he felt the first tear begin to roll down his cheek, and wiped it off savagely with his good hand.

'Did you hurt yourself, Tim?' His mother's face was full of concern, and he pushed past his sister to move closer to her. He could see that his parents had been doing a jigsaw together.

'My hand. Someone skated into my hand.' He held it out and winced as his mother pulled the glove off. He hadn't looked at it yet, and felt a strange sense of vindication when he saw the angry red welt bisecting his palm, already turning a deep purple. He could have sworn he could see it throb.

'Oh, that looks nasty. We'd better put some ice on it.' His mother busied herself in the kitchen, taking the ice-cube holder from the freezer compartment and preparing a tea towel to wrap around the hand.

His father had turned to Alana. 'And you, darling. Did you have a good time?'

'She was talking to a man,' Tim fired off, and was gratified to see his sister look daggers at him.

'Now there's nothing wrong with that,' his mother

said as she tied the icepack around his hand. The ice felt soothing, numbing the pain away, and suddenly he felt guilty for having tried to get his sister into trouble. They were really, he reflected, a bit old for family holidays. He'd already been away with his friends, Inter-railing and to Greece, and now he was eighteen, a proper adult. But neither he nor his sister could afford a skiing holiday alone, and they'd both leaped at the chance when their parents had offered it as a Christmas present. Tim hoped their constant bickering wasn't ruining things for their parents; if he was honest with himself he knew he was jealous of her for her easy way with men.

Talking to girls didn't come naturally to Tim; even with Alana's friends he would be tongue-tied, then flee in shame as he blushed, imagining their giggles in his wake. He'd thought to change things this holiday, to be bold, take the initiative, but the week was almost over, and what had he done?

It had snowed overnight, but the sky had cleared before dawn and the thick crust glistened in the clear light. Tim watched, fascinated, as the tips of his skis broke the surface, sending a fine spray either side as he picked up speed near the forest. The piste bashers had only marked a couple of the wider avenues: the rest was pristine, virgin powder, and the slopes were only now starting to fill up. Tim didn't mind being out alone: he had long since given up trying to ski with Alana, who was a better skier and made a point of tackling suicidal off-piste slopes if he was in tow; and his parents, dithering around the nursery slopes, presented an equally unappealing prospect.

The forest was where he liked to be most, weaving in and out of the trees, taking the sharp turns and small jumps, micro moves through a landscape that reminded him of the fantasy worlds of his childhood. Today the trees were in stark chiaroscuro, their heavy load of snow leaving only the barest outline of branch. As Tim entered the still woodland he heard a thump behind him, echoing softly through the snow, as his arrival disturbed an overladen branch. Otherwise the forest was deafeningly silent, the trees and snow soaking up all the sound save for the sharp slices and hisses of his skis.

The path through the trees rejoined the main piste further down, and Tim took the jump on to the slope at speed, skidding across the broad expanse of freshly compressed snow, feeling the harder texture through his legs, then came to a stop, to look back into the forest before heading to the bottom of the lift. A flash of blue caught his eye, dancing across the slope behind him, and it took him a few seconds to work out what it was. Even then it made no sense: a butterfly, its iridescent wings almost too bright against the snow, tumbled and meandered across the slope, to vanish among the trees.

As Tim stared after it, astonished, two men and a woman schussed down the piste, all in matching ski-wear and expensive-looking accessories. With a start, Tim realised that they were the people he'd seen with the girl in furs the day before. But she herself was nowhere to be seen.

The lead, the other girl he'd seen, pulled up in a flurry of snow that buried Tim's skis, and turned to face him. She had, he realised with a sinking heart, probably recognised him as well.

'Aren't you the boy from the ice rink?' she asked in perfect English, with a pan-European accent that was impossible to place. Her mirror shades betrayed nothing.

Tim nodded mutely, and hoped that the ruddiness of his cheeks in the cold air hid his new flush. Her companions had come to a stop behind her, and rested on their poles, leaning heavily into the snow.

The girl smiled. 'I think Christine feels bad about your hand.' Before Tim had a chance to ask where she was, the girl carried on. 'Why don't you come round to ours later on? Have a drink, it's the least we can do. We're at number 78 rue Berquet, it's easy to find. Come after you eat, say for nine?'

Tim managed to stammer 'OK,' then the girl pushed off and sped down the slope, closely followed by her companions, who'd ignored their exchange throughout.

It had been their last full day in Verbier, and Tim had wandered around the town enough to have a pretty good idea of its layout. He'd told his parents he'd met a friend and was going out for a drink, but they hadn't seemed interested, apart from to make the usual dutiful noises about not coming back too late, not waking anyone up and so on. Alana had raised an eyebrow, but he'd ignored her.

The place itself had been easy to find, but Tim waited for a few seconds before going in, his breath clouding out in front of him. It was too cold to stand still for long, and he stamped his feet, trying to return some feeling to his toes. His mouth was dry, his tongue swollen, and he could hear his heart pounding in his chest. For a moment he considered going back to the chalet, but the thought of Alana's withering sneer filled him with energy and, determined now to go through with whatever the evening held, he rang the doorbell.

The door was opened by one of the men Tim had seen with the girls. He looked Tim up and down a little disdainfully, then seemed to remember something and called, 'Alice!' before walking back inside.

Tim, unsure whether or not he was allowed to enter,

stood on the doorstep, the door still open, and waited. He could hear music, laughter and the clinking of glasses coming from the main room. Then the girl he'd spoken to by the forest appeared.

'For Christ's sake close the door,' she said crossly, barging past him and slamming it shut.

'I'm sorry, I didn't . . .' Tim tried to explain, but Alice had taken his arm and was pulling him into the other room, nodding almost imperceptibly towards a row of hooks in the hall when he asked if he could take off his coat. The girl in furs – Christine, Alice had said her name was – was sitting on a sofa. The two men Tim had seen on the slopes earlier were there too, but neither looked up at him.

He stared at Christine. Her face was whiter than he remembered it, and she was dressed almost formally, in a dark skirt and jacket and a white shirt. But his eyes were drawn most of all to her boots. He'd never seen anything like them before. The heels were sharply pointed and high, the toe a vicious dagger point; but it was the height that took his breath away, the eyeholes snaking all the way up her shin and over her knee, to end a few inches higher. The contrast between the immaculately shiny black leather and the bare white skin of the thigh was striking, and Tim felt a sudden mad urge to cover the thighs in kisses, to feel their texture with his fingers.

'So you're the peeper.' He was already slipping into reverie when Christine spoke to him for the first time. Alice giggled a little, while the men toyed with their wine glasses.

Guiltily, Tim wrenched his gaze from Christine's upper thigh and the dark shadows under her skirt. 'I'm sorry, I wasn't trying to look up your skirt,' he blurted out. At this Alice burst out laughing, while Christine smiled, but there was no warmth in it. He could feel himself falling into her eyes, a glittering icy blue whose pull was impossible to resist.

'I didn't mean now. I meant at the rink. You were getting a good eyeful there, weren't you?' she asked.

'No I wasn't!' he protested, feeling himself colour again.

'Don't lie. What's your name?' There was a harder edge to her voice now.

'Tim.'

'Peeping Tim!' Alice roared out, then dissolved in fits of giggles. One of the men smiled; the other still looked bored.

'You know, women don't like people to look at them like that,' said Christine. 'Not unless they're invited. And certainly not teenaged boys.'

Tim was close to tears now. 'I couldn't help it, you showed it to me,' he protested. He could feel the bruise in his hand throbbing.

Christine's face tightened as Alice tried to suppress another giggle. 'Go into my room. Up the stairs, first on the left. I'll deal with you in a minute.'

Stunned, Tim turned and walked up the stairs. He wondered dully why he didn't just leave; but there was something about Christine that made him stay, partly a curiosity about what would happen to him, but also a desire to please her, to do anything she wanted, a desire he hadn't felt since having a long-forgotten crush on a babysitter nine years before. The memory shook him with its force, the desires of an unformed version of himself forcing themselves into his mind. He suppressed them with a shudder. He was a man now.

The door to the room was open, but it was dark inside and the air smelled stuffy, with a heaviness he couldn't place. He turned on the light, and was taken aback by the look of the bed, the sheets crumpled, pillows on the floor. There was something else next to them, and he bent down to take the crumpled pink fabric in his hands. A torn foil packet fell from the material, and his eyes took in the milky whiteness of the ring of rubber he hadn't noticed at first. But he had her knickers. He was holding her knickers. His heart leaping, he resisted the temptation to throw them down again, and instead brought them up to his nose. He could feel himself thickening as he stretched the gusset over his face then inhaled deeply, sucking in the rich, heady odour.

'What the hell do you think you're doing?'

Tim whirled around, still clutching the knickers in one hand. Christine stood in the doorway, her hands on her hips, staring furiously at him. He dropped the knickers on the floor.

'I was – it was untidy, I wanted to clear it up,' he said, lamely.

She walked over to him, and his head swam with her closeness.

'That's a likely story. You were snooping, like the grubby little teenager you are. Take your trousers off.'

'What? Why?'

'Take them off.' The voice was sterner now, and Tim felt a lump in his throat as he undid the button of his jeans, pulled down the zip and let them fall to a heap around his ankles. He knew that there was an unmistakable bulge in his pants, and crossed his hands over his crotch, praying she wouldn't notice.

'Take your shoes and socks off.'

Tim hobbled to the side of the room, his trousers around his ankles, then sat down and followed her orders.

'Stand up. Come over here.'

He obeyed, meekly.

'Take off your shirt too.'

As he did so, he was aware of the slimness of his chest compared to the other men in the chalet, and it made him ashamed to expose himself. He felt vulnerable, more than ever before, but there was a rising tide of excitement in him as well, leaving him dizzy with exhilaration. It was slightly cold in the room, and he put his arms around himself, feeling the goosebumps prickle on his skin as he began to shiver.

'Did it excite you to see me with nothing on underneath my coat?' she whispered in his ear.

It was hopeless to lie to her now. 'Y-yes,' he replied.

'And you enjoyed sniffing my knickers just now?'

'Yes.'

She was pulling on a pair of gloves as she interrogated him, soft black leather that reached high up on her forearms, and she gazed at his crotch. He felt himself twitch, and dropped his hands to cover himself again.

'Put your hands by your sides.'

Tim complied, straightening his back, staring straight ahead and assuming the army posture of attention he'd learned at school. But the bulge wasn't going away, and he twitched again as she sank to her knees before him.

'I don't want to touch it,' she muttered as she took hold of each side of his Y-fronts, then yanked them down. Tim was mutely passive now; events had overtaken his expectations so quickly and there was nothing left to do except see what happened. He was nervous, but he was responding, there was no doubt of that.

Something cold and unfamiliar touched his sensitive skin, and he looked down to see her winding a length of silk cord around his tight sac, tying the ends off over the base, then looping it over his shaft a few times and standing again to pull him, fully hard now, by the end. It was hardly orthodox behaviour for a first date, but Christine was not like any girl or woman he'd met before. He let her do what she wanted, seeing how far she would take things.

She sat down on the edge of the bed, the leather boots creaking, then lay back, still holding the silk cord in one hand while the other took hold of the hem of her skirt. He stared, fascinated, as the material rose to expose more of her thighs, then further still, inching over the dark fur between her legs.

'Kiss my boot.'

She spoke so quietly Tim thought he'd misheard. 'What?'

'Kiss my boot.' This time there was no mistake. He paused, his mind reeling at the thought of what she'd asked him to do, but when she gave a tug on the cord, he knew it would be unwise to protest.

As he leaned forwards to put his lips to the boot for the first tentative kiss, he saw her gloved hand snake down between her legs.

'Don't look!' she hissed.

The severity of her voice startled him, and he stared at the damp mark left by his lips on the gloss of the leather.

'Lick it.'

The command was accompanied by another sharp tug on the cord, and he stuck his tongue out to taste the leather. He was surprised at how bland it tasted; just a hint of something animal mixed with something old and stately. He could hear her fingers working herself, and felt himself twitch again as he smelled her excitement. He couldn't help looking up, to see her hand burrowing in the pinkness at the top of her thighs, her fingers moving busily. He had never seen a woman's sex before, except in magazines, and he caught his breath as he stole a peek.

'Don't look, I said, dirty boy. Close your eyes.'

Blushing and about to burst with excitement at the

thought of being in such close proximity to a masturbating woman – a beautiful one at that – he returned his attention to the boot, and began to lavish long laps of his tongue from the heel up to the knee and beyond, leaving a delicate tracery of gleaming leather behind him. She parted her legs further to give him better access, and he heard her groan. He would do anything she told him to.

The taste of the leather, the feel of the cord tugging on his thickness and the sounds of her hand rustling under her skirt filled his senses. He was licking more busily now, trying to please her, and felt rewarded when he heard her moan rise in pitch to a squeal as she tugged harder on the cord and her legs trembled, the boots clenched tightly around his head and he wondered whether this was her climax.

Then she was up and pushing him back with her heels. His eyes were still closed, and he felt blindly behind himself before falling back, a heel digging into his chest.

'Open your eyes.'

He blinked once against the light, then pushed his glasses back up his nose from where they'd been dislodged. She was towering over him, one boot to his left and the other pinning him to the ground. He tried not to look at the fur above him, her skirt still rucked up around her waist, but couldn't help noticing the glistening skin on her upper thighs. She drove her heel into his chest harder now, smiling down at him coldly as she tugged more firmly on the cord.

'You want to come?' she asked him, her voice thick with contempt.

He nodded.

'Bet you've never seen a woman like me before, eh?' Every time she ground the heel into his chest, she tugged harder on the cord. It hurt him, but the pain combined deliciously with the full tight feeling in his crotch. He wasn't sure what to do, and reached with one hand to touch himself.

'Don't touch it!' she spat, her expression one of fury. 'Leave it to me, you filthy-minded boy, I'll do it. I'll show you what happens to young virgin men who look up women's skirts.'

She pressed harder with the boot, shifting more of her weight on to the heel, and gave the cord a series of sharp tugs. The feel of the cord, the view between her legs and the boot on his chest were suddenly too much for him, and he felt the surge beginning. It wasn't the sexual encounter he had hoped for; he had thought that perhaps they might take a walk, get to know each other; maybe even go skating together. This was as far as possible from any romantic illusions Tim may have had about making love with this strange, icy young woman. She seemed to know it too, and was revelling in his shock and surprise – and the power she had over him at this vulnerable moment. As he stared at her, the first pulses of a climax coursing through him, her lip curled in an appalling sneer as she pushed the heel of the boot still harder into his skin. The clear white pain fused with his ecstatic release, stars boiling behind his eyes, as he emptied himself, jetting on to the shiny black leather that was still grinding into him.

Then it was over, and she was unwinding the cord, businesslike now. She looked distastefully at the marks of his spend on her boots, sliding slowly down the leather, and reached over for a box of tissues.

'Clean it off.' She didn't even look at him, but just passed him the box.

He gathered a few tissues then began to wipe. He'd never shot so much of it before, and felt pleased that he'd been able to show his appreciation. But he couldn't believe that that was it; surely she'd want him to do something else ... maybe even touch her. He wanted to serve her in some way – even help out around the chalet. Before he knew what he was saying, he'd offered himself.

'I'll do anything for you, you know, if you like.' He pushed his glasses back on to the bridge of his nose and gazed at her. When she snorted, her head shaking dismissively, he felt crushed, and lowered his eyes. He could feel the tears welling up, but was determined not to let her see them. He would show her that he could be strong.

'Get dressed,' she said, without emotion. Still not looking at him, she threw him his clothes. He was shivering, the room seeming much colder since their encounter. The mark of her heel on his chest was red and raw, and he gazed at it before pulling his T-shirt back on.

'I'm leaving tomorrow,' he told her, hoping for some final recognition of what they'd done together. There was nothing. She was facing away from him, her skirt down again now, staring out of the window. It was clear outside, and the crescent of a new moon glittered hard and cold in the night.

'You may leave now.' She didn't turn around. He started to reach out, to touch her, but thought better of it, and walked to the door. He knew she'd still be there, gazing out into the icy blackness, if he turned again at the door, so he stopped himself from taking a final look, and trod heavily down the stairs, confused. What kind of woman was this, who used young men in such a cruel way? He could only liken her to the dark goddesses of the graphic novels he used to read in the sixth form – they were always beautiful and heartless, immaculately dressed and unwise to cross. Maybe Christine had modelled herself on some comic-book icon, some bitch queen or modern-day Vampirella with a heart of steel.

The same mixture of laughter and music he'd heard before greeted him downstairs, but he was sure he wouldn't be welcome among her sophisticated friends drinking their expensive brandies and liqueurs, so he pulled on his coat and silently left the chalet. He was sure the laughter he heard as he walked past the window was at his expense. His face tightened in the night air, and he winced as he sucked the coldness into his lungs. There was no cloud cover, and the temperature was lower than when he'd arrived at Christine's chalet of cruelty. A hard rime of frost crunched under his feet as he walked to the road, and he concentrated on the sound as he trudged back, the mark on his chest throbbing in time to the beat of his heart, his imagination fuelled by the thought that he'd had an encounter with a superior being of the most exquisite, albeit vicious, temperament.

His parents were still up when he got back. The room smelled of wine, and he could tell by their eyes that they were a little tipsy.

'Darling!' his mother called out. 'Did you have a good evening? We weren't sure whether you were coming back, were we?' She said this to his father, who grinned broadly and winked at him.

'It was good, yeah, thanks,' Tim told them, alarmed by his father's conspiratorial air. Surely he couldn't have known? It would be their secret, his and Christine's. He raced up the stairs and locked himself in the bathroom.

Facing the mirror, he stripped down to his T-shirt and pulled it up over his chest. It was purple now, with a halo of blue bruised flesh ringing the deep central mark. He fingered it, tracing the outline of where her heel had dug into him, then tested the skin around the mark, wincing involuntarily when he pressed too hard.

'There,' he whispered excitedly to himself, his finger circling the indentation, fiercely proud. 'Christine was there.'

# A Taste for Salsa
Fransiska Sherwood

Still wearing the black cocktail dress and silver sandals I wore to dinner, I slip out of the hotel and escape into the sultry night. A light breeze caresses my skin – a reminder of lovers past, and the whispered promise of those to come. Stealthily it sneaks inside the open back of my dress and, like an invisible hand, brushes over my breasts and stomach. I shiver. Deliciously. Revelling in my freedom.

All around me I hear the calypso rhythm of crickets chirping. The percussion accompaniment to night's song. I skip over the cobbles, following whatever route my feet dictate. A winding path along narrow streets that Cuba's tourists see only by daylight. At this hour the squat, whitewashed houses are no longer posing for photos in the naked brilliance of the sun. Their facades have been turned a muted grey, the blue doors purple. Sleepy shades that are kinder to the eyes.

Yet these streets now seem more awake than they were during the day. Windows have been thrown open. There are people leaning out of them, chatting with neighbours and whoever might pass. The spicy scents of tortillas and tacos drift into the night, and flutter before me like a thread carried on the breeze, down to the harbour.

When I reach the bay, the air is humming with the buzz of voices and the raucous sound of trumpets and trombones. Coloured lights dance into the sea. In every bar they're playing salsa, samba and merengue. My hips start to rock as I walk, infected by the contagious beat. I just can't help it.

Soon I'm drawn inside. A cavern of a place with a vaulted ceiling that I guess may once have been filled with casks of rum. It's crowded with people, and the air is thick with the heady fragrance of sweat and perfume. A close, hot embrace. I squeeze my way to the counter and order a *caipirinha*, then climb on to a barstood while the barman slices a lime into segments and fills my glass with crushed ice. I sit at the bar and watch what's happening on the dance floor, my tongue electrified by the sour tang of limes and senses dulled by the sugarcane spirit *pitù*.

Here they dance salsa with a wild impulsiveness I've never encountered before. A far cry from the subdued restraint taught back home. But then, how could anything danced in Europe match the rude authenticity of something danced in the Americas?

I stare, mesmerised by the see-saw motion of snake hips clad in tight black trousers that leave nothing to the imagination. Lithe bodies weave their way round each other, charming each other with their hips, as if performing some kind of ritual mating dance to the chock-chock-chock of the claves beating against each other.

Soon my head's reeling and my body's yearning to take part. And it's not just my feet that are throbbing to a salsa rhythm.

I push my way forward and stumble out into the fresh air. Maybe I shouldn't have drunk that *caipirinha* so fast.

I catch my breath. Stars are just beginning to twinkle out of the inky blue sky, trying to compete with the lanterns and fairy lights that adorn the eaves of every bar and club. When they've stopped spinning, I continue over the cobbles down to the quay.

There are boats moored. Yachts, elegant and white, that look as if they don't belong here. They bob in the water as the tide laps against the jetty, waiting forlornly, like lost brides, for someone to come and claim them.

I wander on, tracing Hemingway's footsteps, along a stretch of beach paved at the top by flagstones. I take off my sandals and let my feet bask in the warmth they still give off, my soles tickled by their emery-paper scuff. A sensation akin to a lover rubbing his unshaven cheek against my feet.

I've reached the working part of the harbour. It smells of fish and tar. There are oily coils of rope lying about and briny nets spread out on the flagstones to dry. Battered fishing boats lie on their sides in the sand, waiting for the next high tide. It's not picturesque. Not where the tourists come for their photos of fishermen selling crayfish.

But it's far from dead.

There's a steady stream of people making for one of the warehouses and I can hear music. Is there a bar down here, known only to insiders and maybe the odd, adventurous stranger?

I put on my sandals and follow the throng past workshops and sheds. As I get nearer I can make out the definite strains of a salsa. An eight-beat rhythm of throbs and pauses that's already becoming part of my flesh and blood.

A makeshift sign hangs above the door: Chicago Joe's. I slip inside. The warehouse has been turned into a vast discotheque, the whole downstairs area devoted to the dance floor. A metal stairway leads to the bar upstairs and a suspended section decked out with chairs and tables. I guess it was once used for building boats.

I take the stairs and order another *caipirinha* from the bar. It's cheaper than the first one I ordered. Nothing added on for the tourists. I find a table and sit, looking down at the dancers. A carpet of heads that seems to pulsate in the flickering light.

I'm not left sitting alone for long. A strikingly well-groomed black guy in a tight, white silk shirt slides on to the seat opposite me.

'Hello, pretty lady. Where you from?'

'Holland,' I lie.

'You want to dance?'

Why not?

I leave my drink half-finished and follow him down the stairs. They vibrate with each of his steps and I tread on a hum I can feel through my feet.

He glides on to the dance floor and leads me to a space in the centre. I'd rather be in a less conspicuous place, but I guess with my blonde hair and blue eyes people are going to notice me wherever I stand.

He says his name is Rico. I say mine's Annette.

He slips a firm hand round my shoulder blade, the other takes mine in his. I feel his body poise, ready to side-step on the next intro beat. We move in the same instant, connected via the impulses transmitted by his muscles.

Side, pause, and a backwards rock, and then the same to the other side.

So far, so good. I had a competent teacher – our basic steps coincide. Except Rico can do things with his slim serpent hips that I didn't know men were capable of. He rocks them from side to side like a swing-boat, as if they were attached to a pivot at his navel. I can't take my eyes off them. Hypnotised by the spell they cast. My own hips rock to his motion, my senses in turmoil.

He opens me out, and when he pulls me to him again, I notice what clean, pink fingernails he has. Neat and trim like the rest of him. Sleek velvet skin. A lean, firm body. Hair close cropped on his perfectly shaped skull. A chocolate-coloured Action Man doll.

He tries a changeover, drawing me under his arm so I now stand where he just stood. Then he goes under my arm, back in position. We weave to and fro like this until sweat is streaming down my open back in rivulets and his shirt sticks to his chest, revealing the tufts of hair beneath. Little brown tussocks I'd love to investigate. Run my tongue over. Nuzzle against with my nipples.

I take a deep breath. His sweat smells of body spray. An exotic mix of tropical wood shavings and crushed nutmeg that makes my mouth water despite the exertion.

Then the music changes to an even faster song. I have trouble keeping up with the pace. But Rico's patient. Always leading me back in with the basic steps when I fluff it.

'You dance good.'

I smile. No. You dance good. But I don't tell him.

Then comes a slow number, more like a rumba. Sultry and seductive. This is more my kind of thing. I can match Rico's steps and have time to concentrate on the swing of my hips. We fan out and I meet the gaze of other eyes. Rico's not the only one to have noticed a blonde stranger in their midst.

He pulls me back to him, obviously also aware of the attention I'm drawing. Our hips collide, a painful buttressing that sends a frisson of shock right through me – hurt and want. And through the thin material of our clothes I distinctly feel all that his trousers are concealing. And it's not as squashy as it should be.

Damn it. I'd promised myself no romantic entanglements.

He sends me back out to the side and I dance the steps automatically, hardly conscious of what I'm doing.

And then someone else catches my free hand. Startled, I turn my head from Rico and look into the pair of brown eyes I noticed before.

'You dance with me?' His words sound more like an order than a question.

I look back at Rico, but he's already relinquished my other hand and is reaching for my new partner's lady. I guess they've settled it between them. This new guy seems to be number one here, and Rico knows what he's due.

The guy pulls me to him and I look into a stiff smileful of white teeth.

'You like it here?'

I nod.

'You like to dance?'

'Mmm.'

'You have a name?'

'Annette.' Might as well keep the same one.

'That's pretty. They call me Chicago.'

A stupid name. I suppose he lived there for a while or something.

'You dance good. I watch you.'

I've heard that one somewhere before. And I know he did.

His smile falters for a moment.

'You happy?'

What kind of question is that?

'I make you happy.'

He opens me out, then takes me straight into a changeover. He whisks me round, takes me under his arm. We weave in and out. Until I'm breathless and his grin has spread right across his face.

'I know you like to salsa.'

I smile. If happiness were only a matter of an evening spent with a good dancer!

The tight grin relaxes.

The music changes to another fast song. Chicago rocks his hips as if he were in competition with every man in the room. But then, maybe he is.

He's as good as Rico. Perhaps better. There's something unrestrained about the way he dances. Less refined. Raw.

His hips are just as narrow. But he's not as long and lean. Tight buttocks strain the material of his trousers. His waist tapers to a broader chest and shoulders. He's a head shorter, more compact.

He's not bad looking. Damn good-looking, in fact. In that unruly, brooding, Latino way.

Black stubble is just beginning to break through his tanned skin. Dark curls frame his face and he's got incredible, long black eyelashes. The sort I've never managed to achieve even with lashings of mascara.

His fingernails are dirty.

And he dances dirty. With the hips of a gigolo, making promises I know can never be fulfilled.

We dance salsa until I'm ready to drop, and drooling. In all senses of the word. Never have I been turned on like this by a mere dance. My thighs ache with fatigue, my sex aches from unfulfilled cramps of want.

'You like a drink?'

I follow him up the metal stairs, my legs now hardly able to make the climb. He clicks his fingers at the barman, says something that sends him scurrying to oblige, then kisses my cheek.

'I see you later?'

I nod, dazed. Isn't he going to join me? Is he going to leave me panting on the sidelines, unable to continue, but craving more?

He turns and skips down the steps two at a time, and I lose him in the crowd downstairs. On one side they're dancing the *rueda*, forever changing partners in an interweaving circle.

The barman is making up a cocktail. It's an eclectic mix of blues and greens. Is that for me?

'Chicago Joe's,' the barman says when I ask what it is. The house special. When I go to pay for it, he says it's already paid for.

I take it over to a table. Surprisingly, despite the colour, it tastes orangey.

I slurp the last of it through my straw. I don't feel like dancing any more. My legs are weary, my head's spinning. There was more in that cocktail than just fruit juice. I can't see either Rico or Chicago below. I guess they've moved on. And I don't owe them a goodbye.

With heavy feet I clank down the stairs and out into the night. It's refreshingly cool now. My body tingles as the breeze fans my moist skin. It must be about one o'clock. A big pale moon makes ghosts of the white yachts. The bars on the seafront are still a hive of swarming bodies, and a bubbling concoction of samba, merengue and salsa rhythms is carried to me across the bay. The coloured lights follow its curve, and twinkle like a necklace set with diamonds, emeralds, sapphires and blood-red rubies.

I don't want to go back there yet.

I wander among the fishing boats, down to the water's edge. Wet sand oozes between my toes. I have to be careful I don't step on any lumps of tar or baby crabs.

Then, as I walk past an upturned hull, I catch the acrid smack of tobacco smoke. I'm not alone. Is someone watching me? I turn, but out of the shadows a hand reaches for my waist and pulls me hard against a firm body. My cry is muffled by a pair of rough lips and a sandpaper chin. I struggle to break free.

'Why you run away?'

I recognise Chicago's slow drawl and my panic subsides.

'You stupid bastard. You scared me half to death!'

He chuckles. 'You not want to dance no more?'

'No.'

'Tomorrow?'

I shrug.

His hands slip to my hips. 'Tomorrow is ladies' night. Ladies choose, and their drinks are free.'

'I didn't pay for mine tonight anyway.'

He grins. 'And you choose your man?'

His hands tighten round me and there's something wicked in the glint of the moon reflected in his eyes.

I smile. I don't know that I've made any choices yet.

He fingers the criss-cross straps of my dress, and I shiver.

'You are cold?'

'No.' It was just his touch. But he closes his arms round me and pulls me to him. He breathes into my ear and kisses my neck.

'You are looking for love?'

His eyes search mine for some clue. I can't believe what he's offering.

'Chicago Joe will make you happy?'

He plunges his head into the scooped neckline of my dress, pushing through the folds, searching out the swelling flesh of my breasts.

'Chicago Joe, no!'

He plants little kisses along the edge of my cleavage, then seeks out my nipple with his finger and caresses its hardening point through the slinky material.

'Chicago Joe know what the lady want.'

A spasm shoots through my cervix. 'Don't,' I murmur. But he doesn't take any notice.

Half-heartedly I push him away. Somehow I've got to stop him before this goes too far. But it's so difficult to stop something you want so badly.

He begins to slide my dress up over my hips and a

hand glides between my legs. Before I can even gasp, he's already found my clit and is stroking its hardened nub. I moan with helpless pleasure and my head drops against his chest. He kisses my forehead. Then his finger slips beneath the material of my panties and he caresses my flesh.

There's no going back now. He can surely feel the contractions pulsating through my sex. So he knows how much I want him, whatever I say to the contrary. And it's all happening too fast for me to try to put a stop to it anyway. Even if I wanted to.

Before I know it, he's whisked me out of my panties and is fumbling with his flies. He lifts me on to the curved hull of the boat and, half-lying, half-standing, penetrates me without warning. Fast and furious.

I groan with the violence of his thrusts. It wouldn't take much more to knock me over the edge of the hull. But the wooden slats keep me in place, digging into my back with every push he gives. Branding me in stripes. The pain only heightening my awareness, increasing my pleasure.

Never in my life have I been fucked as hard as this. His love-making is as impetuous as his salsa. And the emphasis is all on his hips. With unremitting force, they ram him into me like a piston. With accomplished precision. And he keeps up the pace to the very end, battering me with frenzied figure after figure. All I can do is respond. My body led by his. Just like on the dance floor.

And never have I come so quickly, so urgently, so violently. So . . . spontaneously.

All too soon, this dance comes to an end. Out of me he draws final gasps and moans to match his own, as spasms of pleasure rock through me, making my flesh ripple.

With a grunt he collapses on to me. Then pulls

himself free and stands. I'm taken by surprise by the abruptness of the ending. Like a song cut off and not followed by another.

I lower myself off the boat, my sex still throbbing.

'I see you tomorrow?'

I shrug, and he chuckles.

'I see you tomorrow. I know what the lady likes.'

'But tomorrow it's my choice.'

He looks at me through his eyelashes. 'I'm hoping you choose Chicago Joe.' He pulls me to him, strokes my hair with unaccustomed tenderness. Lightly he kisses me on the lips. And then he's gone.

I find my panties and go down to the sea's edge. When the ink-black water laps my toes I crouch and wash away the evidence of my transgression. A cool, refreshing caress. Then I wander along the beach to the jetty, my thoughts tumbling over each other in an attempt to get sorted.

'Hi. You want a drink?' A suave, velvety voice comes out of the stillness. I look round and see a dark figure in a white shirt sitting at the railing of one of the yachts, a glass full of tinkling ice-cubes in his hand, his legs dangling over the side of the boat.

'Rico! Is this yours?'

'No, but masser left me in charge, miss,' he says, imitating a Deep South accent. He grins and helps me aboard. 'What will you have?'

His drinks cabinet is well stocked. Whisky, Bacardi, Martini, gin. And more or less everything you might need for any Caribbean cocktail. He pours me a bourbon on the rocks, like he's drinking.

'You have a good night at Chicago Joe's?'

I smile. 'Yes. Did you?'

'Until someone stole my partner.'

'Didn't he provide you with another?'

His smile changes. 'I don't like other men's cast-offs.'

'Mmm.'

We go back on deck and sip at our bourbon, looking at the lights going out on the seafront. The bay now blinking like a toothless smile.

'You're American, aren't you? And your name's not Rico, is it?'

'Your name's not Annette. And you're not Dutch either.'

I smile. 'Just covering my tracks, that's all.'

'That's all I was doing.'

We look at each other for a few moments.

'Gonna get rooted down in this godforsaken place?'

I shrug. 'It's as good as any. Why, are you gonna try to stop me?'

He laughs. 'Chicago Joe your type, is he? You like to salsa rough?'

'Not necessarily.'

He gets up and goes below deck. Then I hear the slow, languid strains of a rumba floating through the hatch.

The dance of love.

He bows and offers me his hand when he comes back up, leading me on to a mini dance floor of polished wood beneath the stars. We test a few basic rumba steps, then he opens me out. I spiral back to him. But instead of leading me into a spot turn, he catches me and pulls me close against his lean, muscular body.

'You dance well for a European,' he says. 'Where did you learn it?'

It was love that taught me to dance. Love of movement, rhythm and music. So maybe it was only a matter of time before I came looking for love among men with salsa in their blood. Men who could dance it the way it's meant to be danced.

We go below deck and he takes me into his cabin. A sumptuous, mahogany-panelled lair. A huge bed with shimmering white satin sheets takes up most of the space. How many women has he bedded here? Captured them with his snakelike hips, drugged them with his spice-laced scent, tormented them with the teddy-bear touch of his skin. I'm not the first to dance with him. He's been rocking and swaying his way through hearts to many a song.

And Chicago Joe, that other lone wolf, has probably danced with every girl in town.

Rico slips the straps from my shoulders and my dress slides over my naked breasts and down to the floor. Like a second skin shedding. Its slinky material caressing me the way Rico now does.

His hands feel like a pair of suede gloves as they glide over my body. He touches every part of me, and my flesh tingles in his wake. When he reaches my hips he gently starts to roll down my panties, peeling the lacy black material from my glistening skin as if something might break if he were too rough.

He kneels and, when my panties touch the floor, looks up at me, admiring the curve of my hips, my taut stomach, the pert rosy nipples that peak above the snowy underside of my breasts. His lips quiver. He likes what he sees. Black and white is his colour scheme.

He traces a pattern on my thigh with his tongue, working his way closer to the lush triangle of hair I know he's aiming for. The flickering motion is exquisite and excruciating at the same time. When is he going to reach my sex? – still trembling from the battering it received from Chicago Joe.

As if my prayers were heard, his tongue seeks out my clitoris and weaves round it. Then his mouth closes over its swollen nub and gently he begins to suck. Delicious spasms of pleasure rocket through me. I was wrong. The dance hasn't come to an end. The next song is just beginning.

I can hardly wait for him to penetrate me. My cervix contracts in anticipation. My sex is humming for more. I wish he'd throw me on to the bed and fuck me like Chicago did. Why doesn't he get on with it?

At last he sets me free. Is he too growing impatient for love? When he stands, his black trousers strain at the crotch. He teases open the fly buttons – slowly, like a stripper, revelling in the agony he's causing me – and lets them drop to the floor. They slide past his hips as if he were bathed in oil.

His cock is erect. Pouched in a G-string made of real snakeskin. The scales reflect the light with an iridescent sheen. His dimpled buttocks gleam like the polished mahogany of his cabin.

Slowly he unties the G-string, goading me to a frenzy, and lets it fall at his feet. I stare. This was worth waiting for. He's magnificent. My stomach flutters at the thought of being taken by a man that size. Surely the ultimate hedonistic pleasure?

I pull myself on to the bed, up towards the pillows, hardly able to contain my excitement. The sheet tickles my skin as I brush against it. A delicate caress. Rico climbs on after me, kneeling above me like a sleek black panther standing over its prey.

I sink my head into the pillow, waiting for him to lower himself on to me. Expecting him, any second, to penetrate. But he doesn't. Although his cock is rigid with desire. Instead, he kneels back and lifts my hips so he can see the pink flesh of my vulva. He strokes the frilly petals of skin. Why the delay? Why doesn't he just enter me? The waiting is becoming unbearable.

'Turn over. Crouch in front of me, on all fours.'

I hesitate, then do so. He wants to take me from behind?

He caresses the round cheeks of my bottom, draws his hands over the curves of my hips. He fingers the opening to my sex, so prominently on display. Then at last, he kneels up close behind me and I feel the tip of his cock probing the delicate skin, as if testing whether it wants to enter me, or not.

Suddenly he pushes into me. Soon his hips begin to rock to a rhythm all of their own. Not salsa. Not merengue. Not samba. Not rumba. A see-saw motion to an incessant beat that picks up time and gets stronger and stronger. Like the rhythm of African drums.

My hips push against him in return, as if the same pulses were running straight through me. We slap against each other, like water against the jetty, sending a spray of shock waves rippling through our bodies with each contact.

The humming in my sex has been overtaken by cramps and contractions. Dull pain that breaks out in spasms of giddy pleasure. Before long I'm again awash with floods of ecstasy. Tides that ebb and flow and leave me completely helpless, clinging to the pillow as if ship-wrecked.

Abruptly he pulls out of me, spattering the snow-white bed covers with his come. I roll over and lie on my back, looking up at the ceiling, gently rocking with the incoming tide, while he gets up to take a shower.

After a few minutes, when I've regained my senses, I slip into a black silk dressing gown and go up on deck. The night has grown fresh. The bay is a darkened curve against a pool of midnight blue. The moon and stars have the sky all to themselves now.

I sit at the boat's railing trying to decide what to do, what I want. It's a difficult choice. At home a jealous lover is trying to bind me to him, stop me from dancing with strangers. But am I ready to seek my freedom with Rico on the high seas? Forever on the run. Or do I want to hide away here among the palm trees?

I don't know which of the two is the better dancer, and which the better lover.

I look over towards the warehouses. A solitary figure is making his way back into town. Chicago Joe. The last to leave after locking up. I watch him as he draws nearer. He looks tired. A wolf limping home to his den now there's no one to see how vulnerable he is.

He draws level with the jetty, and I think he's going to pass on by without seeing me. But something makes him look up. A whiff of my scent on the breeze maybe?

For a moment he halts and stares.

I smile.

He smiles back, hesitantly. '*Mañana?*'

I consider my options.

'...*Mañana.*'

# Academic Attraction
## Mandy M. Roth

'So, what do you think?'

Haley stared wide-eyed at Professor Gregory. The noonday sun filtered in the open screen door and caught the highlights of his blond hair, leaving her gaze tracing the edges of his stubble-covered jawline. She looked around the tiny lakeside cottage in the hope he wouldn't notice her lingering stare. The whitewashed antique furnishings and scattered lanterns lent to the nautical theme without taking away from the quaint Midwest cottage atmosphere. Sure, the majority of the shoreline of Lake Erie in Ohio was attractive but the tiny town of Marblehead seemed removed from the rest of the state. It was beautiful, so serene and secluded that it was easy to lose oneself. 'It's perfect! Thanks so much for suggesting this, Professor.'

'No problem, Haley. And I've told you before to call me Mike. I've always been adamant about that with all my students. I hardly picture myself as a professor, and it's not as though I'm teaching grade school.' He flashed a white smile.

Haley nodded and set her bags down on the hardwood floor. After placing her art box on the tiny table, she glanced out the window at the wooded area surrounding the cottage. 'It is nestled in so tight. I never realised something this beautiful was within driving range from the university. I can't believe how peaceful it is here. I haven't seen anyone since we arrived. I keep waiting for someone to show up and tell me the place is closed or that we're trespassing.'

'I told you that I know the owners,' Mike said with a chuckle. 'They set it up so I can come whenever I want during the off season without interruptions. There's nothing worse than having some summer tourist babbling non-stop when you're in the creative zone.'

Haley laughed and turned. 'Speaking of being in the "creative zone", when do you want to get started?' For a split second, she could have sworn that Mike's eyes darted towards the double bed against the back wall. No doubt she was letting her overactive imagination run wild.

'I thought we'd spend the day out on the pier. This time of day, you can see all the way across the bay to the lighthouse. It's spectacular, and knowing Canada is just beyond it adds to the charm. Depending on the weather, we might even take a boat ride to the other islands. It would be good to get some pastel time in there. It's too beautiful this time of day not to. I'm not sure how many boaters will be out. It's a bit early in the season for them. We can head back out there in the morning with watercolours. We might even get lucky and have some fog roll in.'

Haley beamed. 'That sounds great! So, should I meet you out there?' She bit her lower lip and glanced past Mike's shoulder, not sure where the pier actually was.

'I can wait for you. I mean, the last thing I want to do is spend my spring break organising a search party for you,' he said with a slight laugh.

Haley rolled her eyes playfully and grabbed her art box. 'You just can't stop rubbing in how directionally challenged I am, can you? The entire class already thinks I'm flighty.'

'Well, you have to admit that you still get lost on campus and you're a senior now. Think about it, you've been my teaching assistant for over a year now and yet you still get all turned around in the art building.'

'Sometimes I'm too focused on other things to pay attention to where I'm going.'

He grinned. 'You should cut back on that before you walk into a door – *again!*'

Haley groaned. 'We're not bringing that up again, are we?'

Mike smiled and shifted. 'No, I'm willing to let that one go. But how many times have you done that so far?'

Haley's eyes darted to his groin. *He's my teacher, stop looking. He's my teacher.* She swallowed the lump in her throat when she saw the bulge beneath his faded jeans. 'I, um ... I can't remember.'

'Short-term memory loss from cracking your head too many times,' he mused as he leaned forward to take her art box from her. His hand slid over hers and fire shot up her arm. His thumb rubbed past her wrist and the heat went to her cheeks. 'Are you ready?'

She looked him over, letting her gaze linger longer than it should over his groin again. *Yeah, I'm ready.* Haley nodded and followed Mike out the screen door. It creaked loudly as she walked out, and the wooden porch floor gave slightly under their combined weight. She glanced over and caught sight of something brown scurrying under the porch. She yelped and backed up.

Mike turned and followed her gaze. He cocked an eyebrow and the corners of his mouth pulled up. 'Afraid of chipmunks, are you? Hmm, I've always found them to be quite harmless, but to each his own.'

Haley gave him a droll look and laughed slightly. 'I thought it was a mouse.'

He winked at her and motioned towards a large willow tree across the way from them. It grew half in the grass and half in the sand leading down to the beach. Its large weeping branches hung almost to the ground. 'There's a great spot just beyond there.'

Her attention drew back to Mike's profile and she found herself nodding in agreement as she soaked him in. Haley followed him as he led her past the willow tree and down a narrow path. Various trees and shrubs lined the sides and Mike was quick to point out the blue jay darting in and out of their way. The path opened into a large grassy area on the end of what looked like a small peninsula. Rocks lined the edges of it. It was beautiful and felt so private even though they were in plain view of any boaters that may pass by.

Mike walked over to a large maple tree and pulled his art box and pads of paper out from behind it. He watched out of the corner of his eye as Haley took in the scenic view. He knew she'd love it. That's why he'd insisted they take a 'working holiday' together. Having pulled a folded blanket from his bag, Mike turned and spread it out under the shade of the tree.

He sat down and leaned back on one elbow as he watched Haley peer over the edge at the water. When the slightest of breezes caught her long floral skirt, his heart slammed in his chest. It looked almost sheer on her with the spot the sun was in. The clear outline of her long legs and tight ass made his cock hard. What was he thinking bringing her here? Not work, that much was for sure. It's not like he made a habit of attempting to seduce students. But, something was different about her. Her very presence left him with an erection, and her sultry laugh had almost caused him to cream his jeans on numerous occasions.

This week away with her was wrong for so many reasons but he'd planned it all the same. The hopes of getting to sink himself deep within her outweighed the fear of the university officials finding out. Of course, if things went according to plan, he'd have her and keep it a secret too. No need to get the administration all worked up if he didn't have to. He had to admit that part of Haley's lure was how forbidden she was. From the moment she'd stepped into his classroom three years ago, he'd wanted her. The idea of having her rose-coloured lips wrapped around his cock while her blue eyes stared up at him had been the theme of many a workday fantasy.

He'd even taken to masturbating with the image of Haley spread beneath him, with her long chestnut hair fanned out on the bed and her legs wrapped tight around him. And the thought of her naked breasts being close enough to taste, touch, suck, he could hardly control himself. The last thing he wanted to do was sketch some damn lighthouse. No. Mike wanted to fuck the hell out of the little beauty next to him for the next week and then steal away after working hours and fuck her some more.

His body tightened to the point of pain when Haley pulled her sweater over her head. Her white blouse lifted, exposing her toned stomach to him. The thought of nibbling her ribcage on his way down to between her legs made him smile.

Haley glanced over and gave him a puzzled look. 'What's so funny? You're not still laughing at me being afraid of a chipmunk, are you?'

'So, you're admitting you were scared of it now, huh?'

Heat crept through her cheeks and he wanted desperately to see that happen while he fucked her. She approached the blanket slowly, her eyes fixed on him. As she sat down, her skirt got tucked beneath her and pulled high, exposing the rounded curve of one ass cheek.

Mike growled and wiped the palm of his hand across his pant leg. Every ounce of him wanted to slide his hand up her silky thigh and see if she was as tight as he thought she was. Before he knew it, his hand was on her, touching her smooth skin, feeling the heat of her body. Haley gasped. He took hold of her skirt and pulled it gently over her, covering her from his view. 'Sorry, your skirt was ... um ... tucked up a bit.'

She gave a small nod and pulled it all the way down. Now that he'd seen a view, he knew he'd have to have a taste, and soon. His penis jerked and dug painfully into his zipper. Relief couldn't wait. Quickly, Mike stood and forced a smile on to his face. 'I, erm ... I left something back at the cottage. Will you be OK out here for a little bit?'

Haley looked up sceptically at him and nodded. 'Sure. Will you be gone long?'

Judging from the size of his erection, it would take one hell of a thrapping to relieve the tension in it. 'Maybe, but I'll do my best to hurry.'

He walked down the path towards the cottages and waited until he was well hidden before stopping. From this vantage point, he could watch Haley draw as he relieved the tension in his penis. Unbuttoning his pants, he freed his erection. It bobbed obscenely before him and he grabbed hold of it. He wasn't gentle. Taking hold of his tight balls, he pulled any remaining loose skin back as he brought his other hand up. With a tiny bit of spit on his hand, Mike worked his dick once, twice, three times over before he found himself staring intently at Haley's back.

He built himself up to greater arousal, greater stiffness, massaging himself while watching her. She glanced nervously behind her several times. Knowing she couldn't see him as he stroked himself turned him on even more. Haley leaned back and closed her eyes. The sight of her resting was too perfect. The sun caught the highlights in her hair and she radiated beauty.

When Haley shifted slightly on the blanket, her blouse opened, exposing a perfect set of perky breasts. Her nipples were darker than he'd have guessed and he couldn't wait to draw one into his mouth as he rode her. Mike could only imagine what it would be like to touch one, to hold one. Did Haley ever touch them? Did she ever play with herself? Did she ever think of him?

Mike grunted and jerked his hips as he focused on her. His gaze never left her body as he tightened his grip, working himself harder, faster. Haley smiled lazily in his direction and, for a moment, he wondered if she could actually see him. Dismissing the thought as silly, he continued to pump himself until he felt the build up that led to the explosion.

He cried out, his mouth falling open as he hit his zenith. Come shot forth from him, hitting the tree in front of him. He used one hand to steady himself while yet more semen spurted out; he had certainly worked up a load.

When he had spent all his fluid, he tried to tuck himself back into his jeans but he was still too erect to fit comfortably. He needed to fuck Haley and soon. He couldn't go on with this endless self-pleasure. He wanted to see her face in the rapture of arousal – with him the cause of it. He was almost certain that she was as horny as he was, and he decided he'd step up the pace a bit.

He shuffled his feet and rustled a few branches to signify his return. Haley sat up and adjusted her blouse. Slowly pulling a sketch pad on to her lap, she looked off towards the lighthouse.

'How's it going?' he asked, his voice slightly strained from his massive exertions.

Haley smiled up at him. 'Mmm, it's great. I was just enjoying the view while you were gone.' Her gaze went directly to his groin before raking slowly up his body.

Nervous that she'd seen him, Mike glanced back towards the spot he'd chosen to hide in. When he saw the tree he'd stood behind in plain view, his heart hammered in his chest. He looked down at Haley, worried she'd not only think him a pervert but assume he was out to get inside her pants. While she would be right in assuming that, it didn't make the desire to take her appropriate.

'Sit down. You're missing out on some great light,' she said, smiling slightly. 'I absolutely love it here. There's no place I'd rather spend my break.'

He slid down next to her and grabbed a pad of paper. He stared at her profile, waiting for the right moment to say something to her. Had she seen him masturbating? Suddenly, the idea that she'd seen him stroking his cock excited him.

*This is beyond wrong. Tell her to go. Leave yourself.*

Haley turned and locked eyes with him. His concerns flooded away. It seemed as though the sounds of the lakeshore intensified tenfold while they stared at each other in silence. The water continued to make slapping sounds against the rocks at the base of the pier and the sound of birds chirping nearby reminded him of the blue jay they'd seen on the way out here.

Haley watched Mike as he slid his shoes on to go. After spending the afternoon sketching on the pier, they'd decided on setting up near the woods to draw for a bit. As it grew dark, they'd headed back to the cottages and ate. Haley was surprised to find that Mike was quite the cook. The pasta he'd made was divine. Watching him eat it was even better. Each time he took a bite, she'd imagined his lips over her sex. By the time they were done with their second bottle of wine, Haley's panties were moist and her body was in a state of need.

After dinner, they'd moved to the extra long lyre-shaped white sofa. Haley was shocked to find such an expensive piece in a lakeside cottage, but it worked well. Its scrolled arms and soft pillows welcomed her as she stretched out for a bit and, before she knew it, Mike was tickling her feet, which had somehow ended up on his lap. She pulled them away fast and he leaned forward to grab his own shoes.

'It's late and you're tired,' Mike said softly.

Haley nodded despite the fact that she desperately wanted him to stay. The thought of him sliding his lean body in and out of hers made her stomach flip over in excitement. She shifted awkwardly and glanced at him through partially closed lids and was silent as he walked towards the door. When she heard the screen door shut, she exhaled. The need to run after him was great but she held tight to her position. Begging her college professor to stay and fuck her, while erotic, was not acceptable student/teacher behaviour. He was her role model and the best instructor she'd ever had. Being attracted to him was an accident – although a very unfortunate one indeed.

After a few minutes, Haley stood slowly and pulled her blouse over her head. With ease, she worked her skirt off. She headed towards the bathroom, in hopes of soaking in the tub to relieve her sexual tension. When she opened the old wooden door, something scurried past her foot. She screamed and jumped backwards. A tiny grey mouse darted past her.

'Haley?'

The sound of Mike's voice brought her back from the edge of hysteria. Turning, she found him standing in the doorway. The feral look on his face reminded her that she was only in her undergarments. Much to her surprise, she made no effort to cover herself. She waited, sure that he'd back away, leaving her to masturbate yet again, before notifying the university that she was to be removed from his classes. When he took another step towards her, a wicked smiled covered her face.

'I can look around for the mouse, if you'd like,' Mike said, his eyes never leaving her.

Giving into her desires, Haley reached between her breasts and unhooked her silk bra. The cool cottage air made her nipples stand on end. She glanced up at him, hoping that she hadn't scared him away. The moment his hands went to his shirt, she smiled. When he too lifted his shirt over his head, exposing his tawny chest to her, she gasped. He was even more amazing than she thought he'd be. His body was toned, well defined. She had to pace herself to avoid running to him. This moment had played out a billion times in her head. Each scenario different, yet the outcome was always the same – the two of them naked and ready to fuck. He was off limits. Right? God, how she longed to be with him, to see if he was different from the men, or rather boys, she'd grown accustomed to. Mike was in his mid-thirties, sixteen years her senior to be exact. The very thought of the sexual tricks he'd learned over the years excited her.

He stared at her with hungry eyes. It was now or never. She'd taken that next step. She'd bared her luscious breasts to him and he'd be damned if he'd pass up the opportunity to have her. It was wrong, but his body didn't care. She stood stationary by the bathroom door. Her breasts were fully exposed to him and her tiny white silk panties barely covered the thatch of dark hair on her mound.

He took another step towards her, unfastening his jeans as he went. His cock needed little encouragement to be ready. It had been prepared for three years. Haley tipped her head and her long chestnut hair fell in waves over her shoulder. It slid over her breasts as he reached for her. Pulling her into his arms gently, he let a wolfish grin spread over his face.

When she didn't pull away, Mike drew her tight to him. Her soft curves pressed against his firm body felt so good, so right. His penis ached for relief and, currently, it wanted to find salvation only in her silken depths. Bending down, he brought her chin up to look into her blue eyes as he fondled one of her nipples. He squeezed it between his fingers gently and put his lips near her ear. She shivered and he couldn't help but chuckle. 'Mmm, forbidden fruit.'

'What?' she asked breathily.

Before she could protest, Mike dropped his mouth down on hers: His tongue found its way in and hers rose to greet it. Within seconds, they were touching, petting, tugging on one another – as though they'd never get enough. Haley bit at his lower lip and moaned when he grabbed her ass and squeezed it tight.

He rolled her nipple between his fingers and bent down even further. When her dark nipple came into focus, he slid his tongue out and over it. He eased off it and blew slightly, smiling as it reacted to him. Teasing her nipple, he licked it quickly and rubbed his lips over it softly. She moaned and her hands came to his hair, pulling his head tight against her chest. Mike drew her nipple into his mouth and growled. Sucking gently, he worked her other breast with his hand as he edged his body down more. He pulled off her nipple and it hardened even more. He smiled up at her. 'So ripe ... like berries for the picking.'

Haley ran her tiny hands over his cheeks. She cupped his face and stared down at him, her eyes full of lust as he went to his knees before her. Her brow furrowed. 'Mike?'

Tugging at her panties, he slid them down her thighs. The tuft of neatly trimmed dark curls that lay beneath smelled of sex and of Haley. He drew in a deep breath. His eyes fluttered. Licking the front of her hip, he continued to work her panties down her legs. He eased them off her and tossed them aside. Eyeing the prize, he feathered his fingers back up her smooth legs.

Parting her folds, he licked along the outer edges of her sex. Haley jerked slightly and he grabbed tight to her ass with his other hand to keep her steady. Kneading her ass cheek, Mike continued to let his tongue glide over the rim of her slit, lightly skimming her clit.

'Mike,' Haley panted as she clutched his head tighter. She swayed her hips, easing herself into his face.

He smiled into her as her juices oozed out of her sex. Lapping it up, he growled at how good she tasted. So sweet, like peaches and cream.

She moved faster, pressing herself against his lips. Varying the degree at which he sucked on her bud, Mike felt Haley's legs begin to quiver. Her orgasm moved over her rapidly and he eagerly relished the juice that trickled from her body.

'Mike ... please.' She pulled on his face.

Reluctantly, he gave into her and stood. The lure of her mouth was too great and he clamped his over it, seeking her tongue, her permission to continue. She bit playfully at his mouth, skilfully dodging and receiving his tongue at all the right moments.

She encircled him with her hand. He wanted to throw her on the bed and ravish her but she broke their kiss and dropped to her knees before him. Reaching down, he touched her cheek lightly and she nipped at his fingers lightly. 'Honey, I need to be in you.'

'You'll be in my mouth.' She worked her hands into the front of his jeans and began to slide them down his hips. When his cock bobbed before her face, she laughed. 'Who'd have thought "the teach" was going commando?'

'No, Haley ... don't refer to me as that. Here, with you, it's just me ... just Mike. Don't remind me how wrong this is. Not now.'

Nodding, she met his gaze. Her blue eyes were hungry and he wanted to be the one to satisfy her. She moved his pants down a bit more. Wrapping her hand around his thick shaft, she smiled in delight, moaning her pleasure. Mike mirrored her noise as she ran her hand up and down the full length of him. She let her tongue flicker out and over the head of his cock before taking him fully into her mouth.

'Ahh ... easy, baby, easy ... Haley, you have to ... oh, that's it. Right there. Deep throat me, baby. Take me all the way down.'

He closed his eyes in ecstasy as she took him all the way in. When he felt her gag reflex kick in, Mike almost shot come down her throat.

'Oh, Lord, that feels so good.'

Haley continued to move over his shaft. Each time he hit the back of her throat, they moaned simultaneously. It was even better than he'd imagined, watching Haley on her knees sucking him off. His fingers were wrapped in her chestnut hair while her blue eyes stared up at him. Her hot mouth worked him to the brink of orgasm. Quickly, he pulled her off him. She protested but he didn't listen. He'd waited three years to have her and now that he had the opportunity, he wouldn't miss out on it.

Mike picked her up and carried her to the heavily carved walnut bed. Laying her down across the covers, he couldn't help but think her even more beautiful then. Her long hair fanned out on to the pale-blue comforter just as it had in his fantasies and his chest grew tight. She was so beautiful, so perfect, so willing to let him have his way with her.

'Mike,' she whispered.

Her sex called to him, the taste of it still fresh on his mind and tongue. Unable to control himself, he leaned forward to sample her again. Parting her velvety folds, he inserted a finger into her hot wet channel, bringing his lips to her swollen bud and drawing it gently into his mouth. The taste of her was divine. A meal he'd never grow tired of eating.

Haley bucked beneath him as he varied sucks and licks on her clitoris. She clawed at the bed and rode his face while he fingered her. So tight. So hot. So his. As she writhed under the weight of his caresses, she hit her summit. Still he didn't stop his onslaught. He lavished a series of long licks over her slit, making her wiggle more. Nectar oozed from her and he moistened his lips with her scent.

She tugged on the sides of his face and when he met her eyes, he saw the need in her face. 'Please, Mike.'

The knowledge that she desired him as well sent him flying. Sliding up and over her, he eased himself between her legs. He came to a rest above her, in a semi-push-up, the head of his penis positioned near her cleft.

She twisted slightly, causing the tip to enter her tight core. His arms tightened as he strained to keep from fully sheathing himself. He took a few calming breaths, wanting this to last and last. It took all of his resolve not to take her roughly, ravish her until he was sated. Well, as sated as he could ever be with this luscious young temptress. She was his addiction. No question about it. A very wrong addiction though. One that could ruin his career.

'Fuck me, Mike,' she begged.

Unable to resist her any longer, Mike did as she wished. He thrust himself deep within her until he was all the way to the hilt. He smiled; his little Haley was every bit as tight and wet as he'd imagined; maybe even more so.

Pulling almost all the way out, he locked gazes with her and smiled. She closed her eyes and he grabbed her chin lightly. 'No, I want you looking at me while we do it.'

A grin spread across her face and she ran her hand down the length of their bodies. His cock had a spasm when she wrapped her hand around it and he fought hard to control himself.

'If you hold me, I'll never last, and the thought of diving into your tight little pussy isn't helping my control any.'

She released him. He slammed into her, making her cry out and grab his arms. Mike pumped rapidly, causing the brass lantern light on the bedside table to wobble. Breaking it would be a shame, but stopping what he was doing would be much worse. Her channel gripped him and his penis bulged with the need for release. Afraid of coming too soon, Mike slowed his pace and began to make small swirling patterns with his hips. Haley responded by clawing his back.

'Right there, oh yes, Mike, there!' Her cheeks were now rosy and her lips swollen. She was so close, teetering on the edge of culmination. She wrapped her legs around him, allowing him deeper penetration. 'Ah, you're so big,' she purred. 'Too big, Mike.'

Mike rolled to the side, pulling Haley with him. Waves of silky long hair surrounded his face. Looking up through the chestnut veil, he saw her shocked look and chuckled.

'You could have warned me,' she said, her voice low, sultry.

'I didn't want to hurt you, baby. This way, you can control the pace and I can watch you fuck me. Besides, a gentleman always allows the lady to go first.'

Her brow furrowed. 'Hurt me? If that was hurting me then you have my full permission to hurt me any damn time you like.'

'Really?' A sly grin spread across his face and he made a mental note to hold her to that promise.

She straddled his waist and slid her body over his slick cock. Her eyes widened as her body did its best to accommodate his size. She'd had close contact with a number of penises, despite her tender years, but by far, Mike's was the most impressive.

He ran his large hands up her sides and cupped her breasts. Tweaking each nipple slightly, he sent slivers of pleasure running through her. 'Do you like that, baby? Do you like it when I squeeze your nipples?'

Haley rode him, rubbing herself against his lower abdomen and drawing in deep breaths as she took him fully with each stroke. Nodding, she leaned forward and captured his lips with hers. The new angle provided additional stimulation to her bud and her legs tightened. A tingling sensation emanated from her toes and she rode him harder and faster. She sucked hard on Mike's tongue. He let out a muffled cry beneath her as her core milked him with a fierceness she'd never experienced before.

Mike pulled at her hips, driving her down on to his erection even more. His body went rigid beneath hers and she had half a second to decide whether or not to stay on him.

Haley began to roll off him and he clutched tight to her hips, holding her in place as he came in jarring waves. Her eyes widened as she took every last drop of him deep within her body. She broke their kiss and moved to slide off him.

Mike's eyes widened. 'Tell me you don't regret it

already, Haley. Please tell me that look is the one you wear after mind-blowing sex.'

She laughed. 'I most certainly do *not* regret it. I was just going to let you get some sleep.'

He shook his head slightly. 'You're joking, right? I'm not done with you. Hell, I may never be done with you.' He wrapped his arms around her and held her close to his chest.

She nuzzled her cheek against him and ran her fingers through his chest hair. Eventually she eased herself off him and collapsed back on the bed. 'I need a shower,' she said.

Mike kissed the top of her head and ran his hand gently over her back. 'A shower can wait. We need to talk.'

She smiled down at him and waited for him to continue.

'You know that we have to keep this – *us* – a secret, right?'

Haley bit her lower lip and nodded. Running her hand over his collarbone she let out a soft laugh. 'I won't tell a soul about us. You have my word,' she said, kissing his chest.

'Mmm, now that we have that little discussion out of the way ...' Mike flipped her on to her stomach and rose to his knees behind her. She tried to turn and look back at him. He caught her and positioned her face forward. A dark sea chest propped in the corner caught her eye. A large black iron anchor was propped next to it, keeping the nautical theme and making the moment all the more special. Mike's firm grasp brought Haley back to the moment. Pulling up, he brought her to her hands and knees. 'No. It's my turn to control the situation. I want you to take every bit of me, from every angle.'

'Mike?' Her eyes widened as he thrust a finger into

her tight channel. Her vaginal muscles seized hold of it, and she didn't need him to tell her how wet she was. When she felt the tip of his penis probing her, she moaned. 'No more, Mike. Please, I can't do this. I need a break.'

'Mmm, you're a hell of a lot younger than me and if I'm ready to do it again, so are you.' He thrust himself into her with one long stroke. She yelled out and pushed back against him. 'That's it, baby. There you go. Yeah, take it all the way. You like that, don't you? You like my dick crammed in you.'

'Mike ... yes ... ah ... Mike.'

Easing his pace, he found a spot that stimulated him just right and made her moan. Haley arched her back and he ran his hand up it, coming to a stop at the base of her neck. He gripped her neck lightly and bent forward to kiss her back. He ran his other hand around to her cleft and she jerked slightly when he plucked her ripe bud. She tightened around him and he had to stop moving his hips to avoid finishing.

'Ohh ... Mike ... there, oh ... there.'

Mike rubbed her jewel again, in hopes of eliciting additional pleas for more from her. He caressed her sex gently, tenderly, while she began to rock her hips back, forcing him deeper into her. His sac slapped against her as he drove with full force. Haley's body shook and then he felt her orgasm ripping through her. Unable to stave off his own, he came with a start into her, soaking her with his essence. He lay still, sated, his body pressed on top of hers, his breaths coming in shallow pants for a few minutes.

Finally he withdrew and she turned to face him. She sat before him on the bed, her cheeks flushed from their love-making and her inner thighs glistening from their combined juices. It took everything in him not to ravish her again.

She cupped his face and pulled him to her. Spreading her legs wide, her gaze flickered downward. 'What do you say to spending the night fucking each other's brains out?'

He arched an eyebrow. 'The night, huh? There's still a hell of a lot I want to do to that tight little body of yours. How about the rest of the week?'

'Even better, Professor.' Haley smiled and pulled his mouth close to hers. 'Besides, I really want good marks in your class.'

He slid himself over her and laughed softly. 'I'll have to think about that.'

'You could always go back into the bushes and *think* about it. Or, better yet, think about it behind the willow tree.'

Mike chuckled. 'You saw that, huh?'

Haley smiled. 'Yes, and I can't wait to touch myself again as you masturbate. I don't think the tree enjoyed the show nearly as much as I did.'

Mike eased himself over her and grabbed hold of his happy cock. 'Good to know.'

# Marks in the Mirror
## Francesca Brouillard

It was ten days before the marks disappeared completely but I kept checking long after that, twisting round awkwardly in front of the bathroom mirror. Those shocking pink stripes held a disturbing fascination. Oddly I felt quite disappointed when they'd gone; there was almost a sense of loss.

*That first time he did it to me the overriding sensation was shock. Pure shock. I felt panic and fear as well, but shock was the main thing. Then the inevitable pain. A smarting, burning, humiliating pain. Anger came later, sizzling orange and confused, bubbling with indignation and spiced with shame.*

*Afterwards, when finally I looked at him, I was surprised to find his face strangely devoid of emotion. It was not twisted or flushed from some sadistic pleasure. Just nothing.*

That same evening as we'd sat opposite each other over supper, a slanting sun turning stray crumbs to gold, he'd behaved as if nothing had happened. Chewing on the remains of a baguette and the inevitable goat cheese, he'd talked about his childhood and hot summers spent there in the Pyrenees, minding the goats with his father.

The previous day he could have captivated me with his stories and I would have asked about his current life in Paris but right then, *that* evening, I was too consumed with anger to even hear his words. The humiliating scene from the morning replayed itself in my head till the very air around me vibrated with tension. I picked at my food distractedly and wriggled; sitting was painful.

As if suddenly aware of my discomfort he broke off his story and looked at me.

'Eva ...' Despite his excellent English he had not been able to pronounce Eve, so he'd taken to calling me Eva, which his French accent made rather exotic.

'Eva, you have a problem with your seat, I think. Would you prefer to take a cushion?'

Was that a smile twitching at the corner of his mouth? I blushed furiously and had a sudden violent urge to hurl the pitcher of wine over him. I stopped myself; I wasn't going to give him the satisfaction of seeing my rage.

I began to wish that Angelline, whose company I'd rather resented the previous day, was still there. Ineffectually adolescent though she was, another presence would have prevented anything happening.

Back here in my office those few weeks on the farm, and in particular the days spent on the mountain, seem so remote as to be unreal. Memories of the rank overpowering smell of goats, hot afternoons on the hillside and the sour odour of cheese wafting up through the floorboards seem to belong to another lifetime. I could almost believe it had never existed.

Almost. But for the marks in the mirror – which have finally gone – and a dark, uneasy feeling, which won't.

As I dash between board meetings and conferences in an expensive cloud of perfume, juggling accounts, investment options and a team of financial experts, I wonder how that slow pace of life and its dull routines had ever appealed to me.

I press the buzzer on my desk. 'Maureen, can you send Jacob through and tell him to bring the figures for October.'

I feel slightly irked at having to deal with Jacob today. I suspect he's been slacking while I've been away and needs bringing back in line. It's always difficult in management, keeping people up to speed. Some of my team, generally the university recruits, think I'm pushy and ruthless, but they're on top money so I expect top performance. Maureen let slip that certain ones amongst them refer to me as the Rottweiler. I took a private pleasure in that.

'Ah, Jacob. Take a seat.'

*I was wrong earlier when I said Louis' expression was devoid of emotion after that first incident. I just wasn't able to see the complexity of his motives then.*

Although the Caribbean is usually more my line, this year I'd decided to go and stay with my cousin and her family in France. The decision was prompted by Naomi, my regular holiday mate, dumping me for her new bloke and my having no one else to go with.

I suppose I'm what some people would call a workaholic. I love the power and responsibility that come with my job; the decision-making, the control, the team of people working for me – it all gives me a buzz and sense of importance. Inevitably, though, I don't have much time or energy for a social life, nor a great deal of opportunity to meet people. Men, I mean. Of course I'm surrounded by them at work, as Naomi constantly points out, and some of them are attractive enough, but they're always the wrong sort; those on my managerial scale are inevitably in their fifties while the younger ones have not yet made the grade. It may sound arrogant, but I couldn't envisage a relationship with a man lower down the hierarchy. It's a matter of status.

Anyway, it was my lack of holiday companion that initially made me think of going to France. My cousin Holly and her French husband have been renovating their farm in the Pyrenees for what feels like decades, and they've recently converted a barn into gîtes and gone over to organic farming. They have a flock of goats and sheep and specialise in producing cheese using traditional methods. I know I'm welcome there – as Holly says, an extra pair of hands is always useful – and the prospect of sun, mountains and fresh air presented an attractive alternative to the dusty bustle of London in summer.

Michel, Holly's husband, met me at the airport in Perpignon. On the drive back we chatted about family, business, and what was happening on the farm; they had two families in the gîtes and a teenager, Angelline, staying with them over the holidays. In addition there were a couple of local guys helping with the animals and cheese-making. One I'd met previously but the other, Louis, now lived in Paris and was just back for the summer.

When I was introduced to him later at dinner he nodded at me curtly and caught my eye for just long enough to make me feel I'd been weighed up and found lacking. This perfunctory dismissal irritated me, and I would have had nothing more to do with him had it not been for a certain dangerous allure beneath that supercilious exterior.

I spent the first week hanging around the farm and chatting with Holly. Our afternoons would be spent preparing the evening meal, which formed the focal point of the day. Sometimes we were joined by the families from the gîtes or neighbours, but it was always a large and noisy, sociable occasion. These were the only times I saw Louis, and despite a few attempts at conversation, I always felt tense around him and experienced a disconcerting fluttering in my belly.

When Holly asked me during my second week if I'd like to spend a few days in the hut on the mountain I was delighted. I remembered it as a stone ruin sheltering below a crag, but it had been repaired since my last visit, to enable someone to stay with the goats over summer. Louis would be relieving the current shepherd, and Angelline had asked if she could go along.

I was both pleased and disappointed with this arrangement. The whole goats and mountains and back-to-nature thing had a very romantic appeal; it was the stuff fantasies are made of. However, the combination of an adolescent chaperone and a man about whom I felt ambivalent detracted somewhat from this idyll.

After a couple of days at the hut Angelline started her period and wanted to go back down to the farm, a feeling I could sympathise with given our rustic sanitary conditions. I rather welcomed this development at the time, thinking that a few days alone with Louis might ease the awkwardness between us and even lead to something more promising. What naivety! Away from the sociable environment of the farm he barely bothered responding to my conversational overtures, and my few attempts at charming him with a nice meal or compliments were completely ignored. Even when I offered to help with the milking he showed little grace, just issuing curt instructions and criticising my clumsiness.

Perversely, though perhaps predictably, the more he

ignored me the more I felt attracted to him. I began having erotic dreams that lingered long after waking. Dreams that took me to the edge of a precipice and left me poised there on the verge of orgasm. Dreams from which I woke to find myself lying in a sweat, my hand between my legs. Dreams that filtered through the thin dividing wall that separated me from his sleeping body and tortured me with their elusive desire.

It was these dreams, surely, and the fractured sleepless nights, that drove me to the shameful act that triggered that first 'incident'. How else could I account for finding myself in the cold pink of dawn, crouching behind a tree, spying on him? I'd slipped out of the hut a few minutes after I heard him leave, pulling a jumper over my pyjamas and making straight for the wooded crag above the stream. From there I knew I'd be able to see the small pool we used for bathing.

From my hidden vantage point I heard the scrunching of pebbles under his boots as he came into view. At the water's edge, he stooped to take off his shoes and socks then tugged his sweater over his head, in that way men do, from the neck. His body was lean and functional-looking; you could see the sharp curves of muscle carved by work rather than work-outs.

His hands dropped to his belt. I swallowed and ran my tongue over my cracked lips. Surely he could hear my heart thumping? He slid his pants down, stepped out of them and waded into the pool. The pale buttocks tensed and hollowed as the water crept icily up his thighs, and I could almost feel the goose pimples on my own body. He bent over and splashed water over his head and chest. When he stood again I could clearly see the black stripe of hair that ran down his belly and fanned out above his penis. Behind my own pubic bone a muscle tautened. If I'd hoped to find vulnerability in his nakedness then I was to be disappointed; as I watched him wash, his brisk, unselfconscious movements evoked the unpredictable power of a stallion.

I left as he was dressing.

As I reached a rocky outcrop above the hut I found myself suddenly face to face with Louis. He was sitting nonchalantly on a boulder beside the path. Waiting. My mouth went dry.

'Ah, Eva!'

I tried a smile and wondered whether to feign innocence. I didn't get the chance. He stood as I approached, grabbed me by the arm and shoved me up against the rock. There wasn't even time to struggle. He twisted me round and forced me over till I was face down on the rock. I felt the hard coldness against my chest and an edge grazed my hips through my pyjamas. When I tried to raise my head he pushed me down roughly.

Did I scream or fight back? I don't know. I remember being aware of sharp pebbles digging into my breast and the hollow, empty-belly feeling of shock. Then terror rose like a suffocating balloon in my throat, threatening to choke me. What was he going to do? Please don't let him rape me! That was my first thought. Oh please, God, don't let him do that! I tried to think of things to say. Should I plead? Apologise?

I felt his hand brush my bottom and pull up my sweater. Was he going to bugger me? No, I would die! It was unthinkable.

That's when I felt the first blow. I screamed, though it was more from shock than anything else; he'd slapped me across the backside as if I were a naughty child! Perhaps that was it; it was just a joke. I was being smacked in punishment for spying on him. He was going to teach me a lesson. Perhaps it was even his idea of a come-on.

The second and third slaps swiftly dispelled that notion, scalding my buttocks with glowing humiliation. If this was a joke then he was far too heavy-handed. This hurt! Seriously. The next slap left my backside burning as if a hot iron had been put to my flesh. I was crying now, loud gulping sobs broken by yells with each slap. Any resistance I might have shown dissolved under his punitive palm.

There were, I think, no more than half a dozen spanks on that first occasion, yet they were enough to keep me spread helpless over the rock for several minutes after he'd stopped.

When finally I stood up, dishevelled and tear-stained, I was too embarrassed to look at him. I hated him. I hated him for witnessing me in this state; for seeing my shame, my indignity, my humiliation. Perhaps I hated him more for this, oddly enough, than for the ordeal he'd just put me through.

And when I did eventually look at him ... I saw nothing.

That night I lay for a long time debating what I should do. I could hardly pretend nothing had happened. Maybe I should confront him and have it out. It would be too embarrassing to tell Holly and Michel. I could just pack my bags and leave, but that would be cowardly. Besides, he'd think he'd got the better of me.

Eventually I drifted off into a restless sleep where lustful hands overpowered me, pinned me down, and pleasured me in unimaginable ways. Hot mouths licked me, sucked me, pressed against my sex and nibbled me. Although I couldn't see them in my dream I knew they were his hands, his mouth.

When I woke I was sticky between the thighs. I didn't pack my bags.

\* \* \*

I'd thought I'd feel an overwhelming relief to get back to the farm and Holly and normality, but somehow it was an anticlimax; everything felt rather bland and mundane. As before I only saw Louis at meals, where he was polite but distant, and this in a peculiar way irritated me. It was as if he was pretending that nothing had happened. At the same time I was angry with myself for colluding with him. By saying and doing nothing I was permitting the 'incident' to become our secret, as if I'd consented to it.

Holly could sense that I was on edge at the farm, and asked if I wanted to spend my last week at the hut. I knew Michel was doing a stint on the mountain and I reckoned a few days of his easy-going good humour would restore my equilibrium. I was beginning to relax after a couple of days of his company when Louis appeared. He'd come to relieve Michel who was, apparently, needed on the farm.

Was this a pretext? Had Louis volunteered to relieve Michel because he knew I was up there? There was no way of finding out. My stomach had leaped with excitement at the sight of him, but the feeling was quickly soured by anger and a dark, creeping dread that tiptoed close to fear. I could have gone down, of course. But maybe by then I couldn't.

The following afternoon, Louis startled me as I was washing up. I'd been nervy since he'd arrived, and his very presence made me clumsy and awkward, so it was no surprise, when he burst through the door unexpectedly, that I dropped a plate. It smashed around my feet with a sickening ring, and I froze.

Everything after seemed to happen in slow motion. Louis put down his bag, walked over to me and bent to pick up the broken pieces. I stood there, unable to respond, unable even to think. He placed the pieces in the sink then took me by the arm. My heart banged against my ribs and my legs became rubbery.

I could have resisted, I suppose, or run away, but I didn't. I allowed myself to be led to the table and, when he instructed me to lean over, I obeyed. As his hand pressed down between my shoulder blades, flattening me against the tabletop, I felt a jolt of anticipation shoot up my thighs and into my sex.

My loose cotton skirt gave scant protection against his ruthless hand. Though I managed to suppress my cries initially, the repeated slaps soon had me crying aloud as each muffled thwack branded my backside with the imprint of his palm. It seemed to go on endlessly, the sound of his hand and the sharp shock of pain followed by the deep purple throbbing of my bruised flesh. Hot tears burned streaks of shame down my face and formed undignified puddles on the table.

I couldn't bear to face him when he stopped – I felt too humiliated – but he took hold of my chin and tilted my head till I was forced to look at him. His expression was disturbing. It made me feel naked and vulnerable, as if he had some hold over me. I looked away quickly.

*I was wrong earlier when I said I couldn't see the complexity of his motives in his face. It was that I was scared by what I saw.*

The next few days passed without incident. Louis was out most of the time with the animals, and I wandered over the hills or lay reading by the stream. During the evenings we co-existed uneasily in an atmosphere of sexual tension and stilted conversation. Neither of us made any allusion to the spanking.

When my last day arrived I felt both relief and a strange disappointment, as if something hadn't quite lived up to my expectations. Louis and I were awkward around each other, trying to maintain a physical distance that the hut didn't really permit. It made me stupid and clumsy, so that I bumped into things and dropped my clothes as I packed. Inevitably disaster ensued. I knocked a jug of milk with my elbow and sent it splashing into the sink. A silly accident that didn't really matter, but I knew what would follow.

I looked at Louis. I almost wanted something to happen; the tension between us, like the air before a thunderstorm, had grown electric. He held my gaze and my skin tingled. Slowly, without taking his eyes from mine, he lowered his hands to his waist and began to unbuckle his belt. My heart quickened. He pulled the belt from his trousers and ran it thoughtfully through his hands as if testing its suppleness, then nodded towards the table.

'Bend over, Eva.'

My mouth was dry and I noticed my hands were trembling as I placed them on the table under my cheek.

'Pull your jeans down.' His voice was low, controlled. I made to stand up to undo my jeans but he pushed me back down, forcing me to struggle awkwardly with the zip while my hips were pressed up against the table. I managed to wriggle them down over my backside then felt him tug them further down. My briefs began to creep up between my buttocks, a trivial detail under the circumstances, yet something about the intimacy of it heightened my sense of vulnerability.

I tensed as the leather cut the air with a whistle and cracked sharply on my flesh. There was a timeless pause, then a searing stripe of agony painted the world red and emptied my lungs in a gasp. My whole body shook with the shock, and I would have collapsed had I not been laid out on the table. I tried to raise myself to protest, but felt his fingertips lightly on my back. Obeying his unspoken command I submitted and gripped the edge of the table. Again the cruel crack of leather as another lash drew a weal across my backside and a scream from my throat. Please, no more! No more! I bit my lip to keep the words inside and tasted the hot saltiness of blood mixing with my tears. I sensed him raising his arm again, and dug my nails into the table. An eternity passed. Had he changed his mind? Had he decided it was enough? I breathed out cautiously. Then it fell. Cruel. Scorching. A savage arc across the other two lashes, leaving me too exhausted to sob. I was unable to move for a long time. Finally he helped me stand and made me a coffee with brandy.

When eventually I reached home after an agonising journey, I took a long bath and examined myself in the mirror. My backside was scored with three raised red weals. It was ten days before they finally disappeared.

It was such a relief to get back to work. The huge backlog of accounts kept me late in the office and exhausted enough to sleep soundly all night. Lunchtimes – when I took them – I spent obsessively in the gym trying to shed the weight I'd put on from all that goat cheese. Everything fell so neatly back into its time-allotted slot there was no available space for my mind to consider the disturbing events that had taken place, or for my emotions to run riot with my body.

The buzzer on my desk goes.

'Someone to see you, Eve. Says it's personal. Are you busy?'

'Yeah, but send them through anyway, Maureen. I'll deal with it.' It would probably be one of the juniors needing leave for a grandmother's funeral or something.

I'm checking a summary of accounts so I don't look up when the door opens – I'm also slightly annoyed they haven't knocked.

'Hello, Eva.'

My body responds to his voice before my brain has even processed the information. There is a tightening in my groin and my stomach somersaults. My pen falls to the floor. I start to rise but he stays by the door and I am left in an awkward crouched position behind my desk, unsure whether to go and greet him or sit back down.

My mind searches desperately for an appropriate response. I must say something but nothing seems suitable. I don't even know whether or not I'm pleased to see him. In the end I just come out with a rather strangled 'Louis!'

He leans back against the door and looks at me with the sort of half smile that shows he is fully aware of having the advantage. It's too late to go over and embrace him, the moment has passed, and my hands are trembling too much to extend in a handshake. I must take charge of the situation. This is my office, for god's sake – he can't just come in here and set the rules! Not that he has actually done anything, but my thoughts have become jumbled and incoherent. And all the time he is just watching me. I try a smile.

'So what brings you here, Louis?' It sounds so artificial and smug I feel myself blush.

'I've come to see *you*, Eva.' His arms are folded across his chest and he looks quite relaxed. Inside my blouse I have broken out in a sweat, yet there are goose pimples down my arms and breasts. I have a sudden panic that my nipples are visible and giving off all the wrong messages, so I cross my arms and lean forwards on my desk. Take charge, Eve. Say something.

'Are you over here on business, then?' What a stupid question.

'No. I'm here to see you.'

'You mean you've come specially? All the way from the farm?'

'I'm back in Paris now. For work. But yes, I've come to see you.'

My heart thumps inside my ribs and I'm not sure if it's panic or something more frightening. Get a grip! He has a small smile on his lips but I don't think he's mocking me. I attempt a light-hearted laugh but it sounds hysterical, like a woman on the edge.

'I've come to see if you're happy now you're back in England.'

'Of course I'm happy. I've a great job, a nice home ...' It comes out too fast, too gushing. Whoa, Eve, stop trying so hard. Slow down. I clear my throat, take a breath.

'I've every reason to be happy, haven't I?'

His face doesn't alter – still that little smile – but he looks at me steadily, as you might look at a child you were waiting for to admit the truth.

'I felt that perhaps you had come to France to get away from something.' His voice is soft and even, his accent seductive. 'Or maybe to find something.' The question mark is in the raised eyebrow, the slight tilt of his head inviting confession.

I have a sudden desire to touch him, to run my fingers along his cheek, to press myself against him.

'No, I'm perfectly content with my life, thank you.' My voice is all prim and uptight. I hate myself.

'*Eh bien*, I shall say goodbye, Eva. It seems I have misread the situation.' And he turns to open the door.

What have I done wrong? Which was the wrong answer? I feel like I've been given a test, which I failed, and now he's leaving. No second chance.

'Wait!' There's desperation in my voice. He looks round at me but doesn't move.

'Louis . . .' I must say something to detain him. A little longer at least. 'Please . . . just come in . . . don't go yet.' He shuts the door, leans back and waits. I can't think what to say. Everything seems either too trivial or too dangerous. I play for time.

'Have you seriously come just to see me?' I try to make my voice light and casual. He doesn't answer but continues looking at me. Waiting. I glance down at my hands and notice they are tugging at the hem of my shirt.

'I . . . Why are you bothered whether I'm happy or not?' I must keep talking to keep him here. Yet why? I'd thought when the marks went, those last signs of his hold over me, I'd be able to forget him – that I'd *want* to forget him – yet here I am making a fool of myself in an attempt to stop him leaving. Still he says nothing.

'I'm, er . . . glad you are here, anyway.' Do I sound trite and insincere?

'Eva, why do you have such a problem talking to me? Don't you know what I want?' He frowns at me and butterflies create havoc in my belly. 'Don't you know what *you* want?'

I feel as if my body desires one thing while my common sense tells me something else entirely. I drop my head into my hands. Don't make me think about dangerous things. Leave me to my busy, important life. I don't want complications. I want to stay safe and in control.

'You need me, Eva.'

I look up, shocked. Perhaps I've misheard. But he holds my gaze, challenging me to deny it. Suddenly the messy confusion of my emotions focuses into one angry, clear thought – the bloody audacity of the man! The sheer pigheaded cheek of him, to imagine that I, with my prestigious job and respectable salary, should need him: I am livid.

'Need you! Why on earth should I need a . . .' I search furiously for a suitably cutting insult. 'A pervert!'

He tilts his head slightly. 'Ah, so that's what you call it in English.' His voice is still soft and quiet but I sense an air of danger behind it. I feel myself redden. He strides up to the desk and leans over me.

'So you think I have strange desires? Maybe you think I like to humiliate women. To punish them, eh? Is this how you see me then, Eva?' There is an impatience to his voice now, a passion, and I'm nervous. My eyes shift along the desk to the buzzer.

'Well, Eva, is this the sort of man you think I am?' Suddenly his hand is under my chin, tipping my head back till I'm forced to look at him. A tremor runs through my body at the contact, but I'm not sure whether it's due to fear or lust. He holds my eyes in his till I shake my head. I know it was an unfair accusation, but in some ways it was preferable to the alternatives – the things I can't admit.

*I lied earlier when I said I was scared by the motives I saw in his face. I was scared by what they showed me about myself. Scared to discover I had a perverse side to me. Scared too that someone else could see it.*

He lets go of my chin but remains leaning forwards over me.

'Have you never asked yourself why you let me do that to you? You could have stopped me. You could have told someone. You could have packed your bags and left. But you didn't. Why not, Eva, why not?'

I have no answer. I can't even formulate a reason to myself. Perhaps I don't dare. He stands up abruptly and walks back to the door. I have a sudden panic that he might just walk out on me. Go. Forever. I open my mouth but at the door he stops. Then he leans back against the wall, folds his arms and waits. There is a long silence. I realise I'm terrified he'll leave now. It is as if he's lifted the lid off a deep, deep well and left me perched on the edge.

When he finally speaks his voice is hard.

'Take your shirt off.'

The command catches me off guard.

'Take your shirt off, Eva!'

When I don't respond he lowers his hands to his belt. No! Not here. My hand flies to the buzzer on my desk in alarm. He can't do that to me here, in my own office.

'Maureen?'

He pauses, holding me in his gaze, and for a moment time is suspended; then, without taking his eyes from mine, he begins to unbuckle his belt. I swallow. I desperately need to assert myself. This is *my* domain, where *I* should be in control.

'Eve? Did you call me?'

Yet inside me is another equally compelling force. A dark, unspeakable desire I can't admit to. Neither of us moves.

'Eve, is everything all right?'

Slowly he continues undoing his belt and pulls it from round his waist. A pulse throbs between my legs and I press my thighs together.

'Eve! Is anything the matter?'

'Sorry, Maureen. No, everything's fine. I just want you to divert my calls and ... and ...' He is running the belt slowly, calculatedly through his hands. 'And, Maureen, could you see that I'm not disturbed. Thanks.'

He folds his arms and lets the belt dangle from one hand.

'Take it off, Eva.'

Slowly I begin unbuttoning my top. I slip it off my shoulders and lay it on the desk.

'Now the bra.'

I'm suddenly shy. Although he's seen me stripped of my dignity he's never seen me undressed before.

'Stand up!'

I push my chair back and rise.

'Take off your bra.'

I reach behind me, unhook it and, after a pause, let it fall forwards, freeing my breasts. They feel swollen, conspicuous. I feel his eyes on them and look away, embarrassed. As he approaches me I want to cross my arms over my chest but I don't dare.

'Lean over the desk.'

I obey.

'Pull up your skirt. All the way. Now remove your pants.'

I do as he says, struggling to get my underwear over the spiked heels as I rest forwards on my chin and breasts. His hand is on my back, but lightly, not pinning me down; he knows he doesn't need to.

The anticipation sends a thrill through my body that makes me shudder involuntarily, and I'm afraid he will construe it as a tremor of fear or, worse, desire. Though I have to admit it, my dread of the lash is laced with an excitement I know is sexual.

I hear the whistle of leather then the harsh crack of contact that turns my world red. I stifle a cry. Louis leans forwards, takes my shirt and shoves it in my mouth. The second lash lands directly over the first, and I choke a humiliated cry into my shirt. I bite down hard as I hear him raise the belt and bring it down again. It licks round the crease of my buttocks with a force that ricochets round every nerve ending in my body. I know I can't take any more; he will have me begging to stop if he raises the belt once more. But already I can feel the blood rushing between my legs; the gooiness inside, even as my eyes blink back the tears.

As the throbbing radiates out in pulsing waves I picture the raised welts he will have painted on me, the secret signature of his power. I will relish them later in the mirror, those angry red imprints that confirm his control over me. I wonder how long they will last.

My face is wet with tears when he stops. He steps back then moves my chair away from the desk and into the centre of the room.

'Sit down but keep your skirt up.' I lower myself gently into the seat, biting my lip to avoid crying out in pain. The wood is cold against my burning backside. Soothing.

'Open your legs. Wider!' He is leaning against my desk, the belt beside him. His voice becomes softer now, almost husky. 'Now touch yourself.'

I try to imagine how I must appear to him, blotchy-faced, dishevelled and naked but for my heels and the skirt bunched around my waist. My widespread legs and bare breasts, heavy with the extra pounds I've put on recently, must make me look tarty and brazen. I put my hand to my pubes and rub gently. His eyes follow my movements. Under my fingertips I feel my clitoris respond.

'Inside, Eva. Push your fingers up.'

I tilt my hips back and press my fingers into the warm silkiness of my slit.

'No – inside, properly. I want to see you fuck your-self.' The vulgar phrase sounds funny with his accent, somehow less aggressive. I push my fingers deeper, and they slide in easily. I am wetter than I thought. He strides over and I feel his hand grab my wrist. With something almost like tenderness, he raises it to his face and puts my fingers in his mouth, one by one. His tongue curls around each one in turn. I begin to melt. Suddenly, almost roughly, he takes my hand from his lips and pulls me to my feet.

'Put your hands against the wall,' he commands.

He pushes me so I am facing the wall, and makes me lean forwards on outstretched arms. Then, thrusting his knee between my legs, he kicks my feet outwards till I am splayed apart. I have barely found my balance when I feel his hand tighten on the back of my neck as the hard end of his cock shoves into me. There is a moment of exquisite pleasure as I feel myself forced open and entered, then a sharp pain as his pelvis slaps against the raw flesh of my buttocks. I cry out. The grip on my neck tightens and he pushes himself yet further into me.

I tilt my hips, offering myself up. The pain heightens the thrill of being penetrated, and desire envelops me in concentric circles of pleasure and pain as I submit to him. Finally I am able to succumb to that dark, inner self that wants to be overpowered, dominated, controlled. I groan.

He pulls out slightly and I feel my backside throbbing.

'Is this what you wanted, Eva?' His voice is a whisper, almost a hiss. I don't reply. He slaps me sharply on the side of my buttock.

'Is it, Eva? Isn't this what you wanted all along, for me to fuck you?'

I nod.

'But you need something else as well, don't you, Eva?' His voice is silky now, seductive, and he slides his cock easily back into me as he talks. 'You need to feel my power over you. *Ma puissance*. I must first become your master and teach you to obey.' He begins to move slowly in and out of me, making me gasp when he presses against my tender flesh.

'You are like the animal that needs to be disciplined before it can be rewarded.' As his movements become faster, deeper, I feel my own body responding. 'Like a wild creature that must be broken and dominated before it can be tamed.'

He reaches up and starts squeezing my breasts. The tension that has been gripping my body for weeks is suddenly concentrated in the muscles that suck his penis into my dark wetness. My hips thrust against him, embracing the delicious pain of contact. He pinches my nipples and I sense him beginning to swell inside me. Suddenly a dam inside me bursts, tearing a scream from my throat. I feel his teeth bite into my shoulder, then I explode as he floods me with his juices.

The mirror will be criss-crossed with the red welts and teeth marks of my lover tonight. Perhaps this time they won't fade.

*I was wrong when I said I was scared by what I saw in his face and what it showed me about myself. What scared me was seeing that he knew, right from the start, what I was like. He knew exactly what I needed, what I desired, what he had to do.*

# Summer's Seduction
Celia Stuart

'What the fuck were you thinking, driving to the Grand Canyon?' A ribbon of black asphalt shimmered in front of my eyes as I plodded along the side of the road, my sweaty feet slick inside my running shoes. 'Who the hell goes to the Grand Canyon in the middle of summer? July! It's 120 fucking degrees out here! Whose brilliant idea was this?'

I stopped ranting and walking long enough to wipe my face on my shirt and catch my breath. Sand, browns and deep reds painted a landscape of green cactus fields and distant mesas. Any minute now I expected to see Billy the Kid come galloping up on a dusty horse. 'Lucy Jean, you've lost your mind!'

Of course, no one answered my rant, so I shook my head and pushed on. The cacti were busy ... being cactus. My three-year-old Chevy Impala was busy, steaming. And the jackrabbits were busy ... jacking.

Some vacation this had turned out to be.

Corporate restructuring – the ultimate in multi-tasking – had finally made it to Oklahoma. Downsize, reorganise and give one person three jobs. But I wasn't sure I wanted to stay. After I found myself screaming at a stranger in the grocery store, I decided to buy myself some time with a vacation. My bosses had nodded their heads in understanding, saying they'd be happy to wait, but I'm not sure I believed them or cared.

Brilliant. Just brilliant.

I continued to walk, intermittently pulling my sweat-soaked T-shirt away from my body and fanning myself. *Dry heat, my ass!* Even my panties were soaked with sweat. *Ew!*

I couldn't just fly and buy a package tour (with lecherous old men in plaid shorts and screaming, sticky children). Oh, no! I had to drive myself and take *the scenic route*.

The scolding continued, my blood pressure and my temperature rising with each hot, heavy step, until I was too tired to do more than whine. By the time I finally reached a gas station, I nearly cried. The sight of it had pushed me on for the last quarter-mile.

Instead of an oasis from the heat, I found a locked two-stall garage with an office attached – no way could it be considered a store – piles of old tyres stacked on one side of the building, and ancient gas pumps, everything coated with an inch of reddish-brown dust. Not even a dog to bark and warn someone of visitors, or a water hose. And locked doors separated me from the soda machine. I briefly contemplated breaking the window, then realised I had no change to buy a drink with. With a sigh, I dropped the rock in my hand and circled around the far side of the low-slung building.

Even the flimsy bathroom doors – and access to sinks that had water – were padlocked. I gave the bathroom doorknob one final rattle then pushed on while eyeing the tyre graveyard. Knowing my luck a snake would come sliding out of one of those piles of tyres and bite me. I'd die right here, at a deserted Arizona gas station, rot, dry up and blow away before anyone knew I was missing.

Imagine my unadulterated joy to find a tidy little grey house tucked out back complete with a hanging basket of bright flowers by the door and a tiny windchime that oddly set me at ease.

'Hello!' I normally spent my days surrounded by the hum of computers, the ringing of phones, copy machines, radios, *people*. So the total and complete absence of sound nearly sent me into a panic. 'Hello!' I screeched at the top of my lungs, wandering closer to the house. 'Anybody home?'

Nothing but the wind. I climbed the narrow steps to the tiny porch and guiltily looked around. Nobody. Anywhere. Then I tried the doorknob, which turned easily in my hand.

'Orgasmic,' I muttered to myself as icy-cold air lured me inside. It was downright chilly and my nipples tightened painfully while sweat evaporated at the speed of air – air-conditioning, that is.

I shut the door behind me and cautiously looked around. A bar separated the pale yellow kitchen from the living area where I stood; the complete absence of knick-knacks, the functional but ugly brown living room carpet and brand new recliner screamed 'bachelor pad'. But even bachelor pads had water. I walked straight to the sink, flipped the lever and watched clear, cold water pour out for a minute before sticking my head under the faucet and drinking until my belly hurt. Then I rinsed my face and arms off and dried them on my grimy T-shirt, and took a look around.

Everything was tidy and dust-free, the kitchen linoleum spotless, no dishes in the drainer, or mail tossed on the counter. With its shiny chrome, bright-red seats and sparkly Formica top, the little dinette set tucked under the kitchen window looked like something my grandmother might have owned. The sofa was as old as the carpet, while the oversized television looked brand new – *now if that isn't just like a man* ... One bedroom sported a cheerful yellow crochet bedspread on the queen-sized bed and a French provincial-style dresser – also free of clutter. The second bedroom was as dark as the first was light and cheery, the bed covered with a navy spread, the furniture dark and heavy. But in here photos of someone's family at various ages hung on one wall.

Feeling as if I'd disturbed someone's sanctuary, I guilty tiptoed out and shut the door behind me, collapsing on the scratchy couch and pillowing my head on my arms with a jaw-cracking yawn.

The sound of the front door slamming yanked me upright, and I pushed stray hairs off my face, trying to get my bearings. *Goldilocks had dozed off.* But it wasn't the three bears that woke me up. *Hot* registered somewhere in my sleep-fuzzed brain. He was hot. Tall, thick and tanned ... and glaring at me from beneath the brim of his baseball cap.

If he was a serial killer, I'd happily go to my death – especially if he let me shower first.

He removed the cap and slowly hung it up, never taking his deep-green eyes off me. His short, neat hair was a direct contrast to the two-days' growth of beard on his rugged face, faded blue T-shirt and jeans, and grease-caked workboots. And he looked rather grim, despite his full sensual lips.

I suppose I'd look grim too in his position.

'Mind telling me what you're doing asleep on my couch?' The deep rumble of his voice sent a shiver racing up my spine and my nipples hardened with a sudden case of nerves.

No woman ever wanted to look her worst in front of a man, whether they're a hot prospect or not. And I, of course, looked the *absolute* worst in my sweat-stained, sleep-rumpled shorts, my fair skin coated with more sweat and grime and my red hair, freshly washed this morning, now stuck to my head in a makeshift ponytail. My mouth tasted like I'd licked my way across the desert. And he was hot.

'I fell asleep.' I swung my legs off the couch and sat fully upright, awake enough to realise how stupid my answer had been.

'Obviously. What are you doing in my house?'

'I broke down . . .'

'That your Impala about five miles back?'

'I walked five miles?' I stared up at him, my jaw slack in shock.

'No wonder you fell asleep. What the hell were you doing off the main highway?'

I continued to stare at him for a minute, then hung my head, hoping he'd shut up long enough for me to pull myself together. 'Please stop interrogating me!'

'Why didn't you use the phone and call for help?'

'Because I'm a fucking idiot!' I finally hollered, glaring up at him.

The frown on his face disappeared but he still looked stern. 'Give me your keys. I'll tow your car in and take a look at it. Help yourself to the shower. I assume you have luggage?'

*No, I always travel with no spare clothes.* 'A suitcase and a tote bag in the back seat.'

'You can get cleaned up while I'm gone and I'll bring your bags in. Take the yellow bedroom.' The way those green eyes casually raked over me reminded me I was currently a far from desirable specimen of womanhood. 'I'm Greg – Greg Summers, by the way.'

Feeling chastised and humiliated, I stood up and dug my keys out of my pocket, handing them over with a mumbled thanks and 'I'm Lucy Jean.'

*Why did I go and tell him my middle name when I'm the only one who calls me Lucy Jean?* I scolded myself all through my shower. One of the hottest men I'd ever seen in my life and I'd screamed at him. And here I stood, using his shampoo and conditioner, his shower and his spare bedroom, like some sort of demented Goldilocks, testing everything in sight. I found my suitcase and bag on the bed when I came out, the house silent but for the windchimes outside.

Overwhelmed at the predicament I'd put myself in – just because he owned a business didn't mean he *wasn't* some kind of a freak – I started crying in the middle of towelling myself off. After all, Norman Bates's mother had owned a motel.

Shaky with exhaustion, it was all I could do to drag on my robe and stretch out on the bed for a nice long cry. And another nap.

The smell of food woke me up, something spicy that made my mouth water. For a minute, I couldn't remember where I was. Then, as I stretched, flexing my calves to work the soreness out, it all came back. My feet were tender because I'd spent my morning walking in the Arizona desert.

Only to be found curled up on his couch by the mysterious Greg Summers, a knight errant who came complete with tow truck and wrench. Eyes closed, I smiled and stretched, enjoying the slide of my silky robe against my skin and the warm tingle of awareness between my legs, my months-long sexual dry spell, brought on by an almost perpetual bad mood, seemingly gone. What else did Greg come with? The room was cool and the house quiet. No phone, no television, no assistants buzzing, no one demanding a report, no deadline. Just me, Greg and my reignited libido.

He was definitely my kind of vacation souvenir. My robe had nearly come open and cool air caressed my bare skin from my legs, across my stomach and up the valley between my 34Cs. I skimmed my belly with both hands and my puckered nipples tingled, sending heat trails to my pussy. Smiling to myself, I tweaked the sensitive tips, pulling my knees up at the same time.

Surely I had time for a quickie before dinner.

About the time my hands reached my pubic curls, I was interrupted by a throat clearing. The object of my fantasies stood at the end of the bed, his eyes searing my bare skin as they flickered from my face to my hands cupping my mound. I wasn't apologising for masturbating in his spare bed – or near masturbating. Despite the heat in my face, I smiled and shrugged, encouraged by his twitching lips. 'Can't blame a girl for trying.'

'Save it for dessert,' he quipped, turning and disappearing through the door.

Dessert, huh?

'You rescue damsels in distress and cook dinner too. Nice.' With a smile, I shoved another forkful of meatloaf in my mouth.

Greg cleaned up nice too, very nice. Jeans and T-shirts were obviously invented for men like him. Rugged men who didn't give a damn about how they looked but looked damned fine in anything they put on. He'd shaved the stubble off to reveal a firm, square jaw and washed away the day's heat and grime to show off a surprisingly intelligent set of eyes.

'Man's gotta eat.'

There's a lot to be said for the strong silent type, but I'm not sure what. Maybe I should have asked him to take me to a hotel. I tried again. 'So, how'd you end up out here in the desert?'

He paused, a buttered piece of roll halfway to his

mouth, and scowled at me. Obviously, something he was good at. 'I think the better question would be, how did *you* end up out here in the desert?'

'You always let strangers you find sleeping on your couch make themselves at home and feed them?' I countered, suddenly angry. I could scowl just as good as him.

'What in the hell are you doing driving around by yourself like that? You're a hell of a long way from Oklahoma, little girl!' He threw his roll down and it landed in a puddle of gravy on his plate.

'You snooped in my car?'

'Damn right I did, Lucy Jean Cavanaugh of Oklahoma City, Oklahoma. You always masturbate in strangers' beds?'

Lips pursed, I threw down my fork, scooted my chair back and crossed my legs, suddenly wishing I'd worn my robe to dinner instead of denim shorts and a T-shirt. 'I'd masturbate driving down the highway if it suited me,' I quipped tartly. 'What the hell are you so mad about anyway? Your turn, you grouchy old bear. Why are you out here?'

'I like wide open spaces.'

I snorted and tossed back, 'I was on vacation, when I broke down.'

'Never.' He sipped his tea, keeping his eyes on his glass.

'Never? You mean, you've never taken in a stranger? Then why did you?'

'I like redheads,' he said. Eyes on his plate, he quietly added, 'And you're a real redhead.'

'You noticed.'

'I notice lots of things.' His voice was low and rough as he finally looked up at me, the anger in his eyes now replaced by something hot that made me clench my thighs together.

'Such as?'

Outside the window, night blanketed the desert, hiding the stark scenery. But in the kitchen the air changed, suddenly electric, and I resisted the urge to reach up and smooth my hair in case it were standing on end.

'Your skin.' His voice was a low, hypnotic rumble that pulled me out of my chair.

'How long's it been?' I walked around the tiny table, stopping beside his chair, and peeled my shirt over my head, letting it fall to the floor. My bare skin goosebumped and my nipples tightened as Greg focused on my breasts.

'So long I don't even remember –' he whispered, looking up at me '– what it feels like to have a woman wrapped around me, under me, clawing at me.' He turned to face me and spread his legs, pulling me closer as his fingers worked at the button-fly of my shorts. 'I wanna lick you, see if your skin tastes as sweet as it looks.'

'I haven't had sex in five months,' I softly confessed, pushing my hips towards his face, '*good sex* in at least eighteen.'

'My favourite part of a woman's body?' He leaned forwards and pressed his lips against the soft spot just below my belly button, then licked it with his warm tongue. 'Right here,' he whispered against my skin. 'So soft.' He kissed and licked that tender area again, then sucked at my belly button, teasing it with his tongue.

I sagged against him, weak-kneed and tight-nippled, burying my fingers in his thick silky hair. My shorts fell off my hips and I kicked them free, and pushed my belly against his mouth, amazed that something so tender could have such deeply felt results. My pussy was swollen and tender as the lowgrade fever of need I'd woken up with spiked.

I wanted more. I wanted him to go down on me until

I came. I wanted to claw him so hard he'd never forget what a woman felt like. And I had no idea why, or where my sudden burst of lust had come from. Beyond a sudden impulse to have sex with a stranger. But sex with Greg would be more than the back-alley stranger-sex variety.

His fingers slipped under my panties and they followed my shorts. Suddenly, he looked up at me, the expression on his face pure panic, his fingers digging painfully into my hips.

'What?' A shiver of fear drew me back from that hot needy place and I realised my impulsiveness could easily bite me in the ass.

He stood up and yanked his T-shirt off, revealing a long lean torso that rippled with muscles. 'Turn around.' He nudged me towards the kitchen sink, and more than a bit of fear tickled me now. There was no way I could fight him off and ... 'Lean over,' he ground out. I nearly choked on my racing heart at the sound of his zipper and his jeans being pushed down. I couldn't run, bare-ass naked in the desert for –

He latched on to my neck, chasing my fear away with his warm mouth and the feel of his hard cock pressed against the cheeks of my ass. Both oddly gentle.

With a sigh, I propped my elbows on the edge of the sink and bent over, aware of his callused fingers between my thighs, gently stroking me until I squirmed against him. He moaned into my neck and I arched my hips to better accommodate the thick cock that followed his teasing fingers. Then he was inside me, hot and hard, plunging and stroking, stretching me and it didn't matter that I couldn't claw his back. He rode me, pumping furiously, fucking me 'til I couldn't catch my breath, 'til I reached around and dug my claws into his ass, laughing and squealing.

'You like my pussy, Greg?' I panted, tilting my head so I could see him.

He groaned in response, his face red and tense with the effort of maintaining any control, and kissed me, a hot erotic play of tongue that made my pussy clench and I tightened my legs as the combination of heat and friction pushed me that much closer to my climax.

'Do it, Greg. Fuckmefuckmefuckme,' I growled. 'Harder, baby ... yeah ... like that.'

I focused on the huge harvest moon that bathed the darkened landscape in a pale eerie glow. There was nothing but us, caught up in the most primal act in the world, struggling towards the pinnacle of human pleasure.

'You feel good,' he growled in my ear. 'So good. So tight. You like that, Lucy Jean?'

I couldn't even work out a reply, or protest his use of my middle name, just a continuous set of high-pitched squeals and harsh broken laughter that coincided with each thrust until I came, any semblance of order gone as I wriggled and ground against his cock, praying for the longest orgasm of my life. I rode it for all it was worth, tuning out everything but the sharp pleasure. And the feel of Greg's chest hairs against my back, just how deeply my nails were latched into his ass, how tense I was under the weight of him, his fingers strumming my clit. Then his orgasm as he shouted a long drawn out sound and his own rhythm grew as offbeat as mine. Until we slowed. And I sagged against the kitchen sink, on very shaky legs.

'What the hell did you do to me?' he ground out, rubbing his face in my neck as he slipped from me.

I turned to face him, sagging against the counter. 'I guess that's what they call kitchen-sex,' I teased, struggling to catch my breath.

He wasn't amused. Instead, he bent over and pulled his jeans up, his lips set in a grim line.

I'd been insulted before, but this definitely took the cake.

Angry because I'd been royally fucked, my ass was cold and I stood in the middle of some man's kitchen with sex juice running down my legs. I waved a hand at the table of cold food. 'So now what? We finish dinner?'

'That shouldn't have happened.' He ran both hands through his hair and blew out a heavy breath. The scowl was back on his face.

'That wasn't your idea of dessert, Greg? Isn't that what you said? Save it for dessert? Hell that was the entrée, honey!' Two steps put us chest to chest and I ran my hands across his heavy pecs, the crisp hairs tickling my fingers. 'What are you so afraid of?' I leaned forwards and sucked one of his nipples into my mouth, gently nibbling the sensitive skin, while never taking my eyes off Greg's face.

'I knew a redhead once,' he gasped, frowning. 'I caught her in bed with my best friend; they ran off together and took my dog.'

'You're making that up.' I stood up straight and pressed my breasts against his chest, winding my arms around his neck.

'I knew a redhead once. She was nothing but trouble,' he murmured, a reluctant grin tugging at his lips.

'I'm not her, and since I'm missing the Grand Canyon, and all, the least you can do is show me some Arizona hospitality.'

Then I pulled his head down to mine and kissed him. He was surprisingly passive – reserved – his mouth still over mine while I sucked at his full lips and hungrily teased him with my tongue. At least he wasn't unresponsive. But I wanted more.

Finally, he yanked my hair back hard enough to make me wince and returned the favour, kissing me back then nipping at my lips in retaliation before we both had to finally come up for air.

'I ordered the water pump for your car but it won't get here until Thursday.'

In other words, we had two days, and I wasn't about to look a gift-fuck in the mouth. 'I'd say let's get naked and crazy but we're already naked – at least I am.'

'You are a crazy woman.' He released my hair long enough to throw me over his shoulder, ignoring my shriek of surprise as we headed down the darkened hallway.

He was right, I was a crazy woman, stuck in the desert with a man I knew nothing about who made me want to fuck like a rabbit. When I woke up the next morning, Greg was gone. And I had no idea how long he'd gone without sex but he obviously had a lot to make up for. I gingerly crawled out of bed and showered again, ignoring the strange impulse to go pantiless and opting for a short, loose sundress and bikini panties instead.

Muscles I'd forgotten existed screamed in protest as I stepped into the kitchen. Outside it looked like the sun had been up a while, and it occurred to me, I hadn't wondered what time it was or worried about getting anywhere. All I could seem to recall was it was Wednesday and tomorrow the part for my car would arrive. I'd be back on the road by Friday, at the latest. I suppose the silly side of me would be sad to leave.

I dug through the refrigerator and cabinets then scrambled eggs and fixed toast while wondering what living with Greg would be like, out here in the middle of nowhere, no neighbours, no internet, no traffic … just quiet.

I took my plate out on to the tiny back porch, the

wood already warm under my feet, and sank into one of the plastic chairs, wondering what Greg was up to. How the hell could he stay in business out here in the middle of nowhere? And it really was the middle of nowhere.

From where I sat all I could see was sand, cacti and more cacti that faded into the distant blue haze of a mountain range.

Again it hit me that I didn't hear a thing. I finished eating my breakfast with only the early morning sunshine for company until the silence was finally broken by the sound of footsteps on the porch and Greg came around the corner.

'Morning.'

'I helped myself to breakfast.'

'*Mi casa es su casa.*' He leaned against the porch railing, dressed in coveralls, which he'd pulled off his shoulders to reveal a white tank top and his tanned muscular arms. The smudge of grease on his forehead was endearing.

He squatted beside my knees and looked up at me, his eyes gentle. 'How you feeling?'

'Tired,' I replied with a smile. 'You?'

'About the same.' The smile he gave me was nearly as endearing as the grease stain. He didn't look quite so ... world-weary, I suppose.

We had definitely smoothed the hard edges off him last night.

And me too, apparently. 'Sore too. A little.'

He apologised with a grimace of obvious regret. I set my plate on the little plastic table and leaned over, cupping his chin as I did. His stubble was rough under my fingers, his lips smooth under my mouth, against my tongue. I licked them with a soft moan and delved deeper. Loveplay at its finest, the kind you only experience when you're new to each other and still feeling your way.

Despite my soreness, I found myself aroused at the realisation that we could fuck right here under the late-morning sun and no one would ever know. It was more of a turn-on than actual foreplay. Greg must have read my mind – he moved between my thighs while we continued to kiss. I licked and sucked at his lips, aware of the warm sheen of sweat on his shoulders, the heat of the sun soaking into my back, and his fingers kneaded my inner thighs, his thumbs digging deep, gentle circles into my skin.

'You're sore, remember?' He pulled back, looking up at me, and I shrugged. 'Stay here. I'll be right back.' He disappeared inside, reappearing a minute or two later with a quilt. Where had that come from? 'Stand up,' he ordered. I did and he spread it out in the chair. No way could that cheap plastic chair hold us both – not even on a good day.

Before my mind could wander too far, he reached for me, reached under my skirt and pushed my panties down. A frisson of heat spiralled out from my stomach. I was ready for whatever he had in mind, my sex already slippery. He ground against me, his big hands biting into my ass and the rough material of his cover-alls chaffing my hungry clit.

With a soft laugh, I yanked his T-shirt over his head, but he backed away when I reached for his zipper.

'Sit,' he ordered.

I did, wriggling like a puppy in anticipation. Again, he knelt between my legs, pushing them wide apart and propping one on his shoulder. I heaved a deep sigh of anticipation and relaxed, pulling up my dress to watch. His lips tickled my thighs with soft kisses and I resisted the urge to spread myself open for him. Instead,

I reached up my dress, cupping my braless breasts, my half-open eyes on the scenery in the distance. I squeezed them, pinching my nipples hard and moaning at the heat that streaked straight to my swollen clitoris, which Greg was now gently blowing on. His thumbs held my lips apart and his attention was almost reverent. I let my leg fall open wider, propping my foot sideways on his shoulder as our eyes met.

'What are you doing under there?' he demanded, his eyes narrowed.

'Wanna watch?' I offered, giving him a playful smile.

'Take it off,' he gruffly ordered.

I struggled out of my dress, despite my awkward position, then sat naked in the sun. Naked as the day I was born and suddenly as free.

I tweaked my nipples again and moaned but hung on, my eyes on Greg's face. His eyes were still narrowed into slits, his thumbs still held my pussy lips apart and my juices trickled down to tease my ass.

'You like that?' He reached up, swatting my hand away, and pinched one for me while his other hand gently massaged my aching mound. I wanted him inside me, I wanted to feel his fingers and tongue on me, but he didn't. Instead, he continued to worry my nipple.

'Yeah.' I grinned, pinching my other nipple in kind.

Little electrical impulses of desire danced across my skin to my ever-swelling clitoris. My own scent tickled my nose, the warm musky scent of sex, desire, need. 'I feel like I'm being fucked by the sun,' I moaned.

His eyes warmed, a smile teasing his stern lips and creasing the edges of his eyes. My fanciful side imagined we were the last two people on the planet. Then wondered if this was how Zeus had seduced young maidens, as a beam of sunlight, teasing and tantalising with the gentlest of licks.

My eyes drifted lower and I propped my other leg on Greg's broad shoulder, easing back in the chair as Zeus and he ate my pussy. He lapped at me, spreading my juices everywhere, then pulled my tender bud between his lips, sucking hard and stroking it with his soft tongue. I moaned as the rest of me turned to jelly, my arms and legs weak, my head lolling back.

Greg wrapped his arms around my upper thighs, holding them in place and leaving his fingers free to work their magic. His thumbs massaged my tender nerve-filled lips while his tongue lapped at me, then intermittently circled and danced across my clitoris, the coil in my belly winding tighter every time.

The urge to watch warred with the urge to stay like I was and let him do as he pleased, until the gentle probing of a finger at my ass caught my attention, and my head snapped up. Greg's head nearly blocked my view, his breath warm and ticklish on my skin as one thick finger slowly slid inside my ass and stopped. The slight discomfort faded and I relaxed, reached down to stroke his hair, and tilted my head to the side and watched. He looked up at me, his green eyes hot, and pulled my sex lips back so I could see ... everything. His fingers, plunging in and out of me, stroked both tunnels simultaneously, and my aching, swollen clit. I giggled, licked a finger and ran it lightly across the puffy nub.

'No,' Greg panted, leaning down and blocking my view again, as he pulled it into his mouth. It was too much.

I'd never been much of a one for anal-play but this ... this was something else altogether. My belly tightened as low-level shockwaves rippled through me, increasing in intensity. With a near-hysterical laugh, my grip on his hair tightened, my other hand roughly tweaking a nipple and not letting go as I arched off the chair, riding his face and fingers, suddenly drenched and slick with sweat as an amazing orgasm rolled through me. My body wound tighter and tighter with each wave, my eyes focused on his head between my thighs as Greg held me in place, teasing both holes, biting and sucking at me until I came a second time, my screams of laughter and cries for more turned to pleas for mercy. I was too tender for *more*.

He untangled us, gently resting my legs on the porch, then buried his face in my belly and wrapped his arms around my waist, his breath hot on my sweaty skin.

We stayed like that, listening to nothing for the longest time, a light breeze drying our skin and carrying off the smell of sex.

'Do you always laugh when you have sex?'

'Never.' I smiled down at him, my hands gently stroking his sweaty hair as I leaned over to kiss him. I loved the taste of me on his mouth, the smell of me on his skin. I had no idea where my giggles during sex had come from and they had nothing to do with being ticklish.

Finally, he stood up and silently pulled his shirt back on, his hard-on prominent under his coveralls. I stopped his retreat with my leg and grabbed the loose waist with my fingers, pulling myself upright and unzipping him as I went. 'Where you going, Papa Bear?' I drawled with a smile.

'Papa Bear?' He grinned again. 'You don't have to.'

I did, freeing his cock from the white cotton briefs and licking every thick inch, teasing the head and moaning as he tensed against me. Then setting a slow steady pace with my hand and mouth, jacking him off and sucking him at the same time while his hands played in my hair and he whispered to me.

'I liked fucking you in the kitchen last night.'

I smiled up at him, despite my full mouth, and gave the head of his shaft an extra-hard suck.

'I like it when you laugh too. Crazy, but it turns me on.'

I purred but didn't stop, the salty taste of him pushing me onward.

'I was gonna let you play with yourself last night ... but I figured you'd freak. Aw, God. You liked that finger in your ass,' he grunted with a thrust of his hips.

I moaned and reached for his sac, massaging it with my fingers.

He groaned, his hips thrusting faster, his balls tightening in my hand. 'Suckit, Lucy ... suckit ... suckit ... suckme' was followed by '*ohyeah!*' at the top of his lungs and I let my hand finish the job as he came, spurts of hot semen splashing my bare chest.

With another giggle, I milked him dry while he watched, his chest heaving.

'If I started every day like that I'd never get a damned thing done.' He pulled his coveralls back up with a red-faced grin and dropped to his knees beside me.

'Yeah you would,' I teased, wiping my chest with my panties. I had no plans to put them back on anytime soon.

'Sorry I can't stay and play, darlin', but I do have work to do. So be a good girl 'til I get back.'

'Can I stay like this, Papa Bear?' I lazily drawled. My legs still felt weak and I wanted to take a nap where I sat, using the sun as a blanket.

'Suit yourself, Goldilocks,' he replied, standing up. His eyes seared every naked inch of me. 'Might wanna put some sunscreen on those lily-white titties though.'

I snorted with laughter, watching the roll of his ass as he walked away with almost military precision. Then I looked at my tits, cupping one in each hand and smiling. They *were* lily white ... with pretty puffy pink nipples. I gave them both a pinch, then went in search of sunscreen, dancing naked through Greg's house as if I had every right to.

Back outside, I applied a coat of SPF 30 everywhere I could reach, then propped my feet on the extra chair and dozed, my mind wandering miles above me. I think I now understood the allure of nudist colonies. Not that I had any intention of joining one, but there was something very primal and natural yet wicked and erotic about sitting outside buck-naked for the roadrunners and buzzards to see.

I woke up hot, sweaty and horny again. How long had I napped? Where was Greg when I needed him? Working, of course. I felt seventeen again ... OK fourteen and newly aware of my body in a way I hadn't been in a while. Sex – and even masturbation – had become a means to an obvious end, a chore, and I realised how my life had spun so far out of control, become so not fun, not simple any more. Until now.

I looked down at myself, at my nipples that tingled and tightened under the hot sun. I brushed my fingertips across them, studying them, the little ridges, the blue veins under my pale skin, how the tips of my nipples were darker than my areolae. How there seemed to be an electrical connection between the sensitive tips and my pussy that swelled in proportion to my sudden desire for myself.

I cupped my breasts, kneading them, wondering what Greg felt when he touched them. What it would feel like for his mouth to suck them again. Bite them. What his stubble would feel like against the tender skin. I pulled my puckered nipples with my fingertips, pulled them out and squeezed them hard and smiled at the tightening in my belly. Then I released them, scooted the extra chair closer and let my legs fall open. The sun warmed my tender lips, teasing me, luring me to spread my legs wider so it could fuck me again.

I slid my fingers down my belly and massaged my aching lips, spreading them and staring at myself. My ass still stung from Greg's earlier loveplay, but not in a bad way; in a way that made me want it again.

I spread my legs even wider, catching a glimpse of my swollen bud under a light dusting of curls. I needed to shave again. I loved shaving myself. Even the thought of it turned me on. There was nothing like lying in a hot tub, legs spread, pussy slick with shaving cream, the razor's caress as tender as a lover's. I licked a finger and ran it across my slit, briefly debating whether to go in search of my vibrator (hidden in the bottom of my suitcase) or just use my fingers.

Laziness won. I held myself open and slid two fingers down to my wet juicy hole, experimentally playing with myself, teasing my most tender spot. With a giggle, I licked my fingers, and repeated the process, wondering what Greg thought of the way I tasted.

At that, I slowly pushed two fingers in as far as I could reach, then added a third and did myself while I watched, until my ass clenched and my hips pushed upward towards the sun.

Zeus and some unknown sun god watched me while I watched myself, my hips convulsing against my fingers, drenched with my juices, my sweet, swollen clitoris begging for mercy while I laughed and moaned, riding it to the very end. The poor thing had seen more action in twenty-four hours than it had in the last six months.

I leaned back in the chair, leisurely licking my fingers one by one, and stretched with a satisfied catlike sigh.

'You are the horniest damned woman I ever met,' came a voice from behind me.

I jumped then smiled over my shoulder at Greg, wondering how long he'd been behind me. 'It's this sunshine. What do ya'll put in it? Can I get some to go?'

In reply, he set two large glasses of tea at my elbow and gently cupped my tits with his big rough hands. 'You gonna eat out here, dressed like that?'

'Is it lunchtime already?' The sun was hotter now, less friendly and more irritating as it glared down on me from the pale-blue sky above, but I wasn't ready to put any clothes on.

'Half past twelve.' He disappeared, returning with two plates that contained perfect triangles of bread loaded with leftover meatloaf and mayo and surrounded by chips. Then he sat and pulled my legs on to his lap.

Neither of us commented on the fact I was bucknaked and had been practically since I'd gotten up. As if it were the most natural thing in the world, and I suppose it was.

'You're starting to burn,' he observed in between bites of his own sandwich.

'I'll go in after lunch.' Nothing said I had to put clothes on. Maybe a bath and a date with my razor. It'd make a nice surprise for Greg later. A bald slick pussy to play with.

'So how in the world do you end up with enough business out here to *stay* in business? Are you independently wealthy?' I teased, popping a chip in my mouth. A chip I nearly choked on at his answer.

'I'm a deputy-sheriff,' he said softly, eyes on my face.

*No fucking way. A cop?* I sat still, very aware of my nakedness.

'I knew I shouldn't have told you.' With a shake of his head, he stood up and carried his plate into the house. He wasn't getting away so easily. I followed him into the kitchen, shivering at the chilly air and cold linoleum under my feet.

'Wha-why shouldn't you have told me?' I crossed my arms, aware of how ridiculous I must look standing there giving him an inquisition in the nude. 'Beyond the obvious, I don't care, Greg!'

'What obvious?' He threw his half-eaten lunch in the trash and turned to face me, his arms crossed and the scowl back on his face.

'Hello!' I held my arms up and turned from side to side. 'I've become a nudist.'

Greg's scowl slowly faded as his eyes lingered on my chest. 'Being a deputy in a small town is like being a minister,' he said softly. 'Folks expect you to be a saint. I date women in Buffalo Falls and I'm terrified to make a pass at 'em. Worried over what they'll say or tell their friends about that nice Deputy Summers.'

God help me, I giggled, but he did have a point.

'I'm on vacation. Just watching the place for a friend.' Then another thought struck me, one that made me frown. 'Are you really working on my car?'

'I know my way around under the hood.' We both grinned and I scrambled for a solution to our mini-dilemma.

'We've got what? Twenty-four hours, two days tops?' I sauntered closer and backed him against the counter with my wickedest smile, unzipping his jeans.

'Yeah,' he murmured, cupping my bare butt cheeks.

'So what's say we forget about the real world and treat this like the vacation it is, and I promise never to tell a soul that Deputy Summers has a damned fine pussy-eating technique and the biggest dick in all of Arizona.'

With a chuckle he asked, 'Does this mean I get to watch you run around naked for the next two days?'

'I think I was a nudist in my last life. Maybe some Amazonian tribeswoman with a bone through my nose and a tiny animal-skin skirt,' I quipped in lieu of a reply, my fingers wrapped around his cock.

'Deal,' he replied, giving me the first genuine grin I'd seen in days.

The next two days passed way too fast to suit me. I ran around naked most of the time, my mind and body equally free for the first time in ages. Greg and I had sex at will, including in the bathtub after I shaved – and he watched – and in the garage, the big doors open, the occasional car flying by on the highway and sending a chill of tension up my spine at the thought of getting caught.

Then I drove back to Oklahoma City, quit my job and packed up, ready to do something, try something new with my life, while Greg became an important lesson.

And a bittersweet memory.

# Night Crossing
Deborah Knightly

Penny put out her cigarette, climbed into her car and started the engine.

Judging by the number of vehicles, the night-time crossing from Portsmouth to Cherbourg in February was not a popular one, and if it wasn't for her crippling fear of flying, Penny wouldn't be there herself.

The traffic moved slowly up the ramp, and she tapped impatiently on the steering wheel. She was edgy, and keen to get this tedious journey out of the way so that her fun could begin. While she waited she re-tuned the radio, away from its normal talk-news station, in the hope that some music would put her in the holiday mood. She stopped at a heavy rock show, and the beat thumped sensuously through the car. It was invigorating although a little brash for her tastes, but she persevered. After all, she sighed, I am on holiday.

When Angela had suggested the Girls should have a weeklong reunion holiday in Cap Ferret, Penny knew she had to go, whatever it took. They had all met at university when they shared a corridor in a hall of residence and, at first, Penny had felt like an outsider. She didn't have the money to join in with many of the things they did, but the Girls always loved to tell her about what they had been up to, and she even acquired the nickname 'Aunty Pen' because she was such a good listener. Always dependable, she was the one they had trusted with their secrets.

Since then the Girls had done well and enjoyed many kinds of success – high-flying jobs, marriages, 2.4 children – and Penny was pleased for them. But sometimes she noticed them looking at her with 'poor Penny' expressions. Here she was, 29 years old, working as a bank clerk and rarely dating. She was happy the way things were, but occasionally she suspected they might think her way of life was second rate.

She imagined they might even pity her for the fact they could fly to Bordeaux tomorrow, while here she was at almost midnight with a six-hour ferry crossing and nearly five hundred miles of road ahead of her. Although maybe that particular pity was justified, she mused.

Her thoughts were still elsewhere when she heard a knock at the car window; a man was inspecting boarding cards. Penny wound down the window and stuttered an apology while she searched for the card in her bag.

'That's all right, love.' He grinned. 'I don't mind waiting.' She found the card and turned to hand it to him. He was staring right down her cleavage. Her V-necked cardigan was buttoned up to the top, but from his vantage point above her he had a clear view between her breasts. He caught the look of surprise on Penny's face as he took the card, and he laughed as he waved her in. 'Make sure you get in good and tight up behind, love.'

He was still chuckling as Penny drove up to the car in front. She wasn't sure if she had imagined the innuendo, but she felt the colour rising in her cheeks all the same. Not that she was indignant – she liked the attention – but she never knew what to say in these situations. She stopped the car and watched in the mirror as he walked away. He had nice eyes, she thought. And, talking of tight behinds, his bum wasn't bad either.

Penny picked up her handbag and left the car, heading up the stairs into the body of the ferry. To the cafeteria for coffee first, she thought, and then sleep. They weren't due to dock until almost six o'clock in the morning, so this was going to be a long night.

The cafeteria was surprisingly busy, but Penny managed to find an empty table in the corner and settled down with her cappuccino. She had actually asked for a black coffee, but the tired-looking woman behind the counter had got it wrong, and she didn't like to make a fuss.

She pulled a book from her bag and looked at the scantily clad woman pouting provocatively on the cover. Penny hesitated. She had bought the novel at the last moment, an impulse buy from a stand in the ferry terminal. Maybe she should have gone for something more demure, a courtroom drama or a historical romance perhaps. Reading this kind of thing in the privacy of her bedroom was one thing, but out here, in the brightly lit glare of the restaurant, was another. She glanced about. The other passengers were busy eating and drinking, and not remotely interested in her. It's just a bit of fun, she reasoned, and that's what holidays are for. She smiled and turned to chapter one.

An hour later she finished her coffee, closed her book, and made her way to the rest lounge. It was a large room, with rows of seats arranged in blocks of four, and it took her a few seconds to adjust to the dim lighting. It was very like an airline cabin, she thought. She stopped at the steward's desk, and looked around while she waited for him to notice her. Only a small number of the reclining seats were occupied.

'You can sit anywhere you like – it's quiet tonight.' The steward, a spiky-haired lad of about eighteen, barely glanced away from the monitor he was staring at as he passed Penny a ticket. 'That will be fifteen euros.' She handed over the money and pointedly thanked him, even though he never took his eyes from the video game on the screen. 'And manners cost nothing,' she added under her breath as she walked away.

'Pardon?' Apparently she wasn't as quiet as she had thought, and he had heard her. Penny blushed.

'Nothing,' she mumbled, and then immediately she wanted to kick herself. Why couldn't she just say what she thought? Why couldn't she say what she meant, ask for what she wanted? Penny was still irked by her own mousiness when she took a chair next to a window. She dropped her handbag on the floor at her feet, slipped off her shoes and tilted her seat back. I should work on that, she thought.

Half an hour later she was still wide awake and shivery. She sat up, and noticed for the first time that there was a blanket pushed into the pocket behind every seat. She pulled one from its place in front of her and settled back, spreading it over her lap. Immediately she felt warmer and more relaxed.

She closed her eyes and contemplated the week ahead. No doubt her friends would excitedly tell her tales of glorified erotic encounters, some of which might even include their husbands, while she would not have anything to tell them.

Nothing had changed, really. At university her love-life had been mainly confined to drunken boys who always seemed surprised to see her on waking, and who had scuttled off before they had even had break-fast. It wasn't that Penny didn't like sex – she did. But the idea of dating work colleagues filled her with morning-after horror, and she was sure that the bank had a rule about romancing customers. Although, if they had more clients like the boarding card guy, she might be tempted to break it, she thought. She smiled to herself as she recalled his cheeky face and tight bum. She wriggled in her seat.

I knew that book was a mistake, she thought to herself, but then she reconsidered. Sometimes, when sleep was eluding her, she found that giving herself an orgasm was the best solution. Balling all her tension between her legs, she could then release it in a gushing climax and without fail she would soon be dead to the world. But usually she was not trying to sleep in a public place. She opened her eyes and looked around. She could see only one middle-aged man, and he had his eyes closed. If that was all she could see then she figured that no one else could see her. Under the blanket she pulled up the front of her dark woollen skirt. No one stirred. Well, this is certainly something new, Penny thought, and not mousy at all. She smiled to herself as she slipped her hand into her knickers.

Her pubic hair was short and soft, and she reached down further between her legs. She gasped as she found the small hot spot that held the key to her release. Her fingers seemed to draw the wetness from within her, and soon she was slick with desire. She had a sudden urge to taste herself. Taking her hand from under the blanket, she slipped two glistening fingers into her mouth. That was when she noticed him watching her.

She froze. The middle-aged man was not sleeping at all, but looking in her direction. He was about 20 feet away, in the otherwise empty row of seats. Penny stared at him, unblinking, like a rabbit caught in the headlights. But instead of looking shocked and horrified as Penny assumed he would if he had realised what she was doing, he was smiling. He glanced down at his own lap, and Penny followed his line of vision. He was rubbing the bulge in his trousers. She opened her mouth in disbelief and noted that her fingers were still resting on her tongue. She pulled them from her mouth and unconsciously licked her lips. Her confused brain was confronted with the taste of her own sex and the sight of a stranger who seemed to be masturbating in front of her, and the effect was instantaneous. Her nipples stiffened. Penny looked away, aware of the throbbing between her legs but unsure what she should do. Then: what the hell, she thought. This was the kind of thing she read about in books and magazines but which had, so far, been lacking in her own life. She smiled, and again she looked towards the stranger. By then, he had gone. That's a relief, she thought, but she couldn't help but notice there was some disappointment there too. The idea of a New Penny was scary, but also incredibly tempting.

Seconds later she was surprised by a voice at her side.

'Is this seat taken?' It was a ridiculous question in the deserted lounge. She looked up. The stranger now stood only two seats away from her.

'No,' she said, and clutched her hands together in her lap, feeling the hem of her skirt through the thin blanket and wondering what was going to happen next. It was only a request for a seat, but it was loaded with meaning. He was already removing the jacket of his suit. Folding it neatly and placing it on the seat at the end of the row, he sat down.

'That's good.' He loosened his tie and looked at Penny reclining next to him. In an attempt to gain some control of the situation, she sat up so that she was at least physically level with him. As she moved her arms to push herself into a sitting position, the blanket slipped, exposing her hoisted skirt and naked legs. She was horrified, but immediately the stranger was at her feet.

'Allow me,' he offered, and he lifted the blanket, slowly trailing his hand up the length of her leg, and along the inside of her thigh. His fingers brushed her crotch, and Penny shivered involuntarily, grabbing the blanket as he moved his hand away. He smiled at her.

'Thank you.' Penny returned his smile, trying to look sophisticated even though her mind was speeding. Stay calm, she told herself. What do I do now? Look perky? Sexy? Smile? Oh Lord. Finally she remembered to breathe again, and found her tongue.

'It's nice to have some company.'

'Yes. Sometimes these night sailings can get a bit ... lonely,' said the passenger. He moved his seat into the recline position so that it was level with Penny's and pulled another courtesy blanket over his own knees. 'So it's always a pleasure to find a like-minded traveller, don't you think?' He was not as old as she had first assumed; maybe only about 35, and actually quite attractive. Penny wanted him to think that this was nothing out of the ordinary for her, and she did her best to appear casual.

'Yes. It makes the journey pass much quicker, I find.'

'Not too quickly, I hope.' He was watching her intently, and Penny held his gaze as he picked up her right hand in his and, bold as anything, placed it under his blanket, on top of his erection. Her heart was beating fast, but instead of pulling away, she swallowed her apprehension and rested her hand on what felt to be a fair-sized penis that was straining against the inside of his fly. He moved his hand over Penny's, and closed his eyes. 'How does that feel?' he asked.

'Feels good to me.' Surprisingly good, thought Penny, as she stroked the stranger through his trousers.

'Me too,' he said. 'Unzip me.' He lifted his hand, and waited expectantly for Penny. She quickly weighed up the situation. With the exception of the stranger whose groin she was now rubbing, there was no one else around to see what they were up to. Penny wanted some fun. She had fantasised often enough about what she would do if an opportunity like this presented itself, and now it had. This was her chance to find out. She pulled down his zip and his eager penis sprung into her hand. She closed her fingers around it, then moved her hand up the shaft, running her palm over the sticky tip.

'Tickets, please!' Penny and the stranger immediately stopped moving and turned towards the steward's voice. He was some distance away, the top of his spiky head visible above the chairs. He moved slowly between the occupied seats, and Penny remained motionless. The steward stopped, and appeared to be chatting and laughing with another passenger. The stranger was getting restless.

'It will be ages before he gets to us.'

'Yes, but even so . . .' This was, after all, Penny's first time at salacious activity in public.

He urged her to continue. 'Come on, don't stop now.' He shifted in his seat, and manoeuvred his trousers down some more so that he was completely free. The steward was still joking with the same passenger, and Penny agreed that they were in no immediate danger of discovery. She decided that her best bet was to do a good job of the task in hand, so that they weren't in this compromising position for too long. Her hand slid easily up and down the full length of his erection, and as Penny concentrated on the rhythm she didn't immediately notice as his hand went under her blanket. Apparently he wanted to return the pleasure. She jolted when she felt his fingers pushing the gusset of her knickers to one side and pressing down lightly on her most sensitive spot. Penny moaned appreciatively, then he increased the pressure and she caught her breath.

'You have a lovely touch,' she said. And you know just where to use it, she thought, comparing the stranger to most of the fumbling boys she had been with.

'And you have a lovely pussy,' the stranger replied, and Penny felt herself swell with pleasure. No one had complimented her like that before, and she liked it. She opened her legs a little wider.

'Tickets, please!' The steward had moved on, but Penny could still see him on the other side of the lounge. Again, he stopped to trade banter with a passenger. We've still got plenty of time, she thought.

Penny closed her eyes and gripped the stranger's penis firmly, wanting to bring him to orgasm in the hope that he could do the same for her. He certainly seemed to know what he was doing. One moment he was gently teasing her with his fingertip, and the next he pushed a finger into her wet and willing body before returning to the softer touch. Penny struggled to stay quiet in the hushed lounge as she felt her climax rising. Judging by his groans, her stranger was also getting close. As his orgasm approached his touch on her own body became more insistent and Penny lifted her hips to meet his hand.

'Yes, yes!' Penny might have been talking to the stranger, or to herself, but either way she didn't want him to stop. Somehow she managed to stifle her cry as she felt her orgasm start, beginning where he fingered her and spreading out across her body in hot ripples. She arched her back and tensed her muscles, coming in a surge that coursed through her body. As her own peak subsided, Penny barely had a chance to breathe before the stranger closed his hand over hers, pumping himself harder and faster. She opened her eyes and watched as their hands moved under the blanket. Suddenly he stopped moving, and Penny felt his penis pulsing in small, discreet spasms as he came. When his cock was finally still, he let her hand go.

'Tickets, please!' At that moment the steward arrived at the end of their row, his voice strident in the quiet of the lounge. The couple moved quickly to retrieve tickets from bags and jackets, and cover any signs of what had just happened. Penny felt slightly dizzy when she realised how close they had come to being interrupted. She felt for her ticket in her bag, and handed it over. '*Merci.*' The steward handed back the stubs, grinning widely at Penny. 'And thank *you*.' Her first guilty thought was that he must have known, but she had seen him on the other side of the room, and he had been friendly with the other passengers, so she smiled politely as she put the ticket away. More likely, she realised, that he was still smarting from her earlier remark on his rudeness. The steward moved on and the pair busied themselves sorting out their clothing. The stranger scooped up his blanket, pushing it back into the pocket. He stood up and put on his jacket.

'It's been a pleasure to meet you, and I hope that we bump into each other again sometime.'

'Maybe we will.' Penny smiled, decidedly more relaxed than when they had met. 'Enjoy the rest of your trip.' I certainly will, she thought. As well as having some excitement, now she had something to tell the Girls. And it had been so easy! Before long, she left her seat and walked to the exit.

'*Bon soir.*' The steward was still grinning at her when she passed his desk, and Penny wished he would just go back to playing his game. She made her way to the nearest staircase and headed for the observation deck. She needed a cigarette.

She inhaled deeply and looked out across the dark expanse of water. She exhaled the smoke and smiled, feeling pretty good about what she had done. If one of her friends had told that tale she would have thought that it was a sleazy thing to do, and not the kind of experience she would like at all. But the reality was that she had liked it a lot. Penny looked at her watch. Two-thirty. The air outside was cold, and pinched her face. Maybe she should go back inside and try again to sleep. She dropped the butt of her cigarette into the sea. Resting her forearms on the railing, she leaned over. She was certainly tired, and she closed her eyes, lost in the sound of the boat cutting through the waves. She didn't hear the crewman walking towards her, and the first she knew of his presence was when she felt his hands on her hips. Penny abruptly stood upright and turned to face him. He lifted his hands in the air benignly, not wanting to scare her.

'Hey. It's OK. But you want to be careful, standing around like that. A guy could get the wrong idea.' He smiled, and at first she thought he was the boarding card man, wearing that same ferry line top. He wasn't, but he had the same cheeky grin. Even in this cold weather he was only wearing a short-sleeved T-shirt, and his arms were muscled and tanned. Penny wondered if his chest was the same, and she felt that familiar stirring between her thighs. She squeezed her legs together.

'I just came outside for a cigarette . . .' She trailed off, and he laughed gently.

'Hey. I'm not complaining. It was quite a view from where I was standing,' he said cheekily. He looked her up and down, his gaze lingering around her breasts before returning to her legs. Penny folded her arms across her chest.

'No. I mean ... I'm sorry, but I'm really not that kind of girl.' She kept her eyes on the ground and moved to walk round the side of him. He put his hand out on to the railing and barred her way.

'Really?' he asked. 'Because from what I saw earlier, you are *exactly* that kind of girl.'

Penny shot him a look. 'Excuse me? I don't know what you think you saw, but –' She was at first confused and then horrified, wondering what he meant and then suddenly realising that he must have seen her in the rest lounge. He read her expression.

'CCTV,' he said simply. And then, just to add some weight to his explanation, 'The steward fed the input from the lounge to the monitors on the car deck.'

Penny thought she might faint. The crewman stepped closer to her and, grateful for the support, she reached out for his shoulders. He slipped his right arm around her waist, and breathed against her neck.

'That's better.' His left hand travelled down the side of her thigh, and then around to cup her buttock.

'No!' Penny's protest might have been more effective if it had not been mumbled into his chest, or if she had meant it. But tonight that stranger had released more than just her tension, and this crewman was right. He knew exactly what kind of girl she was and, in that moment, so did she. She knew that this was what she had been waiting for. Not a relationship or a soul-mate or 'the one' or any *one*. Just this time, this place, this situation. This cock. She wanted him. And she knew that she was going to have him.

Penny could feel his hard-on pressing into her stomach, and her clitoris awoke with excitement. He squeezed her cheek, and began to lift her skirt. The cold air hit her newly exposed thighs and brought her to her senses.

'Not here. We might be seen by someone.' Penny had had enough exhibitionism for one night.

'Or cameras.' He took her hand. 'Come on. This way.' He led her down the side of the brightly lit deck, past the barrier that said NO PASSENGERS BEYOND THIS POINT. They ducked under the lifeboat suspended above them and squeezed passed a bulkhead. Suddenly they were in darkness. Penny nodded towards the steep metal stairway that marked the end of the passageway.

'What if anyone's about?' she asked.

'They won't be.' He edged Penny backwards towards the railing, his hands at her waist, his mouth at her throat. 'It's crew only, and there's no one around at this time in the morning.'

He lifted the front of her skirt and pressed the flat of his fingers against her sex. She could feel that her panties were moist as he rubbed her slit through the thin material.

'Turn around.' Penny had no intention of arguing. She faced the barrier and held it with both hands. She felt one of his hands on her back, gently pushing her down, as the other one raised her skirt to her waist. Bent over, Penny looked down at the sea and licked her lips, tasting the salt in the air. She was impatient to have him. She opened her legs wider as he hooked his fingers into the elastic of her panties and pulled them down around her thighs. She heard his zip and the next moment they both moaned as he slowly entered her. She pushed back on to him, biting her lip as she felt him moving deep inside her.

'Fuck me,' she breathed, quietly at first and then louder. 'Fuck me, fuck me. Fuck me!' She heard herself utter the expletive in a way that she had never done before, and it excited her. Penny was asking for – no, demanding – what she wanted, and getting it. This was the side of her that she had kept under cover for so long, and now it was finally out in the open.

'Harder, I want you to fuck me harder!'

He thrust into her and then pulled back as far as he could before lunging into her again. Each time he withdrew, the head of his penis nudged against her bud and drove her crazy. She tried to open her legs wider, but her knickers restricted her movements. She reached down to where they were stretched around her legs and pushed them down. Stepping out of them, she turned her head to watch as he took her. His jeans were undone, pulled down only slightly. One hand was on her hip, holding her steady as he ground himself into her. The other was holding the base of his penis, guiding his movements. His fingers dug into her skin and she gripped the railing as he pounded into her. Penny groaned as she felt him swell and the low guttural sound that escaped his throat told her that he was about to come.

'Yes, yes! Give it to me!' Penny wanted all of him, and she contracted every muscle in her body, holding and squeezing him. After only a few more strokes he cried out, and Penny moaned in pleasure as she felt him jerking and erupting inside her. His movements slowed and he pressed himself against her while he caught his breath. Penny eased her grip on the railing and closed her eyes.

Then, to her horror, she heard a voice.

'Way to go, bro!' The exclamation was followed by the sound of footsteps coming down the metal staircase next to them. Her first instinct was to hide but she was trapped. Her crewman was still pressed close against her, still inside her.

'Hey, Tom. I didn't see you coming.'

'That's exactly what I saw you doing.' The other

voice, Tom, laughed at his own joke. 'But not your lady friend here. Aren't you going to introduce us?'

The man pulled away and a flustered Penny stood up.

'Sorry.' He sounded slightly embarrassed. 'I don't know your name.'

Penny straightened her skirt and turned towards the two men. Immediately she recognised the newcomer as the boarding card man. She tried to muster some dignity.

'Penny,' she said, smiling politely as if she were at a party. Then she stopped. 'Nice to meet you' seemed the wrong thing to say in the circumstances. But Tom didn't agree.

'Well it's very nice to meet you, Penny. I'm Tom, and I guess you know my brother Rob.' The brothers grinned at each other, and then Tom turned to Penny. 'Nice parking, by the way.' She was flattered that he remembered her, assuming he was referring to their first meeting and not her encounter with his brother.

'Thanks,' she replied, as she considered her next move. Neither of the two men seemed in a hurry to go, and she was enjoying herself and all the attention. Suddenly, possibilities that might otherwise have remained only fantasies were within her reach.

'I believe these are yours.' Tom bent down and picked her knickers up off the deck. He dangled them in mid-air, but as she reached out to take them he bundled them up and held them to his face. He breathed in through the soft material. 'Mmm. You smell good. Does she taste that good too?' He looked at Rob.

'I don't know. We only just met ...'

'And you were gonna leave without giving the lady any satisfaction? Come on, bro! Where are your manners?' He looked at Penny. 'You didn't come, right?' Penny shook her head, pleased with the direction things were heading in. Tonight she had started on a journey that she had waited her whole life to begin, and she needed to reach the final destination. 'Well that won't do.' He walked towards her. Next to his brother, she could see how similar they were. Both tall, with curly hair and dark eyes, but Rob was generally much fairer than Tom. Their bodies were well toned and powerful from the work they did, and they both had winning smiles. Tom had a thick overcoat on over his ferry line uniform of white logo T-shirt and jeans, and suddenly Penny realised how cold she was. She shivered and hugged herself in an effort to keep warm. Swiftly Tom was by her side, slipping his arm around her shoulders. 'Hey. You're freezing.' He was ruggedly good-looking and the fact that he hadn't shaved for at least a couple of days suited him. He pulled Penny close to him. 'That was quite a show you were putting on.' Not for the first time tonight, she thought.

'Then you won't want to miss the last act.' She was bold now, spurred on by her passion. Tom bent forwards and kissed her on the lips. Of all the things she had done tonight, she realised, this felt the most intimate. His kiss was soft at first, and she responded to his touch, kissing him back. He moved a hand to the nape of her neck, gently holding her head as his kiss became deeper and more demanding. She was still inflamed from Rob's attention, and overjoyed when Tom proposed that they should finish the journey together. She had come so far already, now it was time to really push the boat out.

'All three of us,' she said, matter of factly, and then added, 'Somewhere slightly warmer though.'

Rob nodded back towards the lifeboat they had passed earlier and, for the second time that night, he took Penny's hand and led her along the deck. Rob reached up towards the craft and pulled on a thick orange cord. He caught the chain ladder as it fell down, and steadied the bottom rung with his foot. He climbed up easily, lifting the tarpaulin cover and disappearing underneath. Reappearing, he held out his hand to help her. She looked back and Tom was right behind her. Penny grasped the chains as she stepped on to the ladder, clambering up as Tom followed. Without her panties, she knew he must be copping a good look at everything, so she wriggled her ass as she went. She was already growing confident in her New Penny skin.

The lifeboat was lighter inside than she had expected – the covering was thin and let in the light from the deck – but there wasn't much headroom, so they had to crouch. Penny looked around for a good place to position herself. Tom shrugged off his coat and laid it on the base of the boat.

'Come here.' He knelt down and opened his arms as she went to him. Kissing her, he unbuttoned her cardigan. 'We'll soon warm you up.' He brushed his hand over her taut nipples and she gasped into his mouth as it sent an electric shiver down between her legs. 'You like that?'

'Yes, yes, I do.' Tom's hands went to her breasts, squeezing them through her bra. Her nipples jutted into his palms and she groaned. 'You think they're hard? Look at this.' He unzipped his jeans and pushed them down, pulling his stiff cock free of his underwear. He sat back against the side of the craft. 'Don't you want to kiss me?' He grinned at her and pointed his erection towards her face. She wanted him, wanted both of them, very much. And now, when she had finally found her voice, she discovered that words were unnecessary. In answer to Tom's question, Penny tucked her hair behind her ears, and dropped her head into his lap. She swirled her tongue around the head of his penis before opening her lips and taking him into her mouth. No longer unsure, Penny knew just what to do. Stroking his balls gently, she licked up and down the length of him as she felt his hand tightening in her hair and heard his moans of pleasure. It felt good to her, and she knew it felt good to Tom.

Until then it had been Rob's turn to watch, and she had almost forgotten that he was there. Now kneeling behind her, he raised Penny's hips and pushed her skirt up on to her back. He slipped his hand between her thighs and ran his fingers along her naked slit. She shivered at that and moved her knees further apart, allowing him easier access. She lowered her head, taking Tom deeper into her throat. As more of her pink flesh was exposed, Rob closed his mouth over her tingling clit and sucked. Gently at first, then increasing the intensity until she was writhing against his face. She had never felt this uninhibited before, and that feeling, together with Rob's tongue, pushed her closer to the edge. Rob slipped a finger into her and pressed down, massaging her G-spot. She closed her eyes as the waves of pleasure built inside her. She was moving her head quickly now, her tongue flicking over Tom's erection. Penny felt him tense as he prepared to shoot his load. Rob continued to finger her, and now he licked around the rim of her anus. Old Penny would never have believed how glorious it could feel, while here was New Penny revelling in the delicious rudeness of it.

Then, just as she felt the first hot spurt of Tom's come in her mouth, Rob pushed his tongue into her. The torrent of sensations was too much: the pressure of Rob's fingers, his tongue penetrating her virgin ass and Tom filling her mouth, and the final onrush of her second orgasm that night flooded her body.

Penny lifted her head as the feelings engulfed her, crying out as Tom's come sprayed on to her lips and across her face. She was still revelling in it as her own juices released themselves on to Rob's hand and down her trembling thighs. The men at her head and feet held her as her body juddered, and when she was finally still, they collapsed together on the floor.

As the brothers were leaving, Tom, being something of a gentleman, returned her knickers. 'We have to get back to work. You might as well rest here for now – we'll be in France in a couple of hours. I'll wake you up.'

'And bring me some coffee?' Penny asked. 'Black. No sugar.' He left his coat and Penny quickly fell into a contented sleep.

Sure enough, he woke her some time later with a cup of steaming coffee and a smile. 'Land ahoy!' He laughed and Penny thanked him for the drink. 'Not at all,' he replied. 'Thank *you*.' He helped her out of the lifeboat and on to the deck, and waved as he returned to his job. She had just enough time for a quick cigarette before she needed to get to her car, so she walked along until she found a good spot to watch the view as they approached the coast of France.

As the shoreline grew nearer, Penny contemplated the night's events. It had certainly been a departure from her usual decorous behaviour, but she felt relaxed, and utterly satisfied, and more than full of holiday spirit. She couldn't wait to see the Girls' faces when she told them about Rob, and Tom, and the guy whose name she had never even asked. And the CCTV! Even Penny could see the funny side now, and it was far more daring than anything they had ever done. In fact, the more she thought about it, Penny realised that her adventure might be *too* shocking to tell the Girls.

She finished her cigarette, and started to make her way back down to the car deck. On the stairs, she passed the still-grinning steward.

'*Bonjour.*' He laughed.

'Oh, just shut up!' joked Penny, loud enough for the people in front of her to hear.

She was still thoughtful when she arrived at her car. What if she did tell the Girls? She wasn't sure how they would take it. They might see her as competition, or a threat to their already precarious marriages. Or, worst of all, they might not even believe her! Sad Aunty Pen, making up tales to impress the Girls. That would be awful.

She opened the door of her car, climbed in and made up her mind. She couldn't tell them. Everything she had done was, after all, for her own pleasure, and she didn't need the Girls or anyone else to tell her that she had had a good time. This was another secret for Aunty Pen to keep. The difference was, this time the secret was hers.

Penny started the engine and waited for the vehicles to descend the ramp. She turned up the radio and smiled as the sensuous beat of the heavy rock music thumped through the car.

# Hot Soda Springs
## A Colorado Woman

Two women outfitted for winter slid on to the heated seats of the Mercedes Benz roadster. The redhead donned spotless driving gloves, adjusted stacked-heel boots on the pedals and turned the key. Steadfast, she grasped the steering wheel and the gearshift knob. The passenger with long blonde hair stretched impossibly long legs under the dashboard and thumbed through the selection of CDs.

They were headed to a lodge with an indoor pool for an impromptu, middle-of-the-week getaway. It was absolute happenstance he discovered them lying beside the steaming waters. The surrounding mist was so thick you couldn't spread it with a knife. There was no reason to rationalise, explain or begrudge how they worshipped each other mercilessly and completely that afternoon – no reason at all.

Backtracking to the selection of CDs, the blonde-haired woman chose a progressive blues album and cranked the volume. Charming nose twitched and full lips mouthed the words. The scenery amazed and astounded. Azure skies stretched forever beyond the Front Range. Fourteen-thousand-foot peaks shackled a few cloud puffs.

The tacit lull between them was acceptable. Driving Colorado's hidden highways affected brainwaves in the same manner as a hypnotist's watch swung on a gold chain. Legend had it that hard rock miners cut the road after imbibing rot-gut whiskey. Others insisted geology mandated. Legalised gambling drew fleets of tourist buses negotiating the winding lanes, and serious motorists travelled the interstate.

Their destination was built around natural hot springs surrounded by fifty acres of wilderness. The property was situated in the shadow of Warrior Mountain, a stepping stone to the granddaddies Mount Evans and Mount Bierstadt. One hand on the steering wheel and one hand on the gearshift, the lovely driver skilfully manoeuvred the powerful automobile. The CD track changed. Acoustic guitars, drums and imprecise vocals blared from surround-sound speakers. Snow-studded tyres crunched beneath them and the women entertained primal remembrances. Frequenting the pool fuelled fantasies of naked flesh, warm caresses and lingering kisses.

Health baths in the heart of the Rocky Mountains were all the rage in the late 1800s. There had been little change in temperatures since then. Soda Springs was so named because the waters were effervescent. The mineral content of the one hundred and twenty-five-degree water was a purported tonic for a plethora of ailments. Best of all, there was no sulphur in the mixture and the scent was heavenly. As the crow flies, Soda Creek originated three miles from the highway. American Indian Nations revered the spring. One chief called it Healing Waters of the Great Spirit.

In 1860, a developer bought the mine that yielded bubbly water rather than precious metal, and built a luxury spa. A wooden gazebo connected the men's bathhouse with the women's bathhouse at the entrance to the covered swimming pool, wherein the sexes were allowed to commingle. Such was propriety of the days before the unsinkable Molly Brown sprouted wings. It was the time when silver and gold flooded high mountain runoffs. It was the era of grand hotels, opera houses and painted ladies evocatively seeking independence.

It was a time when both of our travelling adventuresses would dress in silk and wear kid gloves and mink hats with lace veils. Arriving at the theatre, they would step from a horse-drawn carriage into the lights of a garish sign illuminated with gas jets. The door attendant took their capes, and to the sound of rustling whispers they mingled with a snickering society. It was a day of low supply and high demand and their luscious pussies exacted a goodly weight in gold nuggets.

The theatre was three storeys of brick and iron. It was the most spectacular and tallest if not the only civilised structure in the dusty township. Under crystal chandeliers, our sultry women stood in their private, carpeted box on the mezzanine and surveyed the pawning men who jousted, so to speak, for their favours. Oftentimes, a simple smile sufficed. It was always their choice and the winner never kept the purse. Every plush seat was occupied and a white-gloved waiter discreetly filled their champagne flutes. The after-theatre party was by invitation only and masks were required.

Last New Year's Eve, our two travellers were invited to a masquerade ball at today's selfsame lodge. They felt honoured to be on the guest list, but considered masked events to be nonsense and an overworked theme. Instead, they defiantly arrived bare-faced and bare-breasted.

Dressed as warriors of an ancient female sect and crowned with outstanding headdresses of feathers and beads, they ascended the gazebo. All that adorned the lithe figures were leather thongs. Unfortunately, or fortunately – however one interpreted the situation – the leather thongs shrank in the waters and cut tightly into the smooth flesh of their buttocks. They won first prize for originality and ended the night in a suite of rooms with each other and with their lovers from across the mountain passes.

The décor of the expensive suite brimmed with faux elegance. Matched pieces of knockoff eighteenth-century furniture filled the rooms. A wood fire burned on a grate in the marble fireplace. Heavy drapes and a mirrored armoire lent to the ambiance. A stray rainbow split from a bevelled edge and illuminated their reflections in the freestanding looking glass. The ornate brass headboard lent itself quite nicely to silk scarf ties. An oil painting in an oak frame was an oddity – it was of a bamboo cylinder of the kind that stood inside a foyer and that was meant to house umbrellas. The container in the painting overflowed with riding switches.

The women's delicate ears perked at the sound of a knock on the door. The men were late, but the weather was questionable and always an excuse. They were both of adequate height. The tallest one had a straight nose, large dark eyes, and a touch of silver at his temples. What the second man lacked in a few inches of height was compensated for in dusty hazel eyes, sandy-coloured hair, and a physique honed by athletic endeavours. His teeth were ever so white when he smiled, which was constantly. Both of them rubbed their hands together in front of the fire. Their faces were tanned from skiing. In fact, they both wore expressions usually shown at the start of a black diamond run.

The women were used to partnership and used to sharing. However, their men were quite territorial – not to say they were machismo – they had yet to discover the finer aspects of togetherness. Sultry jazz, blonde hash, and fresh champagne ameliorated the communal foreplay. The woman with the red hair was a massage therapist by trade. Body parts were not as sensual as what she imagined she could do with a body part. The woman with the blonde hair did not distinguish between what a body part looked like, felt like or could do. The entire process enamoured her – that is, she cherished the dynamics of primal urges when combined with sweating limbs.

Ah, our story digressed. Let us leave that side road and return to the original plot. The driver woman picked the blonde up at her salon. Her girlfriend had finished obligatory bookwork and cut pay cheques. Making budget with income left for savings rendered her in a smug, grateful mood. The deposit was in the front pocket of her daypack under the hatch. Staring beyond the icy waters of the clear creek, she rehearsed trivial details, as in remembering to stop by the bank after the holiday.

Like Morvan and Laura in the movie *Morvan Callar*, the twisted road and the scenery of the canyon punctuated their mood. The passenger looked every bit her gender in a cashmere off-shoulder sweater, which bared a sexy cut-away velvet camisole. Black riding boots and tight-fitting Diesel jeans accented her abandon and wildness.

The driver kept her hair shorter. It was the best way to deal with natural curls that, although meticulously cared for, were prone to tangle when longer. Copper penny ringlets framed her head in a halo. She fancied wearing co-ordinating hues from head to toe – tan suede boots, brown leather skirt, rich amber stockings and mustard-gold layered T-shirts under a sable motorcycle jacket. The fashion statement complimented snow-drifted spruce trees. Looking at the two, it was obvious neither of them would ever be reduced to stereotypical damsels bound by tradition.

Having arranged to meet their gentlemen friends for dinner at the lodge, they left the afternoon wide open. The excursion was intended to rid their bodies of city smog and their minds of rigid reality. They craved freedom. Freedom from conventionality and freedom to be women who revelled in the beauty of flawlessly formed bodies.

Skidding brakes on iced mud in the valet parking area jostled them into present time. Driver and passenger unfurled themselves from the Benz and locked arms. Upon check-in, they paid for the suite of rooms they reserved and for all-inclusive wrist bands. After informing the desk clerk they were expecting visitors, they giggled down the hall and up the creaky staircases to the original section of the hotel.

They deposited their minimal bags in a spacious closet and ordered room service appetisers and wine for later. Stripped to the bikinis they wore under their clothes, they rolled a reefer and exhaled the smoke out the double-hung window. Wrapped in terry robes, they padded the maze of hallways and rooms to the steps going down, down, down to the geo-thermal sweat caves.

Each step took them deeper into a hazy mist where energy eked in increments. They were pros at the routine: a few moments of pure heat and pure steam in the baths; a bit of time in the large pool; a stint in the mudroom; and a return to the large pool. Showers were necessary at most of the stages. Emerged from the depths, they ascended the gazebo stairs to the pool they knew by heart.

Unbeknownst to them, upstairs at the check-in register, an extremely buffed man arrived in a Suburban. He booked a room for the night, showered and sauntered to the pool. The enclave defied the unpredictable frigidity of early spring and was magical to neophyte first-timers. Tropical rubber plant trees grew to the glass ceiling. Flowering bougainvilleas and Birds of Paradise bordered thriving indoor gardens under the dome. Baskets of staghorn ferns hung from ivy-trellised support beams.

It was the beginning of the afternoon in the middle of the week and the entire lodge was delightfully deserted. Warm mist beckoned and humid heat embraced. At the farthest distance from where the hot springs released into the pool, he lowered himself and let his body get used to the heat. Slowly, he treaded his way to the centre. Effervescency prevented his feet from touching the bottom. Whatever noise that existed before was muffled. Whatever mind chatter he arrived with was quieted. He floated on a buoyancy that was a cousin to the great salt sea.

The enchanting sound of feminine laughter surprised him and aroused his curiosity. Accepting voyeurism as a given, he swam closer. Through the mist, he sensed rather than saw two female forms stretched on the rounded limestone edging of the pool. They were unaware, innocent, and exuded a camaraderie of respect. He was content to watch for a while. A woman with blonde hair lay on her stomach. Her arms stretched languidly and her fingers dangled in the water. A woman with coppery curls knelt beside her and rubbed her shoulder blades.

The nymphs were poetry. Changing positions, the red-haired woman groaned in reciprocal appreciation as the blonde pulled and kneaded her sleek leg muscles. Long strands of hair brushed alabaster skin. Sweat and mist lubricated the pair of hands traversing taut limbs. He wanted to join the ritual. Jealous muscles twitched and he yearned to partake of their ministrations. He wondered if they shared the tingling sensation that overwhelmed him.

The answer was clear. He witnessed the transition. Curious fingers moved hesitatingly towards the moist mound of hair connecting gleaming thighs. He heard a sigh and saw firm, round buttock muscles respond to the caress. The blonde's hand lingered and he knew the balmy air awakened their sexuality.

Under the water, he slid out of his racing tanks. The scent of bougainvilleas, mixed heavily with their personal perfumes, entered his nostrils and he hoisted himself up to them. The blonde made eye contact. She blinked and giggled. His uncovered maleness stretched to the dome as if offering a gift. Her friend beckoned him to join them.

Undeniably welcomed, he lowered his chest between their knees and closed his eyes. They slithered their palms down the length of his back and legs. Starting at his toes, they moved mercilessly towards his hips. Their strokes matched in faultless harmony. His body failed to differentiate between their touch.

He internalised a raging battle between the no-nonsense therapeutic muscle work and the surging sexual need that threatened to expose his humanness. Sweat beaded on his face and the misty maidens simultaneously rolled the skin of his ass. He was conscious of fingers reaching underneath him in an exploratory journey. Painfully, he felt his penis engorge with fiery blood. They sensed his agony, turned him over, and massaged with new intent.

Then the blonde placed his head in her lap and traced the rugged outlines of his features with her fingertips. The woman between his legs ran the palms of her hands ever so slowly and ever so firmly down the sides of his legs. He experienced sensations everywhere at once. His chest and groin smouldered under waterfalls of silken hair. Twin forward motions caused him to gasp. Teasing tongues encircled his mouth and penis at the same instant. Pleasure overload created a kaleidoscope behind his eyelids.

Quitting the battle, his mind slipped to oblivion.

Instinctual reactions took command. His thighs twitched and fell farther apart and his testicles were lovingly caressed. Hips lifted upwards and responded to pleading lips, which absorbed the full length of his cock. To extend the inevitable, he placed his hands upon an exquisite set of cheekbones and held the head stationary. He caught his breath and proceeded to gently suck her tongue out of hiding and into his mouth.

The ideal twosome, accustomed to partnership in the wild, shifted positions again – to their benefit as well as to the benefit of their willing captive. Scanty swim attire was cast aside. Raw passion unfurled greedy effects like a distant flash of lightning and limbs melted into a collage of mutual desire. An intense need for satisfaction ruled. The sweetness of the moment dissolved into fog.

Lust unloosed all ties. One of the women lowered herself in front of his face and spread her sex lips apart with her fingers. She controlled the depth of his tongue until he grasped her ass to him and his tongue plunged into her. He savoured her sweet juices and recognised her movement as the ultimate dance of desire. Undulating upon the hungry penis, she peaked and rolled to his side. Mutually, the remaining two satisfied each other.

Still with no dialogue and no names, the now spent threesome rested. Agile bodies silhouetted tropical plants that had no business growing at ten thousand feet above sea level. Steam gathered under the dome that covered the pool, the rubber tree and the Birds of Paradise.

A few measured hours later, the blonde-haired woman's hazel-eyed gentleman friend arrived at their suite. He insisted she go on an adventure with him – alone. In the cab of his Ford truck, she snuggled close. His behaviour was mysterious and he smelled like cedar smoke and coffee. No matter where he took her, they would make mad passionate love – of that she was certain. He was a gaming man and it was part of his strategy to keep her guessing and wanting.

He wondered aloud if she was ready to get wet. She whined that she had left her bathing suit at the lodge. It was no problem, clothing was not permitted where they were going. Intimate arrogance was a turn-on to her and she squiggled on the upholstery. Her hand on his thigh traced the double inseam of his Levis to where it was hot and hard.

Ensnared in the juxtaposition between her horniness and the huge semi-trailers on the interstate, he said nothing. She lay her head upon his shoulder. Her delicate fingers rhythmically pressed his crotch and her yearning was audible. Passion thus ignited, he would have encouraged her, but the highway exit was upon them. He slowed for the off-ramp and she lifted her head. A quick right turn followed a quick left. He downshifted for the steep incline.

He nosed the truck to a stop in front of a steel gate with a padlock and no trespassing signs. A frown wrinkled his noble countenance. He hoped he hadn't pushed the envelope – and Nature – by coming too early in the year. Around the bend, trees were bare and sizable accumulations of snow encased the north side of the road bank. With a boatload of imagination, one could conjure a bud or two on south slope aspen trees.

The close proximity of towering pines obscured the sun and she pushed her sunglasses on her forehead. It was as if they were at a drawbridge to another land. He jumped from the cab and asked her to drive the truck through the gate. The hinges swung easily enough. She played the accelerator and looked mighty fine behind the wheel of the pickup. He replaced the padlock and engaged the drive hubs.

The forest was all encompassing until they crested the rise. It was just the way he left it last autumn. The lean-to made of stone survived the winter. He eased the pickup to a slow stop and sprinted around the hood to open the door. Speechless, she stepped off the running board and into the breathtaking scene. Down-slope water collected in a steaming pool the size of a tilt-a-whirl.

Processes deep within the mountain core created the spring and a dense bluish mist arose from the surface of the water. With no alluvial plain underneath and surrounded by mighty spruce and groves of aspens, the pool was an awe entitled anomaly. Snowflakes melted long before landing and the ground was dry. A circle of moss-covered rocks purported to limit the water's power.

A sword should rise above the misty surface. A wizard with a flowing beard should appear from an alcove and a golden stag from the forest. As a lad, he dreamed of loosening the jewelled hilt, that the world's treasure would return to the good and the righteous. One could only wonder if besides craving and coveting the sword, if that handsome man also foresaw himself with our fair maiden.

In still another time space, she balanced on her feet and raised her arms overhead in a quasi-salute to the late afternoon sun. He grabbed the duffle bag from behind the seats and a cold bottle of wine from the tool box. He unpacked a blanket, a corkscrew and two stemmed glasses. He left the camera for later. She knelt on one knee and drew her hand under the water. It was hot to the touch and bubbly. She desperately wanted to strip clothes off and enter, but she wondered if there were bears.

Laughing, he flung the blanket over the lean-to and returned to her side. He assured her that the bears were still hibernating and that they were safe, alone, and in lust. He placed two fingers under her chin and tilted her face towards his. Gently, and with escalating fervour, he melted his lips on hers. Her tongue explored his; his nudged hers back and back; she wanted his cock to do the same.

He teasingly pushed her away and uncorked the wine. With great aplomb, he sniffed the cork and filled the glasses to the rim. Leaving the warmth of the pool for refills was not in his script for the day. Slivered vapours tentacled outwards and invited them hither. Chattering chipmunks and scolding magpies guarded the boundaries. They shed their clothes and slid under the mist.

She was celestial, just as he had imagined during the long months of snowfall and inaccessibility to his priceless real estate purchase. Her beautiful butt perched on the rock ledge and her long tresses grazed ageless granite. Ash-gold lashes gathered miniscule drops of moisture. Pale limbs contrasted the blue-green backdrop and her cheeks flushed.

The effervescent quality of the water had a way of absorbing nerve endings and absolving overworked muscles. It was his first time in the waters that day and he breathed a sigh of relaxation and liberty. Skin soft as suede met his searching fingers. There was no resistance from annoying swimsuit ties at the point where hip bone joined femur. Her eyelids fluttered and the greenest of green eyes searched hazel eyes as if to ask, *What is your pleasure?*

Around his neck he wore a pouch threaded on a leather strap. He removed it and circled her damp hair. The strap rested between her firm breasts and her entire body shuddered. He opened the pouch. Inside was a crystal ball about half the size of a billiard. He touched the crystal to her nose, her lips and her chin. Clasping the precious orb in her palm, she turned her back towards him in a savoury show of anatomy.

He placed his smooth shaven cheek and sensual mouth so close to her ear, the downy hair on the outer rim tickled his nose. Vapours swirled around her mind. She bit her lower lip. Blonde tresses slicked against her head rendered her profile angelic. He gently pushed her up on to the ledge, spread her knees and traced the inside of her thighs with his lips. Her pussy cried out for more. Raising his head from her riches, he entwined the fingers of one hand in her hair and held her immobile. With his other hand he opened her wet pussy and inserted the crystal ball deep inside. His hand lingered.

She murmured the ball was cold. He guaranteed her she would make it hot and he secured her promise that his treasure would remain intact until he chose to do otherwise. She smiled, her nose twitched, and she submerged out of the range of his arms – yet, the ball remained stuck fast inside her silken depths.

He pulled his mermaid topside by her armpits. They sipped wine and snacked on cheese. The orb magnified the longing in her pussy. His cock remained hard against her, but he made no familiar motions to make love. Frustrated, she jumped from the pool and wrapped her still human form inside the blanket.

The sun was setting beyond the forest. They dressed and made the return trip in silence. Both anticipated dessert and every once in a while she squirmed. He grinned and turned the music louder. Such was his style of gaming.

The handsome foursome dressed for cocktails before dinner. No one was particularly hungry, so they had a toke of the reefer and a few sips of Pinot Grigio. The woman with red ringlets brought up the subject of their first-place costumes at the masked event and the evening that followed.

It was a unanimous no-brainer. They cancelled dinner reservations and rolled dice to determine the winner – never a loser – couple who would beg the honour of the silk ties hanging from the ornate brass headboard. Elegant evening attire discarded, they unabashedly appraised each other and retested the stability of the bedposts.

Imagine the surprise. Not only was the blonde pussy with clipped hair chock full of a crystal but the coppery pussy was also full – hers was made of emerald green jade. They did not want to trade but they did want to see if they tasted the same. The men humoured their explorations and allowed themselves to be bound with the colourful scarves – again. It was their nature to give these two best lady friends whatever they wanted, wherever they wanted it, whether it was a holiday or not.

# WICKED WORDS ANTHOLOGIES –

## THE BEST IN WOMEN'S EROTIC WRITING FROM THE UK AND USA

### Really do live up to their title of 'wicked' – Forum

Deliciously sexy and explicitly erotic, *Wicked Words* collections are guaranteed to excite. This immensely popular series is perfect for those who enjoy lust-filled, wildly indulgent sexy stories. The series is a showcase of writing by women at the cutting edge of the genre, pushing the boundaries of unashamed, explicit writing.

The first 10 *Wicked Words* collections are now available in eye-catching illustrative covers and, as of this year, we will be publishing themed collections beginning with *Sex in the Office*. If you never got the chance to buy all the books when they were first published, you can now complete your collection and be the envy of your friends! Look out for the colourful covers – guaranteed to stand out from everything else on the erotica shelves – or alternatively order from us direct on our website at www.blacklace-books.co.uk or through cash sales – details overleaf.

Full of action and attitude, humour and hedonism, they are a wonderful contribution to any erotic book collection. Each book contains 15–20 stories. Here's a sampler of what's on offer:

### Wicked Words

ISBN 0 352 33363 4
£6.99

- In an elegant, exclusive ladies' club, *fin de siècle* fantasies come to life.
- In a dark, primeval forest, a mysterious young woman shapeshifts into a creature of the night.
- In a sleazy Midwest motel room, a fetishistic female patrol cop gets dressed for work.

## More Wicked Words

ISBN 0 352 33487 8
£6.99

- Tasha's in lust with a celebrity chef – it's his temper that drives her wild.
- Reverend Billy Washburn needs salvation from Sister Julie – a teenage temptress who's set him on fire.
- Pearl doesn't want to get married; she just wants sex and blueberry smoothies on her LA poolside patio.

## Wicked Words 3

ISBN 0 352 33522 X
£6.99

- The seductive dentist – Nick's encounter with sexy Dr May turns into a pretty unorthodox check-up.
- The gender-playing journalist – Kat lusts after male strangers while cruising as a gay man.
- The submissive PA – Mandy's new job fulfils her fantasies and reveals her boss's fetish for all things leather.

## Wicked Words 4

ISBN 0 352 33603 X
£6.99

- Alexia has always fantasised about being Marilyn Monroe. One day a surprise package arrives with a sexy courier.
- Bridget is tired of being a chef. Maybe a little experimentation with a colleague is all she needs to get back her love of food.
- A mysterious woman prowls the back streets of New York, seeking pleasure from the sleaziest corners of the city.

## Wicked Words 5

ISBN O 352 33642 O
£6.99

- Connor the tax auditor gets a shocking surprise when he investigates a client's expenses claim for strap-on sex toys.
- Kate the sexy museum curator allows a buff young graduate to make a thorough excavation of her hidden treasures.
- Melanie the interior designer and porn fan swaps blokes with her best mate and gets up to nasty fun with the builders.

## Wicked Words 6

ISBN O 352 33690 O
£6.99

- Maxine gets turned on selling exquisite lingerie to gentlemen customers.
- Jules is stripped naked and covered in cream when she becomes the birthday cake for her brother's best mate's 30th.
- Elle wears handcuffs for an indecent liaison with a stranger in a motel room.

## Wicked Words 7

ISBN O 352 33743 5
£6.99

- An artist's model wants to be more than just painted, and things get pretty steamy in the studio.
- A bride-to-be pays a clandestine visit to the bathroom with her future father-in-law, and gets much more than she bargained for.
- An uptight MP has his mind (and something else!) blown by a charming young woman of devious intentions.

## Wicked Words 8

ISBN O 352 33787 7
£6.99

- Adam the young supermarket assistant cannot believe his luck when a saucy female customer needs his help.
- Lauren's first night at a fetish club brings out the sexy show-off in her when she is required to wear an outrageously daring rubber outfit.
- Cat's fantasies about hunky construction workers come true when they start work opposite her Santa Monica beach house.

## Wicked Words 9

ISBN O 352 33860 1

- Sarah gets a surprise when she and her husband go dogging in the local car park.
- The Wytchfinder interrogates a pagan wild woman and finds himself aroused to bursting point.
- Miss Charmond's charm school relies on old-fashioned discipline to keep wayward girls in line.

## Wicked Words 10 – The Best of Wicked Words

- An editor's choice of the best, most original stories of the past five years.

## Sex in the Office

ISBN O 352 33944 6

- A lady boss with a foot fetish
- A security guard who's a CCTV voyeur
- An office cleaner with a crush on the MD

Explores the forbidden – and sometimes blatant – lusts that abound in the workplace where characters get up to something they shouldn't, with someone they shouldn't – someone who works in the office.

*Look out for future themed erotic short-story collections at £7.99*

August 05 – Sex at the Sports Club
November 05 – Sex in Uniform